A Dark and Promised Land

A Dark and Promised Land

a novel

Nathaniel Poole

DUNDURN
TORONTO

Editor: Shannon Whibbs
Design: Courtney Horner
Printer: Webcom
Cover design by Laura Boyle
Cover photo © wynnter/iStock

Library and Archives Canada Cataloguing in Publication

Poole, Nathaniel, 1961-, author
        A dark and promised land / Nathaniel Poole.

Issued in print and electronic formats.
ISBN 978-1-4597-2200-2

        I. Title.

PS8631.O633D37 2014   C813'.6   C2014-901025-7
a   C2014-901026-5

1   2   3   4   5   18   17   16   15   14

  Canada

We acknowledge the support of the Canada Council for the Arts and the Ontario Arts Council for our publishing program. We also acknowledge the financial support of the Government of Canada through the Canada Book Fund and Livres Canada Books, and the Government of Ontario through the Ontario Book Publishing Tax Credit and the Ontario Media Development Corporation.

Care has been taken to trace the ownership of copyright material used in this book. The author and the publisher welcome any information enabling them to rectify any references or credits in subsequent editions.
                                                                              J. Kirk Howard, President

The publisher is not responsible for websites or their content unless they are owned by the publisher.

Printed and bound in Canada.

Visit us at
Dundurn.com
@dundurnpress
Facebook.com/dundurnpress
Pinterest.com/dundurnpress

Dundurn
3 Church Street, Suite 500
Toronto, Ontario, Canada
M5E 1M2

MIX
Paper from
responsible sources
FSC® C004071

Thraciae multo cum amore

Glossary of Selected Historical Terms

Bois-brûle   Literally, burnt wood, referring to the darker skin tone of some mixed-ancestry people. Archaic name for Métis that faded from use early in the nineteenth century

Bunjee   Another name once used for the Métis people. It can also refer to the language that developed between Scottish traders and Cree or Ojibwe, which is a creole of Native languages, Scots, and Gaelic

Capote   A thigh-length winter coat with full sleeves and often a hood. Made of leather, wool, or Hudson's Bay Company trade or point blankets. Worn by Aboriginal, French, and mixed-blood peoples in the northwest

Djinn   Jinn or genies; spiritual creatures in Islam and Arabic folklore

Dudheen	Also dudeen; a clay pipe with short stem
Êmistikôsiw	Swampy Cree word for a White person
Flap	Dung
Fuke	Low quality, smooth-bore flintlock trade musket manufactured in Birmingham, England, and exchanged for furs in large numbers by the Hudson's Bay Company. Also known as fusil, fusee, Hudson's Bay fuke, North West gun, or the Mackinaw gun
Half-caste	Also Country Born or Black Scots. Term for mixed-blood people of English, Scottish, or Orkney fathers, and mothers from various Aboriginal tribes such as Cree, Ojibwe, Algonquin, Assiniboine, Saulteaux, and others
Half-breed	Also *bois-brûlés*, mixed-bloods, Bungi, Bunjee, and Métis. Term for mixed-ancestry people of French fathers, and mothers from various Aboriginal tribes such as Cree, Ojibwe, Algonquin, Assiniboine, Saulteaux, and others
Hamla Voe	A bay near Stromness in the Orkney Islands
Hawser	A thick cable or rope for mooring or towing a ship
Home Guard Children	Children of the *Home Guard*, Aboriginal people who encamped near Hudson's Bay Company trading forts due to the availability of food, supplies, work, and later on, trade alcohol. They were often perceived as little more than beggars by the door to many Europeans, but they provided much-needed labour, trade, and wild game for the forts

Ituk	Swampy Cree for caribou
Lapstrake	A clinker-built boat (having external planks overlapping downwards and secured with clinched copper nails)
Machi Manitou	The evil spirit or bad spirit of a number of Northwest peoples including Ojibwe, Cree, and Algonkian
Made Beaver	A standardized unit of exchange within the Hudson's Bay Company where one prime, adult male beaver trapped during the winter equalled one Made Beaver. Late in the fur-trade era, the HBC issued brass coins in denominations of one Made Beaver and fractions thereof
Okimow	Swampy Cree word for Hudson's Bay point blanket
Pipes	It was common among fur traders to measure travelling distances by the time it took to smoke a pipe, rather than miles. So the distance between two portages might be described as ten pipes
Turves	Chunks of matted earth and grass roots
Voyageur	French Canadian word meaning "traveller," and usually refers to French Canadian fur traders in the employ of the North West Company based in Montreal
Whitemaa	Orkney for gull

Book One

Chapter One

Her father calls to Rose from the other side of the door, asking if she is ready. She tells him that she will be there in a moment. She hears shouts and the clatter of running feet in the passage. With a sigh, she arranges her hair as best she can with the cracked and hazy glass.

She is twenty-one and thinned by their voyage; her hair is the colour of cedar, the Pict or Norman ghost in her bones. A smattering of freckles. Full lips, almond-shaped face, the beginning of parentheses lines about a wide mouth. A brown birthmark below her left nipple and on her thigh above her left knee. The possessor of a fine Celtic courage, her father often claiming her to be a descendent of Boudica.

She looks around at the tiny cabin; her home for the many weeks it has taken to cross the north Atlantic. There is little to collect, nothing to leave behind. It is as if her presence here never occurred, and she wonders how something of such importance can show so little evidence.

She has tried to be thankful. After all, the rest of the ship's passengers are crowded together in the hold like slaves. She thinks of her small room as a womb, a safe place from which she will emerge into a new life, but too many times she has awakened in total darkness to a smell like damp coffinwood. Her aroused imagination had thought the groaning and pitching of the ship felt like being lowered into a grave, and so she has spent many nights haunting the abandoned foredeck, querying frosty stars as to what it all means.

Dishevelled bed, rusty chamberpot. Black pods of rat dung in the corners. There really is nothing else, her one small case having already been removed. She reaches out and her hand traces a familiar path over the wall, fingering the carved prayers and incantations left by scores of previous passengers. One in particular she is drawn to, carved like scrimshaw in flowing letters. The first week aboard she had discovered the name *Malvolio* carved above her bed. *Malvolio.* She wonders at the wit of the one who left it there: both foreboding and melancholy, but uplifting in its unexpected reference to art. It had become a friend to her. She will miss *Malvolio*. Pounding again on the door, and it rattles in its frame.

In the passage she meets her father, Lachlan, anxious, with a guttering lantern. The deep shadows on his face make him look like an ape. "Have you spoken to the captain?" she asks.

"The fool has no idea where we are," he says. "Nor how long the tempest will carry on. But we must be prepared to leave at a moment's notice." The ship lurches and Lachlan steadies himself against a wall. Rose hurries to take his arm.

"Careful, Father. Oh, what a horrible noise!" The wind that started that morning as a gentle hum had become a full, demented chorus. Along with the wind came the waves, with the ship's motion making moving about treacherous. "Perhaps you should sit down?"

At that moment, a seaman runs up the passage behind them, chased by a cold wind. "Pardon, luv," he says as he pushes past and disappears down the passage, his bare feet slapping dark wet footprints on the weathered wood.

Rose recognizes the man, a youth from South Ronaldsay, who wanted to "see the world," as he had whispered to her while they struggled together in a secret closet. His handsome face and wit had convinced Rose to offer her own landscape for him to explore. "Oh, darling, ye have such lovely tits," he exclaimed hoarsely, burying his face in her breasts. She smiles at the memory of his naïveté, and when they were done, his fumbling proposal for marriage.

"Insolent man," Lachlan grumbles.

"Please, Father," Rose says. Detecting an irritated tone in her voice, Lachlan looks into her face. "Are you angry with me, daughter?"

Rose hesitates, recalls the past several weeks: foul water, infested bread, and the unimaginable reek of hundreds of people living in the ship's belly. Rampant cholera, the dead unceremoniously tossed overboard with a mumbled incantation. During the long nights, she had often cried angry tears for the civilization left behind.

"I am fine," she replies. "Or would be if this ship would cease its awful tossing." At that moment they feel a new motion: a kind of shuddering and tearing sensation that makes Rose gasp. After so many weeks, all aboard are keenly tuned to the frigate and sense the loss of the rudder.

"My word, what has just happened?"

"Come, let us join the others," Lachlan replies. "Quickly, now."

A rat scurries along a wall; it pauses and sniffs the fetid air, whiskers shimmering in the light of a dying lantern. Timbers creak and another rat emerges from a gap in the bulkhead. They curl about each other. Soon the larger mounts the other and begins drumming. The ship lifts. And falls.

With a great cry, the oak timbers erupt beneath them and the black water of Hudson's Bay bursts into the cabin. Swimming, swimming, the rats are swept away.

Above them, a crowd of colonists and Company men fight their way to the companionway. Again, the *Intrepid* falls, shattering her backbone; a cold wind blows through as the sea pours into the ship's bowels. Scores fall down the companionway ladder.

Rose had not moved, nor had her father or the rest of her people. They were Orcadians, phlegmatic by nature and long used to living under the shadow of death by sea. Most of them had retreated against a bulkhead, shadows from the swinging lantern rolling over them. Those scrabbling in the companionway are young employees of the Company and Highland peasants fleeing the Sutherland and Strathnaver Clearances. Many of the women are on their knees and wet-black rats flow around them, following their prayers skyward.

Pressed against the rusty barrel of a fat carronade, Rose sways with the death agonies of the ship. She feels the cold of the iron seep through her skirt and braces herself with her hands, feeling the wet, slate surface of the corroded metal. Her heart hammers.

Hammocks strung like spiderwebs fill the air between carronades. It had been a long day of rain, sleet, and snow, the deck above running with cold water. Rose stares at a drop forming itself on an oak beam; it swells until fat and pregnant, falling into a silver puddle at her feet, a puddle alive with the tremors of the ship. Another wave pushes the dying vessel farther onto the rocks, and the puddle slides into her shoes.

Jammed by the crowd in the companionway, a Highlander begins setting about his fellows with a cudgel. The violence reminds Rose of the time a stoat invaded her father's dovecot. Escape that way is impossible.

An Orkneyman removes his hat and looks around; he points a thick finger. "There," he grunts. In the shadows between two beams is a small butterfly deck hatch, an insignificant break in the overhead timbers. Salt fogs the glass; the brass is green.

He tries it, but time has frozen it shut. With a curse, he grabs a rammer from beside one of the carronades and swings it against the hatch, spraying glass. Reaching through, he fights with the corroded metal, lifting the hatch open with a shriek. The men stand aside to allow the women through.

One by one they are helped through the opening, eyes averted from their skirts. As Rose struggles through the narrow way, several helping hands push against her buttocks; she resists an urge to kick.

The storm that had blown them ashore is unabated, throwing freezing rain and sleet, wrapping the ship in a ghostly integument of ice. Shards as white as polished bone jut from the ship's spars and rigging, occasionally snapping away to go spinning into the darkness. Sea spray showers them; a boom and roar surround them.

The nets had been flung over the rail and men crawl like black insects down the ship's rolling hull. The boats had been launched, but all are destroyed in the mill of rocks and surf.

The ship heels again and several women slide down the icy deck. Rose grabs for the fife rail; clutching a nest of coiled ropes, she digs at the deck with her feet. Her grip slips on the ice so she drops away, tobogganing into the mass of bodies below her.

Crushed among the cursing, shoving crowd, Rose pushes to her feet, bruised and breathing hard. She sees her father, his head and neck protruding from the hatch like a mounted stag's head. He pulls himself through, and, half-crouching, slides toward her.

"Are you hurt?" he asks.

"No. Father, I do not think so. But I have lost my shoes."

"We must get off this damnable ship. All is lost."

"How shall we do that? Must we swim?"

They look around. High above the deck, torn sheets of canvas stream away, howling and cracking like grey phantoms. Lines have snapped and blocks are swinging; one flies out of the darkness and collides against the back of a man's head with the sound of a melon being broken open. He flips over the rail, black suit flapping like the torn wings of a bat. The last Rose sees of him, he is floating face down and spread-eagled like some kind of nightmarish starfish, drifting with the ebbing current out to sea.

The wreck of one of the *Intrepid*'s boats clutches to nearby rocks, her mast cutting a steep arc with each incoming wave. As Rose watches, the little White Ensign fluttering from her masthead rips and flies away into the dark unknown of Rupert's Land.

"What kind of land is this, what has snow an' sleet in the middle of August?" asks a tousled and coatless young Orcadian; he runs his tongue over thick lips and stares at the white line of surf that marks the shore so close and yet so far away.

"It's home, lad, and it's bloody time we got there," Lachlan says. "Over you go, lass."

Rose swings her legs over, and her feet drum against the hull, searching for the netting. Lachlan follows her. The youth watches a moment and climbs after them. "If I'm to die tonight, I'll die among me own," he says.

They edge down the swinging netting, though what they are to do when they reach the churning water, Rose cannot imagine. Black waves leap at them, spinning with foam. The wind tears at her skirts, threatening to peel her away; the netting is icy and cuts into her numb, red hands. Her mouth tastes of pennies and salt.

They are almost at the water when the youth slips with a shriek and falls into the sea. They watch his head bob on the surface for a moment and disappear. Lachlan curses under his breath. Rose feels his eyes on her, but cannot bring herself to meet them, afraid of seeing her own terror reflected in his gaze. His cold hand encircles her own.

All about them people fall in the water — man, woman, child. The body of a swaddled infant — born on the sea — bobs beneath Rose like a piece of driftwood, its tiny, red fingers curled up under its chin, eyes squinted shut beneath the water. A few bubbles escape from its nostrils as it floats away. The night rolls with the cries of the terrified and the dying.

Rose turns away, closes her eyes and leans against the frigate's hull. She can feel the grinding of the reef, and it reminds her of a time she rested her hand on a dog's head as it chewed on an old knucklebone.

She follows that thread back to some comforting memory. The dog gnawing its bone, the singular warmth of her aunt's massive hearth. The smell of peat smoke and brewing tea; pleasing chatter of old women.

"Rose? … Rose?"

She holds her eyes tight, her hands clutched to the rope as if it is all that keeps her sane. An old trick of hers, to be and not be, to remove herself from some difficult experience by fleeing the present and walking down safe, familiar roads in her mind. She sees flowers in a moonlit garden, a star shining through a petal. At the smallest gesture of breeze, the flower bobs in a semaphore of flashing starlight.

"Rose!"She turns toward Lachlan.

"Get away from the ship as soon as you can," he shouts at her. "Keep away from the rocks. It is not far to shore." He kisses her forehead. "Now!"

Grasping one another's hand, they abandon the netting and fall into the sea.

Her lungs explode with a gasp. She kicks for the surface, but cannot inhale. The coldness of the water wraps itself around her, crushing out her breath. Waves carry over her head. Thrashing on the surface, her mind swirls with sharp lights. She is lifted by a wave, and her hand strikes something rough and hard.

She climbs onto the rock. The weeds are soft and slippery, the barnacles cutting; it feels like climbing into a mouth. Shaking, she sits down, wraps her bleeding arms around her knees, and looks at the dying ship. Smoke pours from an open hatch. With a sharp crack, the forward mast splits: ropes fly and bronze hoops burst. The great spar swoons forward, slicing through the clustered people in the water, dark heads bobbing like kelp floats.

Wind whips Rose's wet hair across her face. She pinches a fold of skin on the back of her hand, but feels nothing. Her shaking is uncontrollable.

At the next wave, she allows herself to be swept off the rock. As before, the coldness of the water seizes her, but she does not fight it this time, accepting just a gasp of air, the smallest of breaths. She kicks toward shore. Her skirt encumbers her, and she attempts to pull it off in the water. Her body has become an unresponsive lump; the fabric tangles about her feet. She chokes, sinking; her legs drag. Her feet find the bottom and she thrusts away the tangling cloth; wearing only her shift she climbs onto the beach, water running off her and darkening the pure whiteness of the snow.

Flames engulf the wreck, and by its light she sees people stumble out of the sea, pushing aside clustered bodies rolling with the surf. A cadaverous light shines on the faces of those who stand watching the frigate burn. Some weep, but one after another, they fall silent.

"Father?" she calls between shaking teeth. It escapes her lips as a croaked whisper. She calls again, louder. A face turns toward her.

"Rose!"

Lachlan runs over and embraces his daughter. "Oh, my wee bairn, I thought I'd lost thee … God's blood, you're freezing." Too cold to reply, Rose slides into her father's arms, hiding her face from death. He wraps her with his wet coat.

Overheated cannon aboard the burning frigate ignites, blowing out the side of the ship and sending several balls whining over the water to smash into the forest, shattering several trees. In unison, all the watchers ashore jump back.

Spotting a Company official, Cecile Turr, Lachlan seats his daughter on the beach and hurries over to him. "We must find shelter for these people, Mr. Turr," he says, grabbing the man by the arm and blowing frost clouds into his face. "We must start a fire!" The man turns his sad, heavy eyes toward him, pulls his arm away and sits on the beach, lowering his face into his hands.

Lachlan fights an urge to shout; helpless, he looks up the beach at a palisade of dark trees roaring in the wind. As he watches, several shapes emerge from the forest. Flames from the burning frigate glitter on polished silver and beadwork.

Chapter Two

Alexander McClure opens his eyes and feels grit under the lids scrape against his eyeballs. He cannot imagine where he is, the smell of muddy pig shit, nauseating and unfamiliar. Fragments of memory whirl in his head like torpid summer fireflies.

He is on his back, his eyes taking in a thin, washed sky; the fort's palisade glows in the first light of dawn like a line of rough-hewn nails fresh from the forge. It had rained during the night; his clothes feel like peeling, wet skin. Distant shouts of men carry from the riverbank and a cannon thuds, startling him. York Fort. He rolls over with a groan.

At this movement, an enormous hog bedded beside him begins nuzzling his hair with its wet snout. Alexander shoves at it, and pain sears through his hand; the knuckles are stiff and crusted with blood. Memories of a brawl hover at the edge of consciousness. Something about cheating at cards.

He reaches for his purse, unsurprised to find it gone. Whether he lost during the fight or an Indian stole it as he lay in filth, he would probably never know. He sees a pair of them squat against the palisade, shadowed eyes watching him. The hog thrusts its snout into his shirt with a contented grunt.

"Get away," he mumbles as he stands up, leaning on the massive, black beast. Limping, he makes his way through the fort gates and slides down the high riverbank, his heels digging twin furrows with a following clatter of pebbles. At the bank, he peels off his clothes and wades into the water. It is cold but not icy, and he dives into its depths, surfacing with a splutter and cough, his long yellow hair streaming.

By the time he emerges, the sun is over the bank and the day is already warm. He spreads himself naked on the shore to dry. His brown body is lithe and slender, with wiry muscles; a form descended from runners, more Cree than Scots. A pale flower on his left thigh bulges with a lump of loose bone. A buffalo's horn long ago ran him through there, and it still bothers him.

He rubs his scabby knuckles. Someone had a busted jaw or an eye that wouldn't see for quite a good while, he assures himself. He can't recall details, but is unsurprised at this: it is common for the fur traders to consume enormous quantities of spirits over many days, often amounting to several gallons. Some wake up in chimneys or in the holds of ships far out to sea. Sometimes they never wake, which is far from the worst fate that can befall a man in Rupert's Land.

The son of a Highlander — a fur trader from Albany Factory — and a Cree woman, Alexander has lived in many places, none very long. As a child, he spent much time in York Fort, an oddity in that most Half-caste bastards lived with their mothers. But unlike most Orkneymen, who only served their contracted seven years on the bay, his father had been adamant that his son be raised as a Christian despite the disapproval of many, including the Fort's factor.

Every fall, he accompanied the brigades to the lands south and west of *Missinipi* — the Big Water — the land of his mother. He was left in her care while his father traded for furs at Indian encampments along the distant Athabasca and Slave Lake systems. In the spring, he always returned, and, after collecting his son, they spent the summer at the Bay.

Alexander loved the intense activity of York Fort, the ships arriving from England, the canoe and York boat brigades from Rupert's Land. There was always so much coming and going, so much drinking and fighting and haggling and trading that it was easy for a child to stand unnoticed and take it all in, even though his hair made him stand out among his Indian cohorts. When things were sorting themselves out in his mother's womb, he had received his father's yellow hair — what little there was: his mother didn't call him *Paskwastikwân*, or Old Baldy, for nothing — and his father's passionate temper. His mother's gift was her dark skin and deep love for the wild lands. He thinks it a fair exchange.

Some Company employees despised Half-caste whelps, and these people he had tormented mercilessly. That he was often caught and beaten made no difference; he would sit in a birch tree all day long for the chance to shit on someone, and more than one night he spent hiding in the forest, the terror of the *Machi Manitou* less than that of his enraged father.

There was a school of sorts at the factory for the servant's and the Home Guard children, but he often managed to be elsewhere when the lessons started. He preferred to haunt the trade store, hiding behind barrels of traps or axe heads, momentarily freed from the torment of adults who thought there was always something useful for an eight-year-old to do. Secreted away and pulling the limbs off captured spiders or flies, he listened to the fur traders attempts at a better deal. They were rarely successful.

Despite their formidable size and armament, they could never get the Company's chief trader to change his mind. A slight man with white hair and spectacles, he never became angry, never exchanged insults or profanities, regardless how sorely provoked.

The rate for *made beaver* was set in London and as immutable as the Commandments, he always explained to the bristling men on the opposite side of the counter, showing them the Official List of Exchange. None of them could read, but the list was imposing, nonetheless; you could argue with a man but not the Company.

Once an agitated Bunjee, with face blackened with grease and charcoal, had burst into the store and thrown a musket onto the counter, loudly complaining that he had been forced to live off muskrats and rabbits for months because his gun wouldn't shoot accurately.

"Nonsense," the chief trader replied with a smile. "The Company's trade guns are the finest in the world. They never fail in the hands of a worthy and knowledgeable hunter."

The Bunjee grabbed the musket and pressed the muzzle against the trader's forehead, just above his spectacles.

"Maybe you right, let us find out ..." he said.

"I see your position," the old trader replied. "I will gladly replace the weapon with the Company's apologies."

It was the only time Alexander had ever seen the old man beaten.

The fur traders that came to York Factory with the brigades were enormous men with long bushy beards and clad in buffalo robes. The Half-breeds wore their distinctive red sashes and beaded and embroidered jackets. Most carried a beaded octopus bag and a powder horn and musket slung on their shoulders. The Half-breeds most often spied him, and, with a wink, gave him a candy. His presence thus betrayed, one of the junior clerks invariably chased him out with a broom.

Very rarely he was invited into the warehouse, most often when someone needed help moving something. He was always amazed at the wealth stored at the factory: guns, powder and shot, powder horns, flints and gun worms, knives, axe and hatchet heads. Pots, pans, and stacked piles of *okimow*, the striped Hudson's Bay blankets; sugar, Brazil tobacco, and awl blades. Tiny brass hawk bells to sew on to clothing and harness that made a delightful tinkle with the slightest movement. Hundreds of pounds of bright glass beads of every colour. Batteries of iron kettles, traded by the pound. There were boxes of fish hooks, nets, ice chisels, lines, sword blades, and bayonets the Indians fashioned into spears.

Compared to the few possession his mother's people carried with them, this was an unimaginable bounty. He would have undoubtedly lifted something but for the fact that the humourless clerk had always searched him when they left the warehouse. He had been too young to understand that what so awed him was merely the detritus of a distant, arrogant civilization.

But eventually autumn wound its way through the land, and heralded by the angry bellows of rutting moose, his father loaded the gear required for a season of trading, returning Alexander to the land of his mother at the forks of the Assiniboine and Red Rivers.

A free, enviable life. But that was before Selkirk came.

"McClure!"

He looks around. Standing at the top of the bank, one of his brigade is looking down at him. "Aye?"

The man gestures with a thumb over his shoulder. "Chief trader wants to see you, and he's the devil this morning."

Alexander nods and waves to the man, who stares a moment and disappears. The summons is expected; the peltries Alexander had traded were mostly miserable summer affairs neatly wrapped with a few prime ones as disguise. The ruse lasted long enough to collect credit and get drunk. Now the reckoning has arrived — as it always did.

He craves a pipe, but can't recall where he has stowed his gear. No doubt it followed his purse. "Piss on it," he says.

The morning is becoming hot, although his thick clothes remain sodden. The feeling as he tugs them on is distasteful, reminding him of how skin slid off a corpse turned liquid by sun and flies. His boots squelch water as he climbs his halting way up the bank to the fort.

~

William Spencer, chief trader, is tall and lanky with a scrawny, loose neck with skin hanging off it like a turkey. His fingers are knobby and he stinks of the sour tallow with which he smears himself to ward off blackflies and mosquitoes. He has a habit of constantly digging his tongue at either corner of his mouth.

"There you are, McClure. It's about time," he says in his irritating whine, sounding as always as if something cold was squeezing his testicles. The chief trader's office is in a flanker, a small triangle-shaped closet high above the central courtyard. Originally intended for cannon, but the guns never arrived from England, so the embrasure behind Spencer is pasted over with Company handbills.

"Aye," Alexander replies, not bothering to remove his hat. "You wanted to see me?"

"I asked for you over an hour ago, McClure. You seem to think that Company time is yours to piss away as you see fit."

"Get to the point, man."

"The point is that you have been living beyond your means, living off the Company's good graces, in fact."

Alexander crosses his arms and says nothing. Spencer's colour rises. Sucking in his breath, he twitches a ledger sheet across the desk.

"What do you say to that?"

Alexander doesn't bother looking at the paper, but continues to stare at the chief trader.

"I'll tell you what it says, you illiterate bugger," Spencer shouts. "You delivered a bundle of *made beaver*, or so you told my ass of a clerk. But there were no more than a dozen pelts worthy of the name and the rest is flyblown shit."

"Is that so?" Alexander says, cocking an eyebrow. "I could have sworn ..."

"And you helped yourself to several pounds' worth of trade liquor, bought on what is now shown to be almost worthless credit!"

Alexander shrugs. "I will pay with next season's furs."

"Not good enough, McClure. I have shown this to the factor, and he wants to talk to you."

"Eh?"

Spencer leans back in his chair and smiles up at the trader in front of him. "Yes. You're more trouble than you're worth, Half-caste. When Himself is finished with you, your balls will be flying from the Company's flagpole.

"You're a prick, Spencer." Alexander says. Furious that shooting the chief trader is not a recommendable option, he strides over and kicks the desk. It careens back, sending the man crashing against the wall.

"McClure!" The factor has entered the room. He is a large man, with florid cheeks and sunken eyes carrying heavy bags. Although a gentleman, he gives the impression of having spent a great deal of time brawling in taverns. His habitual cravat, neatly pressed frock coat, and tailored trousers seem incongruous at York Fort. He is the most powerful man on the frontier — more powerful than a governor — and accountable only to the board of the Company of Adventurers in London. "Get up, you fool," he says to Spencer, still tangled in his chair and scrabbling on the floor. "McClure, you come with me."

Without a word, Alexander follows the factor out of the flanker. It is warm on the ramparts and fat blue bottles gather, lifting and buzzing and settling again on the sharpened posts of the palisade wall. They swirl about each other as if driven by unseen cyclones. A hum fills the air.

They walk slowly, the factor pausing occasionally, looking out over the walls into the distance. Time and again, he looks south-ward toward the roadstead, to the Hayes River scalloped by wind. In all other directions, the landscape is scabby swamp brush, a featureless black-green stretching to hazy distance. To the far west, Hudson's Bay is barely visible, a silver herring on the edge of sight.

There are no ships at anchor, but they are due. Every year they arrive with the season, to take back furs to England and deliver trade stuff, equipment, and supplies. It had been that way since he was a boy, and even wars, local and distant, did not stop the trade. At the first sight of masts, he and his friends used to run to the cannon to wait the salute; the factor's secretary came from the fort, and when the ship at last dropped anchor, the gun was touched off and the children running away squealing. A long time ago.

"I don't need these kinds of petty annoyances, McClure," the factor says, startling Alexander out of his memory. He searches the young man's face and turns away. "You look a lot like your father," he says. "No, don't thank me! You're not even a shadow of him. That man was as strong as bull and yet as honest as the day. He was a great friend of mine."

"He spoke often of you, sir."

The factor grunts in reply and mops his forehead with a greasy kerchief. "But nothing stays the same. Not for him, not for me, not even for you. You aren't your father, but you will have to do. Do you know what's out there, McClure?"

"No, sir."

"Nothing less than the fate of the Company. The Nor'westers have us by the throat. There are three ships overdue and if they are lost, I fear the Company of Adventurers is bankrupt. But it's more than that. Do you know what one of those ships is carrying?" McClure shakes his head. "Colonists. More of those goddamned colonists that we have had to deal with these last seasons. Starving, desperate, ignorant Highlanders shipped here by Lord Selkirk for his fucking colony. They should be transported to Van Diemen's Land, but the Lords will not listen. And so they have become my problem."

Alexander knows about the colonists. For the last two years, boatloads of desperate peasants fleeing the Highland Clearances had arrived unbidden on the shores of Hudson's Bay. Last year's lot had been mistakenly delivered to Fort Churchill, which could not possibly accommodate them, and they were forced to make a starvation trek south to York Fort. Their arrival was not cheered, and, as soon as possible, they were sent on their way to Selkirk's new colony at Fort Douglas, deep in the heart of Indian, Métis, and Nor'wester territory.

Although unbidden and despised wherever they went, Alexander had to hand it to them: they were one hell of a tough lot. "I'm sorry, sir."

"Don't be sorry for me, McClure. Because I am making them *your* problem."

"I don't understand?"

"I will not countenance their staying a day longer than absolute necessity at York Fort. Once they arrive — if they arrive, God help us — you will immediately guide them to Fort Douglas. The very next day, in fact. Take what supplies and men you think you need, but I will want them gone, y'hear me? When that cannon over there fires, that's your signal to pack."

"But, sir, I was hoping …"

"I don't care what you were hoping for, McClure."

"I've never guided a brigade before. And I don't know how to deal with Scottish peasants. No one can understand their chatter, their tongue."

"Then you will learn how. I'm not giving you a choice, man, your father's son or no, you will do this for me. Or you will never again set foot in York Factory or any other Company post for the rest of your days."

Alexander begins to sweat. While he can easily trade with the Nor'westers if he chooses, he holds a superstitious awe of the London-based company and feels almost a filial duty to her. Exile from York Factory would be to lose his only contact with his dead father's world.

But to guide a brigade of foreigners! He knows the route between York Fort and Fort Douglas better than most, but has been content to travel as part of a brigade lead by others, limiting his role to trading furs and manning the sweeps. This is something else entirely.

The fort below them is subdued, too quiet for the time of year. In that the Factor is truthful — nothing will be right until the field pieces by the river are let off in honour of the ship's arrival. It was a cause for celebration, with feasting and heavy drinking following the emptying of the ships. As a boy, he frequently took advantage of the drunken adults, lifting their purses or other personal effects to trade for sweets. Once at twelve years of age, he had stolen a trader's pistol, but when the man awoke, he accused someone from another brigade of the thievery. A deadly fight was in the making, forcing a terrified Alexander to confess his guilt to his father, who hauled him before the furious trader. The man was shaggy and dark, bristling with weapons, and he whipped Alexander's behind and legs with a sharp willow until it broke, while Alexander's Indian friends laughed at him. He ran off in shame and did not return to the fort for three days, forced at last by hunger to apologize to his father.

As he grew older, he had followed his father more often into distant lands, paddling with the others, trading and learning the craft of the wilderness. When his father drowned in Knee Lake, he took over where the old man had left off, as a fur trader on the Bay. But he felt an incompetent shadow of the great, bearish Scot who had dominated his life, especially after the death of his mother.

Yet now, all is quiet. The ships have not come. What is happening in the world that so much he has trusted is in danger of slipping away?

"I don't know what to say, sir."

"Listen, son, if I didn't think it was possible I wouldn't put this on you. You're young, but you're capable. It's a test, all right, but we all have to endure. The Company might not last another year. The ships might have foundered. You might lead the colonists to ruin. I don't need to tell you that life is lived on the edge of death and disaster, but we do the best we can. I have my crosses, and I'm giving you yours. God help us all."

Chapter Three

The Indians silently approach the survivors on the beach. As the Europeans become aware of the strangers, they stumble away. The tallest of the newcomers approaches Lachlan. His shadowed eyes travel over the Orkneyman and glance at the burning wreck. The cries for help are dying away; the flames still growing. The Indian gestures to Lachlan and turns away.

Lachlan grabs the officer sitting on the beach, and hauls him to his feet.

"I think they mean for us to follow them. Quickly, man, there is not a moment to lose."

"What? Oh, yes ..." says the officer, seeing the departing Indians for the first time. "Come along everyone, we must follow the Savages. Smartly now!"

One by one, the colonists fall into line. Moans and soft cries can still be heard. A dark line of them forms off the beach; not all who leave the water's edge make it as far as the tree line before collapsing. A few hold back in fear, but, after the flames find the ship's magazine, the *Intrepid* explodes with a great detonation, the icy water of the Bay instantly rushing in and consuming the hulk. A great hiss goes up, followed by roiling clouds of steam.

Absolute darkness and the silence of the dead chase the last stragglers from the beach, following as best they can, stumbling over the occasional body in the darkness.

The Indians had not waited, and, almost as soon as the Europeans enter the forest, they become lost in the tangled, scrubby trees. They stand together crying for help in God's name, when they find the Indians amongst them again, eyeing them like mouse shit found in the pemmican.

Rose clings to her father as they stumble over half-seen bushes and branches in the dark, snow dusting them. Her awareness has diminished to a small, shrinking core.

The path to the Indian's camp is mercifully short, and soon they come upon a collection of five conical tents of hide stretched over poles; a pale yellow they glow, a weird and unearthly light flickering like a will-o'-the-wisp. Dogs bark and flaps are thrown open as they approach.

The widowed women commandeer a tipi for themselves and the orphaned children. Once inside they sprawl about, several almost naked. The tipi is too small, and those with the strength sit leaning against each other. A few sobs for those who died, and more for those who survived.

Indian women bring in armloads of wood and throw them on the fire. Sparks and a smoky haze, miasma of wet wool, and the sour spice of filthy, lousy bodies engulfs the tipi. The temperature soars. They sit in a huddle separate from the Europeans, and a sheen of sweat appears on their dark faces. They set a copper pot to boiling and toss in a handful of small, hairy leaves. One of them fills tin cups and carries the tea to the survivors. Perhaps a dozen are capable of responding.

She brings Rose a cup, and, propping up her head, holds it to her lips. The scent is earthy and fragrant, but the taste bitter.

She softly speaks words that Rose cannot understand, but there is no mistaking the tenderness in the woman's voice. She chews several of the tea leaves and places them as a damp poultice on Rose's cut hands. Rose smiles at the touch and looks into the kind woman's face. The Indian returns her smile, her brown fingertips tracing with wonder along Rose's white arm. She wraps the cuts in soft cloth.

Another presents Rose with a ribbon of dried meat from a skin bag. While she had never really believed all the ghoulish stories she has heard about these people — stories of infant sacrifice and cannibalism — when confronted by this piece of anonymous flesh, Rose thanks her, and surreptitiously pushes it out under the edge of the tent where it is wolfed down by one of the dogs.

The Indians give them a few blankets and robes in which to wrap themselves, and those who are able, turn away from each other and pull off their sodden clothes. The Indians watch with wide eyes.

"I'll take a cane to your eyes, any o' thee that look upon me," says an old woman in a voice high and weak, her thin jaw quivering. "'Tis not Christian to be seen like this, not afore the heathen." She pulls off her rags, revealing pale, sagging buttocks covered in veins and blue blotches. The Indians attempt to suppress their giggles as they chatter to each other in their own language.

"Look at the udders on her; like a nursing buffalo."

"They are so pale, like a pike's belly."

"Pike with hair, you mean; see the thatch on the old one!"

The wind rattles the stiff hides against the poles, and Rose feels a cold draft wrap around her legs like a snake. There are nowhere near enough furs for all the Europeans and they are forced to share; chilled, naked bodies press against one another in great embarrassment.

Pushed to the edge of a robe, the skinny feet and legs of an emaciated and filthy girl stick out. Rose opens her blanket and the child mechanically slides over. Pressing her cold, knobby frame against Rose, she immediately falls asleep.

Rose too needs to sleep, and wishes her father is with her. She curls up on the bed of prickly conifer boughs and wraps her arms around the child, surprised at how cold and hard she is: utterly without animal warmth, like a tree root. A flea bites her, and mechanically she scratches at the place. She wonders where they are and whether it is near the end of their journeying. Her father said something about Red River. Perhaps this is the same place.

When she closes her eyes, scenes from that night's horror intrude: screams of the dying, wooden feel of corpses that they pushed past on the trail. The smell of the burning frigate. She clenches her teeth, squeezing her eyes against the tears. Her body shakes.

Beside her, the Indians stare into their snapping fire while Vega glimmers down through the smokehole. Out in the forest, a night-hawk *chuurs* and Rose thinks she hears a wolf howl, but it might be a dream.

The next morning dawns cloudy and grey, the light in the Indian's tipi broadening in the dull morning. The child beside Rose is stiff and cold. Rose had cried many tears in the long night, and, looking at the girl, all she feels is an empty sorrow. She pushes the matted hair aside and closes the eyes, muttering a brief prayer.

The air in the tipi is thick with smoke and the low-tide smell of the colonists. Rose vaguely wishes she still had the perfumed handkerchief she had often pressed against her nose while aboard the close, foul ship.

She sees one of the Indian women nursing an infant. They are comely enough, she decides, despite their bizarre colouration. High cheekbones, small, flat noses, and full lips. Black hair rolled up on either sides of their heads, held in place by a strip of leather and a bone pin. White paint and red ochre cover their arms, and white woollen blankets ringed with twin indigo stripes serve as coats. Soft leggings of skin, decorated with beadwork in colourful patterns. Their feet are dressed in slippers of a similar material, likewise decorated. They are very exotic, Rose decides.

"We be forsaken," moans an Orkneywoman from beneath a heavy fur robe. Limp hair hangs in her swollen red face. She jostles her huddled neighbors. "The heathen be eatin' us for certain."

The nursing woman gives her an angry look. "If that was our wish, you already be dead," she says, her comprehension of their language startling the colonists. An uncomfortable silence follows.

An old Indian woman — with hair as long and white as her robe and with a face the texture and colour of old boot leather — leans sideways and farts. She opens a toothless mouth in a broad grin. Everyone begins giggling.

Rose turns to the woman with the infant and hesitatingly introduces herself. The child suckles with great vigour. Its mother stares into the fire. After a long pause she replies, "I am Isqe-sis."

"Thank you for helping us, Isqe-sis. We would not have survived on the beach."

Isqe-sis looks up at her. "No good you die there. Tomorrow take to fort. Much …" she thinks a moment, "gifts for your lives: knives, pots, blankets. This why we do."

"You mean a reward?"

The woman nods.

"I see." Rose frowns. "Is this fort very far?"

"No far. One day's journey."

Rose thinks the utilitarian motives for the Indian's help far from Christianlike, and though it gives her a vague sense of being a hostage, she realizes their value is in being kept alive, therefore it is unlikely that any of them will be murdered or eaten. She had expected to see scalps hanging from the poles of the tipi and is surprised that there is only a few ermine, a white goose, and a pair of skin bags containing the dried meat and the strange tea. Despite herself, she feels vaguely disappointed at how crudely prosaic it all seems.

"Rose? Is that you?" Her father taps on the outside of the tipi.

Standing outside, huddled in their borrowed skins and blankets, they stare with fear at the encircling forest. Twisted black spires leaning this way and that, hung with pale green epiphytes that flutter like nightmarish cobwebs in the thin wind. Shadows lie heavy beneath the trees. The bright skulls of slaughtered animals hang on several boughs, and the clearing looks even more disturbing by day than it had by night.

Another fire had been started, and the old Indian woman walks over to a carcass hanging from a tree. She saws off chunks of meat, impales them on willow twigs, and places them over the fire. The roasting smell is glorious.

The colonists gather around, ravenous. Lachlan asks how Rose is feeling, and she affirms that she is well enough, all things considering.

"Indeed?" Lachlan replies. "Well, my neck's very sore. But after last night, praise the Lord that we are still drawing breath."

Rose agrees with him, though she has no idea where they are and is still uncertain of the outlandish people who have rescued them. With a lowered voice, she informs Lachlan that they spoke English. He looks at her with arched eyebrow, but does not respond.

The wind seems to pass through her robe. She doesn't need to climb a tree to know that the ranks of brush and bole go on for endless leagues. There is something about the chill of the wind, the immutability of it that gives the impression that the surrounding forest is breathing, and is a beast of unimaginable size.

There were the odd winter days in Stromness when the weather turned to the south and the thermometer almost burst in the sudden warmth; she could smell the lush green of distant tropical lands on that breeze, hear the chatter of brightly plumed birds as they swooped from palm to palm.

The air now moving past has that sense of space and distance, but unlike that delicious equatorial ghost, this air whispers of barrenness, speaks of a land cold and empty of anything warm.

After a breakfast in which Lachlan watches the Indians closely, but does not address them beyond a cautious "Thank you, ma'am," when he is handed a spear of meat, the survivors don what remain of their rags and the Indians give Rose a stained capote and a pair of moose-hide leggings. They are much too large for her and she is required to cinch them high up under her breasts with a length of hemp. The Indians have no moccasins to spare, and she is forced to tie rotten and discarded pieces of hide around her feet.

Several colonists return to the beach. Wreckage is scattered far down the strand, and there are many bodies half-buried in gravel or shrouded in kelp. Of the two ships that accompanied them, there is nothing to be seen.

Rose stands listening to the hush and roar of surf. On the blurred horizon, the grey water blends with the equally sombre sky, making her feel enveloped on all sides by the same empty waste. Somewhere out there is her home, countless leagues east. The ship that had died on these shores had been her only connection with everything she has ever known, and it feels as if a part of her has perished with it.

She feels a sudden tumble of emotion — grief, fear, and anger at her father for bringing them to this terrible place. She had been awed by the enormity of the Northern Sea, and struck dumb by the mountains of blue-green-grey ice through which the *Intrepid* had attempted to navigate, but any sense of adventure she carried with her from Orkney — a delicate bird it had proved to be — had perished on the night's killing strand.

Most of all she feels overwhelmed by the emptiness. Her life has been a safe one; she had the time and comfort to believe in adventures filled with courage and extravagant heroism. But their arrival in Rupert's Land changed everything: wonder and hope becoming meaningless, ignoble death. There is no page to turn or cover to close; she is trapped within a story not of her choosing, facing a future utterly beyond her control. Even now, the men gather to decide the course of action, her voice unimportant and unwanted.

"Damned, unnecessary tragedy," her father says, standing beside her in his wrinkled coat and breeches. She is startled to see how gaunt he looks, with shadowed cheeks and purple fans below his eyes. His hands tremble. "That captain was a fool," he says.

"It was an accident, was it not, Father?"

"Yes, Rose, but preventable — ah, look at that damned *whitemaa* there. Get, get, I say!" He runs waving his hands at a gull that had approached a corpse. The bird spreads its long white wings and floats off, *screeing* down the beach.

"We must bury these poor folk," Lachlan says.

"Aye, but with what?" someone replies.

"York Fort will have the tools that we need."

"Perhaps the other ships, they will find us?"

"They have been scattered by the tempest. But perhaps *they* will take us south." Lachlan waves a hand at the Indians.

"Aye," replied a grizzled Orkneyman. "Ah spoke with their chief, the big buck standing there. He says they can paddle some o' us down the coast to the fort. It's nae far, he says, though I dinna much trust him."

"Pray, lower your voice, sir, they understand English."

"So kin me dog, but I dinna worry about it." Several men share a nervous chuckle.

Lachlan looks down at the body. A middle-aged man, naked but for a wrapping of polished green seaweed over his belly and legs. He is on his back, eyes open and staring. Tiny puddles of seawater had collected over his shrunken orbits, and he appears to be studying the sky through spectacles. Lachlan wonders if he had met the man, had spoken to him. He does not remember the face. He reaches over and closes the eyes, wiping his wet fingers on his breeches.

"We cannot leave them here to the *whitemaa* or be washed out to sea. If we have no means to bury them then we must bring them above the tide, cover them with boughs, and stand watch. This much must be done."

"But which of us will go with the heathen?"

"I shall go. And my daughter shall go with me as she has lost her habiliments. The Company officer will know from whom at York Fort we should procure assistance. I do not know whom else. You, perhaps."

The man, a muscular Highlander with a black scraggly beard and weary eyes, nods at him.

The task of gathering the dead is a grisly one, as scavengers have already defiled some of the corpses. At least half of the ship's complement has died, though most are not accounted for in the pale forms scattered on the beach.

As the day lengthens, the clouds begin to dissipate and a weak sun gradually emerges. The breeze dies and biting insects flow down from the wall of trees the way a cool air flows from a height with the coming of night. The Indians start a smudge fire of seaweed, but it doesn't help much against the onslaught.

The men carry the bodies to a spot above the high-water mark as far from the forest as possible, the Indians warning that there are animals who will and can walk off with a corpse or part of one at the turn of a back: bear, lynx, wolf, marten, wolverine, and lion, plus a host of small and furtive beasts happy to snatch a mouthful of carrion.

The women take axes and cut spruce boughs to cover the bodies, the beach echoing with the sound of distant chopping. Although she is not expected to work, Rose feels she would be remiss to not contribute. She stands in a bog and hews at tough, pitch-covered spruce branches while mosquitoes and blackflies crawl over her hands and face. It is more difficult than anything she has experienced, and sweat runs into her eyes. With each step, she sinks ankle-deep into wet peat. Moss hangs from overhead branches, dragging through her hair, and coating it in cobwebs and pine needles.

The axe handle suddenly shatters, the ricocheting head scoring her forehead. Blood quickly begins flowing. She stumbles and sits heavily in the peat, weeping. Isqe-sis yanks the broken handle from her hand and throws it into the forest.

"This what you *Êmistikôsiw*, you Whites trade with us, this ..." and she begins a long diatribe, not a word of which Rose understands, although the anger is unmistakable. Still cursing, the woman presses a handful of the moss to Rose's wound.

"In winter such axe could kill a man or his family," she says. "Bad guns, bad axes, sick clothes ..."

Rose cannot help but feel that although Isqe-sis is tending her, the Indian would just as rather leave her to bleed. She feels a rising indignation; what has *she* done to incur this person's wrath? Was not *she* the offended party? She sees a small, silver crucifix peeking from a fold in Isqe-sis's capote.

"You are baptized? You are Christian?" Rose asks, surprised. Isqe-sis nods.

"How..."

"There is camp of the Black Robes." Isqe-sis waves her arm southward. "Port Nelson. My father had the water magic for me. In the name of Jesus they save my spirit."

Black Robes, Rose thinks. *She must mean Jesuits. So she's a Papist.*

"Are many of you are Christian?"

"Not so many. Most Home Guard, yes, rest Cree, no."

"Home Guard, what is that?"

Isqe-sis frowns. "We are poor people, needing White man's trade." She spits in the direction of the axe handle. "Live York Fort. Not now, not since White sickness come."

"White sickness? What is that?"

Isqe-sis looks away. "Sickness come from Whites. Fever, then death. Sometimes sores on face, hands. Sometimes not. But always fever and death. This why we no longer live at York Fort."

∼

Sitting in the slender vessel and clutching the gunwale, Rose is ill at ease. The boat is several feet long and constructed of woven bark. One man in the bow and another in the stern propel it with short, carved paddles. Her father sits in front and behind her, the big Highlander, Declan Cormack, looking thoughtful as he watches the Indians at their work. Behind him, the Company officer sits in the stern, scowling whenever Rose turns and looks at him.

She feels the movement of the sea through the slight material of the craft and it seems as if they are perched on a feather. They glide up one wave and slide down another in a gentle, regular rhythm. She watches the man in the bow, the pumping of his thin, muscular arms. Red ochre covers the faces of these men, their heads shaved except for a single topknot wrapped in hide.

Each stroke of the paddle is short and sharp; stroke following stroke. No words, no rest, no complaint, and Rose is reminded of an oxen tied to a mill wheel, doomed to forever circle the same spot.

She thinks of the distance between her and her old life back in Stromness, in the Orkney Islands. Their house in Stromness was small and cold, with a solitary hearth inadequate for the job. Built of stone with dark, walnut doors and wainscotting and tiny windows painted closed to fend away the unhealthy night air.

Rooms were usually closed tight to conserve heat in main living areas, and her father's library (her favourite room) grew innumerable moulds. Many dismal afternoons had been spent engrossed in distant worlds, while against the window an ancient and gnarly crabapple tree tapped when the wind blew from the sea, scattering hard knobs across the courtyard in the autumn. The damp, musty smell of books had whispered freedom to her.

At first Rose had found the written world to be preferable to the lived, in part due to the regime that her father imposed on the household, their lives neatly bookended by fears of God and personal anarchy. Simple foods and unpretentious clothing has been her lot, although they could afford far more.

But as womanhood arrived and with it a sense of her own desire and will, she learned to explore ideas with others. The relationships people wove amongst themselves lit a candle in her imagination, and in a city like Stromness, with a busy port and entire populations passing from somewhere to another where, it was possible to explore the meaning of many an intriguing concept with any number of strangers.

It was not excitement that she sought, but the young adult's earnest need to decipher the paradox of what the world presented with a sly wink on one hand, while condemning it with the other. To her, moving anonymously through the city was like rolling over a large stone to uncover the secret, mysterious world inside an ant's nest.

Like one of her fictional heroines, she wrapped herself in stranger's clothes and went down to the taverns along the waterfront and met life head-on. Power especially interested her — the various forms it took, the disguises it embraced. She saw it manifest as physical strength and as a dour uniform, as money and a flashing blade. What really surprised her was how often it rested in a look and a powdered décolletage.

When not fascinated by the struggles of man against man, she often wandered the labyrinths of love. In her stuffy tomes, the poets and philosophers waxed at length on the meaning of that ineffable beast, and she refuted them both. The first was too wild-eyed earnest while the latter too removed from anything that pumped hot blood. As Leeuwenhoek glared down his glass and trumpeted on the unseen nature of things, she felt his ilk no closer to expounding on love's mystery than the contents of a chamber pot.

Sometimes these back-room truancies were hard and brutal, at other times they recalled the delicacy of a chrysalis.

Things could become complicated. One time a Mr. Wells, post captain in the British Navy, was one with whom she had explored the more esoteric and violent forms of passion. He was short and fat, with bright, hard eyes and a face almost as scarlet as the Royal marines that guarded his quarterdeck. Upon receiving his admiralty packet commanding him to India, he informed Rose that he desired her company on the long voyage. Wells had not reached his station by deferring to another's will, and her careful, coquettish demurrals moved him not a whit. He would not be put off by a mere girl, and once word reached her ear that he had commanded she be brought to his ship, in irons if need be, she refused to leave her home.

Although a studious woman, Rose was no church-mouse and this sudden reluctance to go for air or visit her friends raised Lachlan's concerns; he noticed an unhealthy pallor and soon called for a bleeding, a process she loathed as much as being trapped in their home.

But of course, Wells was not aware of who Rose really was or where she lived, and the sailors and press gangs searched high and low for her to no effect. At last, in a great rage, he was forced to sea without his love's interest to warm his bed. Rose felt relieved to see his sails on the horizon, and thought it a miracle that the city was not bombarded as a token of his thwarted passion.

After the danger of Wells, Rose kept much closer to home. But the unrelieved routine of their life quickly grated on her spirit and the old ache, once masked by curiosity and excitement, soon returned. Her father's concern remained high; her complexion did not improve and neither did her mood. She was short with the servants and himself, and a veritable parade of physicians marched through their home poking and prodding her, asking veiled questions regarding her woman's functions.

Rather than seek an explanation within her own soul, she blamed her ennui on the ritual of walking her father to the school each morning and the afternoon tea with her friends. There was the constant turning away of the boorish suitors that every mother in Stromness seemed to send to her door; the banality of the middle class was hers and she would not, could not take to it. It was not long before she found herself once again in unfamiliar alleys and hallways.

Not all of her quests were lascivious in nature. Far from it. She had quickly learned that the bodily passions, while interesting in their own right, left little in their wake besides messy hair and possessive lovers. She was driven by something deeper, more innate. Curious and insatiable was how she described herself when musing on her odd and dangerous behaviour with her friends (some of whom thought her much like a goddess); life was short and living was truly made for the young, and best to just get on with it.

The young man from Ronaldsay was the not her first aboard, but almost certainly the last. It was an impulse fired as much by risk as any real interest on her part; her father had been nearby and that was a true novelty for her as he knew nothing at all of her trysts. She rarely gave her companions much thought; they simply amused her. At best, her feelings went so far as a benign complacency, the way one might offer a stray dog an uncertain pat on the head.

But though her need had not been sated in Stromness, she at least enjoyed the luxury of her unhappiness. Though occasionally placing herself in various compromising positions, she had always enjoyed the luxury of sneaking home for a bath in the small hours (and if by unhappy chance the servants encountered her in the hall or stairwell, they discreetly looked through her in a manner she found quite unnerving, as if she had become a ghost). Father and daughter had been toppled from a comfortable station in Orkney to break bread with the wild and the savage awaiting in Rupert's Land, and she did not much like it: hers was a sensitive heart, one that should not have to endure such trials.

After several hours of following the coast, the Indian in the bow pulls up his paddle and shouts, "*Wapusk, wapusk!*" They crane to look; there is something in the water, swimming parallel with them. A wedge-shaped head leaves a trailing wake.

The Indians veer closer, Rose spotting a large, pale body, indistinct beneath the blue of the water. A black nose and small, dark eyes.

"'Tis an Arctic bear," Lachlan says in awe.

The Indian in the bow nods. "*Wapusk.*" He brings out his trade musket or *fuke* and directs them alongside the swimming animal. They see the great paws swinging as it dog-paddles; it turns towards them, but the Indians veer away, maintaining a careful distance.

"Sometime they jump at you," the Indian says. "And then ..." he makes a slashing gesture across his throat.

They follow alongside for several minutes with Rose leaning over the gunwale, admiring the animal. The bear turns to them again, and the Indian in the bow raises his fuke again; a sharp report and water fountains beside the bear's head. The animal thrashes about, throwing blood and spray. A pall of gun smoke drifts over the canoe.

They paddle up to the bear, and the Indian pulls out a knife as long as his forearm from under his jacket. His grinning teeth white in his scarlet face, he leans over the gunwale and saws at the quivering white neck while the water blossoms red.

The sudden violence shocks Rose. She turns toward her father. Lachlan offers her a damp handkerchief.

"You have blood on your cheek," he says. The Indians tie the floating carcass to the canoe and return to their former course.

After a couple of hours of a rhythm under which it is difficult for the passengers to keep awake, they pass a long, flat point and the Europeans are surprised to find themselves in the mouth of a large river. As they nose into the current, they see that countless scores of waterfowl inhabit these marshes: the air is shrill with the whistling of duck wings, and massive flocks of geese rise at their approach and settle in the scrub behind them. Small shorebirds wheel and circle along the shore like a moving shadow.

The bank deepens until they come upon a peeled-log wharf and a long gangway on piles leading from the high shore; the upper edge of a palisade and a tall flagstaff is just visible. The Indians turn toward shore, their keel sliding into the muddy bank.

Rose steps out of the canoe and into the cold, peaty water of the river. She sinks into the mud, feeling it squelch beneath her hide-wrapped feet. Her ankles protest the cramped seating and once on firm shore she bends down and rubs them. Her leather leggings are dark with the river.

Above them, a gull sails on the breeze, dipping and rising, but making no headway. The Highlander hurtles a rock and the gull drifts away, disappearing toward the distant, opposing bank.

Their Indians pull the bear to shore. They squat in the mud beside it, the animal's yellow-white hide now fouled by the slime of the riverbank. They mutter something in their tongue, as if praying; one of them brings out tobacco and offers it to the animal.

"What is this?" Rose asks, pointing.

The officer from the frigate barely glances at the Indians. He is tall and thin, with sparse red hair and a large nose covered with spidery veins. He stands with his hands thrust in his pockets, eyeing the distant palisade with a gloomy look. When he speaks, his Adam's apple seems to struggle for release.

"It is some manner of heathen ritual," he says. "When a Savage kills an animal, he must ask it for forgiveness, or some such rot. Pay them no mind."

"I assume we are at York Fort, Mr. …?" Lachlan trails off.

"Turr. Yes, it is York Fort, and the factor shall be in a hellfire rage at the manner of our arrival. We must get on."

They leave the Indians to their prayers and begin the ascent up the bank. After so many hours cramped aboard the canoe, it proves hard going for all of them but the Highlander, who scrabbles up like a rat on a mooring line. He reaches the top long before the rest and peers down at them with a grin.

"I think there be three lasses following hard on me, nae one lass and two men."

"I say!" Turr replies as he scrambles over the bank, his face red. "You affront me undeservedly, sir. This is a wretched climb."

"Nae affront intended, Mr. Turr."

They follow the path from the gangway to the gates of the fort. After so many weeks at sea, the exercise is hard going for Rose and she breathes heavily, covering her mouth with her hand. They pass a pair of ancient and rusting field pieces overlooking the river. Turr pats one as he passes.

"These would have been fired in honor of our arrival if fate had been kinder to us," he says with a sigh.

A line of clouds, heavy with the threat of rain, hurry from the west as they approach the fort. They quicken their steps. Heaps of garbage are scattered about the stockade and a skinned ox carcass has been dumped just outside the fort gate. Felled by some strange disease, not even the Home Guard has touched it. The smell of carrion and smoke fills the air. A pair of ravens flap away croaking as they approach.

Several tipis squat outside the palisade. Rose points them out to Turr. "The Home Guard," he says with hardly a glance.

"I have heard the term before. What does it mean?"

"It refers to a blackguardly band of thieves and miscreants who, when not thieving, murdering one another or lost in drink, provide the fort with meat, especially in the hungry winter months. I say, it is beginning to rain. We must hurry."

A high stockade of sharpened spruce sunk into the boggy ground surrounds the fort. The main building — known colloquially as "the octagon" — can only be entered through an archway that faces the main gate of the stockade. They approach on a path of rough boards, a bridge over the soft muskeg. A torpid stream runs beneath them, and bugs glide on its slow surface, their long legs dimpling the water. In some places the boards sink into the peat and brown water gurgles up around their feet. As they near the gate, an emaciated cur bolts at them. Turr gives it a resounding kick and it turns away with a yelp.

The Company coat of arms has been painted on the archway of the octagon: *Pro Pelle Cutem*. Lachlan frowns. "'Skin for skin.' Is it not the words of Satan himself, questioning our Lord? 'Skin for skin; yea, all that a man hath, will he give for his life.'"

"I doubt that is the correct interpretation. You are very well acquainted with the Bible, sir. A chaplain, perhaps?"

"No more than all good Christians should be, Mr. Turr."

They follow Turr inside and Rose and Lachlan are surprised that "The Grand Central Station of the North" is such a shoddy affair:

frost has shattered much the stone and brick foundation and the siding is falling off. The archway is warped and twisted, and many of the timbers are cracked. The smell of sewage and rotten garbage is thick inside the walls.

"Like a bit of old Glasgow," the Highlander says, beaming and clapping his hands to his breast. The sound of an organ carries through a wall.

"They will all be in church, I'll wager," Turr says.

Lachlan looks at him with surprise. "You mean it is Sunday?"

"So it would seem. Well, no point in disturbing them. We can find ourselves something to eat. I doubt I have eaten in days."

They find a long, dark mess, with many tables, a stone hearth, and a massive, black iron stove. Turr lights an oil lamp with a coal from the hearth. He disappears for a few minutes and returns with a cut of fresh moose meat wrapped in a cloth. After banking the fire, he rolls pieces of the meat in flour and fries it in a black skillet.

After they have eaten, they lean back in their chairs, listening to the foraging of mice in the ceiling, and feeling more satisfied than they have in a long time. The Highlander leaves them on a quest for drink.

"We best inform someone about those poor folk back on the beach," Lachlan says.

"It can wait," Turr replies. "This is the first I have felt at peace for many days and I intend to enjoy it a little longer. There is time and plenty to send a boat for the others." He settles deeper into his chair and closes his eyes.

Lachlan is about to reply when the cook hurries into the mess and stops, staring at them in amazement.

"Oh, bloody hell," Turr mutters to himself.

Chapter Four

"Damn it, Mr. Turr, this is the worst possible news; it is quite beyond the pale."

"Indeed, Governor."

Robert Semple gets up and begins pacing in his cramped quarters. "There is nothing remaining of the *Intrepid*?"

"There was aught left but jetsam scattered on the beach. And many dead."

"Cigar?"

"Why, yes, sir. My word, where did you come by them?"

"I brought a box with me, in my personal baggage. Contraband or not, a gentleman must have a smoke with his port, and none of your damned trade twist." Both of them know that because of the ever-present danger of fire, smoking in quarters is absolutely forbidden in the fort.

Taking a deep drag of the cigar, Turr looks around. The room has barely enough space for a bed, a washstand, and a desk overflowing with Company Papers and correspondence. Daylight is visible through cracks in the siding where the chinking had fallen away. A black stovepipe passing through the room from below provides the only source of heat in fifty-below weather. He thinks it an exceedingly mean apartment for a man of the stature of a governor of the Hudson's Bay Company's territories in North America, even in the savage wilds of Rupert's Land.

"How many dead?"

"I would expect about half, including most of the crew, oddly enough. I tried to save as many as possible, but in those terrible circumstances there was only so much I could do."

"I'm sure you did all that is expected of a gentleman and more, my good sir, and I shall mention it in my reports. But a nasty business it is. God damn my eyes, how could this happen? Captain Bowers knew the Bay as well as any man."

"I'm really not sure," Turr replies, staring at his hands resting in his lap. Although he is no seaman, he suspects the captain's outrageous drinking played a hand in it. But he is superstitiously reluctant to sully the reputation of a dead man.

Semple looks hard at him. "Tell me what you think, man. Come, come, I must have something to tell Lord Selkirk."

Reluctantly, Turr describes all he can recall: there was a great deal of ice, much more than normal for that time of year. The farther they sailed, the more limited became their options, and eventually they were separated from the *Resolute* and the *Prince of Wales*. Their rudder was taken by a great berg when they turned their stern toward it to flee. After that, it was only a matter of time before the storm grounded the frigate.

"I doubt it will suffice, Mr. Turr," Semple says, tapping his fingers on the arm of his chair. "There will be an accounting."

Turr sighs, the governor's meaning clear enough: blood will be demanded for the loss of the *Intrepid*, and they have one chance to assign blame as far from themselves as possible.

"I supped with the captain that evening and he seemed melancholy to me. Drank three bottles of claret himself with the meal. Perhaps two ... of course, that was some time before the encounter with the berg ..."

Semple takes a deep drag of his cigar and exhales a cloud of smoke. It curls about the room, tendrils pulled through gaps in the walls. "It would be shocking if drink was a factor," he says, unable to suppress the relief in his voice.

"Very shocking indeed, sir."

"Though I am aware of the irony, I believe I should have another drink. More port? Or brandy?"

"Brandy, if you please."

"Capital stuff. It was delivered by long-boat from the *Resolute* — she arrived yesterday, in case you have not heard. As soon as possible, I turned them about, so they and the *Prince of Wales* are wasting valuable time in a fool's errand scouring the coast for you. Joy on your recovery by the way, and may you live long enough to profit by it."

The governor pours the brandy from a cut-glass decanter into two delicate glasses. Turr stares at the burgundy liquid, the sharp smell mixing languidly with the cigar smoke. He tries, and fails, to keep his hand from shaking as he reaches for the glass.

"The factor will be apoplectic when he learns of the *Intrepid*'s fate."

"I have not yet seen him."

"He is on a hunt, I believe. The man wastes far too much time in ridiculous pursuits," Semple pauses, looking into his drink. "You realize the gravity of the situation?"

Turr nods, understanding quite well. After the previous year's debacles, Lord Selkirk is counting on these colonists. His grand plan of building a new settlement in Rupert's Land greatly irritated many powerful men, and the expected assistance from the Company had not materialized. Squabbling and sabotage had been the order of the day, and from their own people! Their enemies would have a great laugh if they knew.

"A dead Highlander is of little use to anyone," Turr acknowledges, "Although the difference may not be as great as one would expect."

Semple does not smile. "Due to Selkirk's madman Macdonell, the Company's situation here has become quite untenable. His pemmican proclamation has roused half the country between here and Pembina against us."

"Pemmican proclamation?"

"Macdonell's ill-conceived device to raise food for the colony. They cannot seem to provide for themselves, no matter how much help and advice are provided. So Macdonell passed a law demanding a tithe of pemmican from anyone passing through the settlement. Naturally, this was deemed intolerable."

Turr cocks at eyebrow at him, tapping his ash on the floor "Nor'westers?" he asks.

"Of course. And now under the tutelage, threats, and subterfuges of those Canadian devils, the Half-breeds are threatening war, and many of the Indians are unwilling to trade with Selkirk's colony or the Company. With the *Intrepid* lost, thousand of pounds of goods are at the bottom of the Bay, not to mention the strong Highland backs imported at great cost."

Turr watches the governor as he gets up and begins to pace in his little room, startling a rat that scurries along a wall. Semple is a small man with a round, boyish face and large, doll-like eyes, and there is an air of brutish arrogance about him, a spoiled and effeminate demeanour that hints at too many nights in gin-soaked drawing rooms and riding high-bred horses across groomed landscapes. No doubt the man is vicious with a rapier and duelling-pistol, but what good that will do him in Rupert's Land, Turr cannot imagine. A damned American as well, and the ink hardly dry on the treaty of Ghent. After the disaster of Macdonell, this is the best that Selkirk can do? It bespoke of nothing but difficult times for the Company on the Bay.

"We will have to let London know," Turr says.

"Indeed. I will request the factor send a man with a packet informing Lord Selkirk in Montreal, but it will be many months before he receives it."

"Assuming no Nor'wester interference, of course."

"Surely they would not dare intercept our correspondences?"

"They would indeed, if they can. They are a thieving, lawless band of cutthroats hardly better than the Savages among whom they drink and fornicate …" There is a sudden commotion below them: shouts and laughter.

"That will be the factor; I must speak with him. No, stay and finish your drink, Mr. Turr; your turn with Himself will arrive soon enough. Enjoy the peace while you may!"

After the governor departs, Turr remains, savouring his brandy, which he refills from the nearby decanter. Soon the oil lamp gutters and goes out; he does not bother getting up to relight it. His cigar ash glows as a perfunctory mote in the darkness.

Would they dare? he thinks. *How naive; of course they would. As we would in our turn. It is war, after all. Nations or Companies, it makes little difference; the terms are the same with no quarter asked or given. It is a struggle where everything — for us and them — is at stake.*

You and I have not been in Rupert's Land very long, governor, but everything I have heard in London indicates a grave situation; after one hundred and fifty years on the Bay, the company is on its knees. The land is a powder keg and Selkirk's goddamned colonists are likely to prove the stray spark that blows us all to hell.

~

The next morning three York boats leave with the tide to pick up the surviving colonists. Rose, standing on the high bank of the river, watches them depart. Her father has left to speak with the factor and she knows that if he discovers her missing from their cabin unaccompanied by an escort, he will likely beat her. But the smell of the tiny, rancid space reminds her too much of the oppressive journey aboard the *Intrepid*, and she longs for cleaner air.

The wind freshens, bringing with it the promise of more rain, but at least it keeps the insects at bay. Her muddy skirts twist about her and she pulls a paisley shawl over her hair. There are few women's clothes at the fort, but the factor had given her what little he could find. Years out of fashion and a trifle too large, but at least they are not a Savage's rags.

At that thought, she sees the Indian's tipis outside the fort. Smoke from muskeg fires peel away from the tops of several of the nearest. Curious, she makes her way toward them, intending to walk past in a manner that would evidence no interest, and yet allow her to see more closely.

As she approaches, shouting breaks from the willows and a boy rushes toward her, pursued by several others. Blood runs into his face. A large rock strikes the back of his head and he tumbles onto the path. The rock-thrower saunters up and picks the bloody stone off the trail. While his fellows laugh and hoot, he brings it down on his enemy's skull again and again, driving the bloody head into the mud.

She yells at them to stop. They ignore her, kicking at the body until the boy who threw the stone begins sawing at the scalp with a long knife. Rose turns and vomits. There is a stirring in the tipi beside her and a man emerges; she recognizes him as the Indian in the canoe who had shot the white bear.

"What you do?" he grumbles, seeing the mess she has made on his home. He stands next to her, and she backs away.

"Please, they have killed someone, you must get help."

The Indian walks over and gives the body a kick. "He is Stone Indian," he says, as if that answer were sufficient.

"But there has been a murder. We must do something."

"He is enemy. Nothing to do. Scalp maybe. You want?" He throws his thumb over his shoulder and grins at her, the youths watching them.

Isqe-sis emerges from the tipi and begins haranguing the man. He tries to argue, but her volume increases until several faces are staring at them from surrounding tipis. Shrugging, he turns and walks away.

"You feel not okay?" Isqe-sis hesitates a moment, thinking. "Rose?" Rose shakes her head, snuffling and holding a handkerchief to her eyes. Isqe-sis guides her into the tent.

"Come sit. You eat?" Isqe-sis indicates a buffalo robe and gives her a bladder of water.

Rose shakes her head. "How did you get here? You were back at the camp ..."

"Come last night. With my brother."

"I see." She takes a heaving breath, blows her nose into a handkerchief. "They killed him. I saw it; he was just a child. You people truly are ... are Savages!"

Isqe-sis looks at her. "Stone Indian are our enemy," she says. "They kill many of us. This one maybe watch us for their warriors, in secret. A danger to us. Perhaps there will be an attack." She pushes a steaming cupful into Rose's hands. As before, she hesitates over the white skin, moving her fingertips over fingers and hand and up the smooth white slope of arm. She sighs and turns away.

Rose shivers at the touch. "But you are supposed to be Christian. How can you kill if this be so?"

Isqe-sis does not suppress her laugh. "Are the English not Christian?" she asks. "Do the English not kill?"

"In my country, the penalty for killing is death."

Isqe-sis laughs again. "Not here. Christian kill. This camp almost empty, White disease kill many this year. Bad axes, bad guns kill some. Many more musket kill *Ayisiniwok*, my people. Death is in the land here. For Christian English, for Christian French, for *Ayisiniwok*, for Stone Indians. Even for girl with hair like falling leaves."

At that, Isqe-sis begins telling Rose about life in Rupert's Land. It is an illuminating experience, and she soon forgets about the body that lies outside, already stiffening and gnawed by dogs. Isqe-sis tells her of growing up in the shadow of the fort; the manner in which the Europeans misuse them, often trading inferior goods for the most prized beaver pelts. Loving between White men and Indian women is very common, and that most of the children that wander about the fort are of mixed blood. *À la façon du pays*, they call it. This had been recently decreed illegal by the Company, as all of these children were morally if not absolutely legally the responsibility of the Company, one it felt loath to carry. Yet such relationships had a long tradition on the Bay and continued unabated, if more discreetly.

The *Ayisiniwok* women are very loyal to their White husbands, but such sentiment is often not returned, and it is common that a trader or employee will return to Scotland or Orkney after their mandatory seven-year residence at the Bay, leaving behind their local wives and children to fend for themselves.

As she listens, Rose finds herself warming to Isqe-sis, and the dignity with which her people endure that which none but the most depraved Orkneyman would countenance; of family, loves, and lives lost by those who traded with the English on the Bay. It had never before occurred to her that the depravity of the poor could be a moral reflection of the powerful.

As Isqe-sis speaks, it becomes Rose's turn to reach out and run a hand along Isqe-sis's honey-coloured arm. Pale skin, wrapped skin, skin hidden from the rare sun was the norm among Rose's people, and the only colour she ever saw among her countrymen was in the faces of the fishermen and the shepherds — people whose skin turned red and purple with the gnawing of the seasons.

Now it is Isqe-sis's turn to blush at the caress; she pulls her arm into her capote and looks down. Her infant mews, and she lifts it to her swollen breast. The crucifix swings free.

Seeing it, Rose asks about her faith, Isqe-sis revealing a deep passion for Christ, and how she hungers to be confessed. Journeys to the isolated Jesuit mission on the Nelson River are sporadic at best, and she suffers greatly during the long intervals in between.

There is a kind of animism to Isqe-sis' faith, a way of looking at Christ that differs from other Christians — Protestants or Catholics. She sees the holy within not just the Body of Christ, but within all creation. The trees, the soil, even for the lowliest of crawling things she feels a religious respect. Rose wonders how her confessors could approve.

When she takes her leave and sees the body in the muddy path, the warmth she shared with Isqe-sis fades. The killing had been too brutal, too sadistic. The dead boy reminds her that even if some of them are ostensibly Christian, she must maintain her guard against the sanguinary aspect of the breed.

⁓

"These people cannot stay, Mr. Turr. We have neither the provisions nor the accommodations to provide for them."

Although his words are flat, inside the factor is fuming. *Selkirk should have known they would not be able to supply his peasants before he arranged to bring them here*, he thinks. *The man seems to believe that Company resources are his to use as he sees fit. A pox on him.*

"I am deeply sorry for their misfortune," he says without the least hint of concern in his voice. "But they must depart as quickly as possible."

They are standing beside the signal cannon at the entrance to the factory. The wind is blowing hard from the northwest and Turr's thin hair flows from his scalp like red smoke. Several ravens are squabbling over the ox carcass behind them.

"They have had a very difficult time," Turr says. "Many have lost family. They will have an even harder go of it to arrive at Red River before winter."

"It is over late to debate the wisdom and ethics of Lord Selkirk's designs," the factor replies. "My order is as firm as my conviction: they must leave tomorrow."

Below them, an Indian pushes off in a canoe. Two men stand on shore playing out a net, which the man ties to several tall poles sunk into the river bottom. The canoe bounces and pitches in a steep chop set up by the wind running against the flood. While struggling with the last of the poles, the canoe suddenly rolls and throws the man into the river. The Indians on shore laugh.

"Have you decided who will guide them?" Turr asks.

"I spoke with Alexander McClure this morning. He is willing to take them on to Red River."

"The Half-caste?"

"He owes the Company a great deal," says the factor, his frown deepening. "Unpaid credit from last year's season; he brought in few furs and of low quality. I did not give him a choice."

"I see. Well, I will speak to the colonists and let them know."

The man in the river grabs the gunwale of his canoe and kicks toward shore. He stands up, shaking off the water while his companions mock him. With a rueful grin, he sits down as a small liquor keg is brought out and passed along.

"Another thing, Mr. Turr: I want you to go with them."

"Eh?"

The factor shoves his hands into his pockets and stares off into the distance. "I am afraid so. I must have a Company man at the settlement to find out what in blazes Macdonell is doing. The rumours are disturbing, and London wants more than just rumours."

The blade of dried grass he had been chewing blows from Turr's lips. Laughter carries from below. "Perhaps you would consider someone else? Someone younger? I had hoped …"

The factor shakes his head. "I need someone I can trust, a man who can give an accurate report. Besides, there is no one else I can spare." He pats the cannon beside him. "God's blood, I would love to fire this. It does a man good to make a great noise and smoke every now and then, eh, Mr. Turr?"

Cecil Turr nods, not trusting his voice. His hands shake. Without taking his leave, he turns away and shuffles back towards the fort.

Rude bastard, thinks the factor, his heat increasing again. He takes several deep breaths then dismisses Turr from his mind. His musings on the joy of cannon fire had reminded him that the supply ships had not yet arrived from their searching for the lost frigate. He swears volubly at the cannon, a stream of blistering invective. Only a factor for a year, and now this. He is sure he will be blamed.

The flood of furs to the Bay has slowed to a trickle despite recent company expansion inland. The widely scattered forts they built at great risk and expense had come to naught; the Nor'westers were always there first, having bullied or bribed the Indians into long-term allegiances. In their arrogance, they even established a post on the Hayes, a mere three-day journey upriver. The Company is on the verge of becoming irrelevant in its own territory, and even if policy is decided in varnished, smoke-filled luxury thousands of miles away, it is the poor bastard on the frontier who will be blamed. *God rot it, it is just not fair.*

Many more Indians have gathered to join the party on the river, and a fuke is let off. The factor jumps. *Damn it to God-rotting hell,* he thinks. *That fucking sod Spencer has traded too much liquor to the Home Guard.* He turns and stomps into the fort. Several colonists are milling about behind the palisade, staring and pointing at the unique things that catch their eye. The chief trader sees the approach of the factor and turns toward him, smiling.

"You can smile all you like, Mr. Spencer, but I find little to be amused about. Your carelessness has roused the Home Guard, and I want those gates locked, *now!*"

∽

Rose sits on her hard bunk, listening to the yowling and gunfire not one hundred feet away. She had been rereading a dog-eared copy of Richard Allestree's *The Whole Duty of Man, Laid Down in a Plain and Familiar Way for the Use of All*, that the Factor had given her. The commotion had started late that afternoon and carried on well past sunset. After the murder of the Indian boy, she had tried to comfort herself with the book, but the frightening whoops and singing kept cutting through her focus. She has never heard such chilling sounds before, and feels afraid and unsafe, emotions becoming all too familiar. They had been given one tallow candle, and its pale light only seems to deepen the shadows.

When the factor offered a private dwelling, she had been delighted that they would have their own space, a wall to put between themselves and the rest of humanity. But with the horrid sounds carrying from the other side of the palisade she finds herself yearning to be again surrounded by her countrymen.

Lachlan sits on a polished section of a log, staring in fascination at the mosquitoes circling him, tiny wings shimmering in the wan candlelight. At the sound of another gunshot, he gets up and peers out the rickety door. A great fire is burning outside the fort, with sparks soaring heavenward to blend with the sharp, cold stars. Through narrow gaps between the palisade poles, he sees shadows of dancing figures cutting across the fire. The air throbs with dark and compelling drumming.

"I dinna much like our position," he remarks. "We are between our friends and whatever *that* is. Good for our friends perhaps, but nae good for us."

Rose turns to her father. She knows that such lapses into his native accent are a sure sign of stress.

"Perhaps we should return to the Great House — what do they call it, the Octagon? The Indian word for it is *Kitzi-waskahikan*."

Lachlan turns to her and smiles. "Ah, lass, you do my heart glad. You have been in the country naught but two days, and already you are learning the Savage's language. Where did you come by the word?"

"I do not recall, father," she says quickly, recalling her illicit liaison with Isqe-sis. "I imagine I must have overheard it."

"Well, I approve," says Lachlan, nodding. "Judging by that bestial noise out there, these people can only be helped by what we can teach them, and in order to teach we must learn their language and their ways."

Rose gets up and takes her father by the hand. Though her face is shadowed and invisible, he looks up at her smile.

"You regret coming here?" she asks.

"No, but I am uncertain. The little I have seen so far falls fair short of what I had imagined. But listen! That racket is moving closer. Let us flee to the Octagon, or whatever you call it. What do the Irish say? Better a good run than a poor stand?"

They abandon the cabin for the brightness and safety of the Great House and its peeling walls. Disturbed by the carryings-on outside the fort, most inhabitants have abandoned their beds and several traders carry loaded muskets.

They enter the main hall where they encounter the chief trader, who is bullied by Rose's father into giving them a tour. They move from one cold room to another, the way announced by a feeble lantern. Rose's skirts stir a dirt floor thick with rat droppings, bones, and other filth as they pass through the chapel, mess, trading hall, and even a magazine, wherein Lachlan thinks it foolish to locate such capricious stores inside the place where so many people lived: one lucky shot from a devil Frenchman would send the whole place to heaven. They finish the tour in the warehouse.

"These are last winter's furs, ready for shipment to England," Spencer says, approaching the massive, iron-clad doors. The lock clacks loudly as he turns the key, the lantern guttering as the great doors are swung open, like the breaching of a tomb. It casts a moving, fitful light onto stacked bales of compressed and dried beaver pelts. The space is close and musty, filled with the stench of hundreds of untanned skins.

"This is a much smaller load than most years," Spencer says, moving closer to Rose. "It's been getting that way for some time. Just a few years ago, this room would not have space for a bleeding mouse; she were jammed so tight with beaver."

"Is it all just one kind of animal?" Lachlan asks, uncomfortable with the clerk's obvious interest in his daughter. "Do you only trade in beaver?"

"Nay," Spencer replies, not taking his eyes off Rose. "There is also marten and mink and bear. Caribou, moose, and buffalo. Anything ye can slit a hide off is in there. Hell, the Savages would skin mosquitoes if we paid 'em for it. But 'tis mostly the bloody beaver."

Lachlan reaches out and fondles the edge of a pelt; it is both crisp and luxuriantly soft at the same time. "Your profanity is unwelcome in the presence of my daughter, Mr. Spencer. However, I find it amazing that the European passion for hats has been responsible for the civilizing of an entire continent."

"I don't know about that, sir, begging your Lordship's pardon," Spencer says with a grin, showing a black mouth largely devoid of teeth. "Civilized, you say, but just outside these walls heathen are murdering heathen tonight. Not much in the way of civilization in these parts."

Lachlan looks at him. "I take your point, but that is why we are here. We will take civilization to the Savages."

Spencer shakes his head, his greasy hair swinging. "Begging your pardon, but you can't civilize 'em any more than you can civilize a hog. They're animals, sure enough. A whip and a brace of pistols and a good, strong wall between you and them is all that's needed to deal with the Savage."

Spencer hides his contempt for the Orkneyman behind his smile. *You don't know,* he thinks. *You're like every other Scottish and English fop that comes here thinking you know the place after a few days, believing you can change things for the good of King, country, and God. Just you wait, Mr. Schoolmaster. Wait 'til you see some of the things I've seen in the years I've been here. Their whelps cut down with axes, the tortures, the killings. Disease burning through the camps, leaving bloated bodies for the ravens to pick at. Starvation waiting in the next valley empty of deer. You think you know, but your safe home is thousands of leagues away, and when you head off up the river, then you will know the meaning of savagery.*

Yes, you will find out, you and your beautiful daughter. More's the pity. Now there's a girl of the likes I ain't set eyes on in many a year. I wonder what she'd feel like under me ...

"Spencer!"

"Aye, what?"

A man hurries into the room, out of breath. "Meeting in the square, pronto — oh, begging your pardon, sor, didn't see thee standing there. Evening, ma'am." He touches his forelock with his finger. "Everyone is expected in the square. The factor wants to give a little speech."

Lachlan inserts himself between his daughter and Spencer, leading her out of the room.

$\sim$

When the Indians started their fire, Declan McCormack stood a little way off, watching. The gates had been locked when he returned to the fort, but although unarmed, he felt unafraid of the carryings-on. The occasion seemed to be the recent arrival of the two missing ships of their Orkney convoy — no speeches, no solemnity, just boisterous drinking and singing and drumming. He had seen wilder carousing in his time, but without the guns. Now he stands in the shadows and relaxes against a tree, feeling an admiration for the Indians, the vigour with which they dance and the exultation of their unashamed bodies. Several men and women sit staring into the fire, their faces shining in the heat, chanting in a high chorus. The wind blows off the river and stirs the flames; sparks swirl about the dancers to be lifted and swept away.

The chanting affects him viscerally, and for a moment he is disturbed by the feelings that bubble up inside him, dark and sexual and as if from a great depth. He turns away from the fire and pisses against a tree; suddenly, laughing Indians surround him. Clapping him hard on the shoulders, they haul him toward the fire. As he enters the ring of yellow light there is a great whoop as several young men jump up and charge. The drums fall silent.

He fells the first one with a solid punch to the jaw, but then they are all over him, like a tide rolling over a sandbar. They pin him to the muskeg as someone yanks off his breeches and jacket. He shouts at them to leave him be, but those wiry arms are far too strong and he cannot move. Soon he is stretched out naked, flushing with shame.

A short and very thin Indian wearing only a hide breechclout walks out of the shadows. His entire body is painted in red ochre, and his face is skull-white. Raven feathers sway from his topknot. His face and ears and arms are adorned in silver jewellery that flashes as he dances; in that light, he looks to Declan like a God. With a great smile, the Indian pulls out a knife half as long as a sword as he kneels over the Highlander. It flashes in the firelight. Declan turns his face away, closing his eyes.

Laughter and the drumming starts again; the hands release him. He leaps up and runs from the fire; in the darkness he cannot see the pine and collides with it, knocking himself unconscious.

Chapter Five

At daylight, a rumour begins through the factory: an Indian woman and her two children have been killed in the night, hacked down by their husband and father. The company surgeon leaves with his assistant to attend. None of the victims are brought into the fort.

"Thank dear God for the walls, or who knows what devilry might have passed here last night," Lachlan says, standing in the yard with the rest of the colonists. It is still early, and the light is low, the expectant hour before dawn. The eastern sky glows red and violent, as if raging over the night's killings. A few scrawny chickens wander the yard: vague, white ghosts in the shadows. A rooster crows. The breeze is cool and whispers of hard days ahead, although it is still high summer.

Turr, standing nearby, bristles at Lachlan's comment. His cheeks are blotchy, and in the dim light his sunken eyes seemed like fly-blown holes. His hair is a barely-discernible orange buzz about his head. He had passed the night in his room commiserating with a vast quantity of trade liquor, to no avail. His problem — being sent away — had not changed in the night, and it feels like little men are hammering on the inside of his skull, seeking a way out.

"God rot the walls," he says, waving a hand at the timbers. "When the Home Guard decide to take York Fort, York Fort is taken, forthwith."

Lachlan stiffens. "Indeed? Then why are the walls there, pray?"

Turr rubs his eyes. "Because better a fool's illusion of security than fear's demoralizing chill."

At that moment, Alexander emerges from the octagon. His gait is an unusual hop-drag, the right limb obviously lame. He is dressed in a rough, buckskin jacket with long tassels and an elaborate blue and white beadwork of flowers embroidered on the chest, arms and back. He wears knee-high moccasins and has a pack slung over his shoulder. In his hand is a carbine and his face is dark. To those watching he looks like a Savage, and a few move away.

"Hard night, Mr. Turr?" he says with a smile, touching his cap as he passes.

"Aye, hard night, all right," a trader says. "Just ask his doxie!" Several Baymen guffaw. Blushing, Rose straightens a crease in her skirt.

"Time to load the boats," Alexander says quietly, looking down, as if informing the grass. "For anyone planning on voyaging to the Forks."

"Who is that?" Lachlan asks. "And where is this 'Forks'?"

"*That* is Alexander McClure, our Half-caste guide for the next two months," says Turr with a scowl. "And you had best learn the land, Mr. Cromarty. The Forks refers to the meeting place of the Red and Assiniboine Rivers. That is the location of Fort Douglas and the heart of Lord Selkirk's settlement, to which we are all headed, God help us. But he'll leave whether we are aboard or not, so I advise everyone to gather their things and follow as quickly as possible."

The colonists hurry down to the river, carrying their meagre possessions. As they pass the gates, Rose edges closer to her father and looks for signs of the trouble from the night before. The ring of a burnt tipi still smolders and many Indians sleep on the ground, apparently where they have fallen. The sharp odour of vomit shadows the reek of the decomposing ox, and they — at least those who still have them — cover their noses with handkerchiefs and hurry past.

A pale form is lying on nearby muskeg and two men approach. A moccasined toe prods it and the figure stirs, groans, and rolls over onto his back. Everyone stops and stares. The man stares up at the brightening sky, as if something of profound import is written in the early red-tinged clouds.

"That's Declan Cormack, by God."

One of the Baymen gets down on a knee; propped by his musket, he says something to the Highlander. Declan seems to consider this for a moment.

Grinning, the men help him pull on his damp clothes and lift him to his feet where he stands gently swaying. His forehead is marked with a great plum of a welt, and his hair, wet with dew, hangs sodden and limp on his face. Bits of moss festoon his head and beard, and he looks as wild as a satyr. He hobbles over to the crowd, where many give him a dark and disapproving look. He walks a little apart as they continue towards the river.

The factor supplied enough provisions to last several weeks, after which they will have to rely on their guide and a hunting party of Home Guard who have been hired to provide for them as they journey south. The factor had coldly explained to a furious Governor Semple that York Fort simply did not possess the resources to provision so many people for such a long journey. The Indians will provide for them, just as they provide for the fort; the colonists would not be in any better or worse position than if they remained on the Bay. Semple does not see it that way, but he has no authority over the factor, and has little choice but to comply.

The Company supplies them with six York boats: flat-bottomed, lapstrake-hulled, double-enders that for more than 150 years had transported passengers and cargo to and from the fort. The boats are more than thirty-six feet long and equipped with many long sweeps and a sail. Alexander divides the colonists to allow four men in each boat, to assist four experienced rowers. There are not enough rowers at York Fort to man each boat with a full complement of seasoned crew; the colonists will have to pick it up as they go along.

The Indians follow in two canoes. Among them, Rose sees Isqe-sis sitting behind her husband, accompanied by two other women and a child. She waves, but Isqe-sis, according to her tradition, ignores her, paddling forward, her baby lashed tightly to her back.

Once the boats are loaded, Governor Semple comes down from the fort. He is dressed in a double-breasted black tailcoat with a knotted burgundy neckcloth and black top hat and white pantaloons tucked into Hessian boots. The Indians watching from the bank are deeply impressed and they point at him, speaking among themselves.

The great man sits in his place in the bow, and, one by one, the boats are pushed from shore. The sweeps dip and the rising sun illuminates the golden water running off the oars as they lift from the river. As the last boat leaves the riverbank, a deep boom echoes from the fort.

"At last, he gets to fire off his damned cannon," Turr says.

As the current takes them, the oarsmen lean into their sweeps; the factory flagstaff soon disappears behind one of the many low islands in the river's mouth. This close to the Bay, the Hayes is broad and slow, the far bank a line in the distance.

The sun shines on the brown water and tossed by a morning zephyr, myriad dazzling jewels appear to spangle its surface. Rose sits in the stern of her boat, just in front of their steersman and Half-caste guide, her father beside her. The women are scattered between their husbands, trying not to get in the way; each stroke of the long sweeps covers a six-foot arc and the rowers must stand to lift the oar and then use their weight to pull as they sit down. The heavy sweeps are thicker than a man's thigh, and although at first the rowing is clumsy and inefficient, the oarsmen soon synchronize themselves, white foam appearing at their bows.

It is hard work for those accustomed to it, and torturous for those who are not. Loaded with crew, passengers, provisions, gear, and equipment destined for the colony, the York boats weigh several tons, and maintaining the speed demanded by their guide requires all of their efforts.

There are many channels and islands to navigate and Alexander keeps the boats in the back eddies whenever possible. He has been up the Hayes many times, and knows the secrets of the river. The tide can be felt many miles upstream, and he knows when to rest and when to row, when to pole and portage, and when to drag the boats with lines from the shore.

Now they must row long and hard to make up for time that will be lost in the portages. If the wind is fair and strong, they will raise their sail and give the oarsmen a rest, though opportunities will be infrequent.

Breakup is in late May and the ice returns early, so dawdling on the river is a luxury they can ill afford. There are miles of northern forest they need to pass through, lands devoid of both men and often the game required to sustain them; although many make the long voyage between York Fort and Red River or Pembina or even further places without mishap, it is neither easy nor taken lightly.

Alexander looks down at the bedraggled peasants they are ferrying to the Forks of the Red and Assiniboine Rivers and knows that by the time they reach the safety of Fort Douglas they will have known hunger, cold, torment by insects, and perhaps much worse.

But now, at the beginning of a new voyage, he feels cheered, as he usually does when setting out. Although recently arrived at York Factory himself, there is little to keep him there, and he is content to turn about and return to the land of his mother.

He reaches into the pocket of his jacket and pulls out dudheen. Cupping his mouth with his free hand, he shouts to the canoes that have pulled far ahead of the York boats. The paddlers in the nearest ease their stroke, and the flotilla of Hudson's Bay craft come upon it and slowly pass by.

As the canoe drifts alongside, McClure hands the pipe to the man in the stern. The Indian is wearing a bent top hat and a scarlet British army uniform, rent and smudged with dirt and smoke, though the bright brass buttons sparkle in the sunshine. A long Hudson's Bay fuke protrudes from between his knees like a phallus.

The Indian drops his paddle and barks something to his wife. She quickly passes him the *wanatoyak* — the slow-burning birch burl stored in a bucket filled with sand. The man dips a twig into the bucket, and, bending forward, blows on it; with his lean hands wrapped around the precious embers, he looks as if praying. Smoke curls from the bucket, and a flame leaps from the dry twig. The Indian thrusts it into Alexander's dudheen and inhales deeply, clouds of smoke billowing. Satisfied, he passes it to Alexander, who receives it with a nod. So inspired, the fellow pulls out his own pipe and lights it as well. He picks up his paddle, and the canoe again pulls forward of the flotilla, the scent of tobacco smoke in its wake.

Drawing deeply, Alexander leans back on his scull and half-closes his eyes.

Rose squirms on the hard thwart, wishing for a cushion. She casts about and her eyes fall again on Alexander. She had watched the interchange between him and the Indian, and as he smokes, she feels resentment at his obvious ease: the oarsmen labour with great effort at their task while this character props himself on his stick, happy as a priest cloistered with a keg of wine. *What makes him so special?*, she wonders. *Steering the boat cannot be that difficult, judging by those closed eyes and that half-smile.*

She considers him: handsome enough face, although she wonders what it looks like beneath all that masking hair. Broad nose, the cheeks lightly corrugated by a distant bout of smallpox. The hulking shoulders and arms of those who used their bodies thoughtlessly, as tools. She had marked his limp, it seeming incongruous with the man's obvious strength.

She knows him, or thinks she does; had met many others of his ilk. Men amazed at their personal powers, believing them to be as astounding to others as themselves. They rejoiced in their skills with pistol and rapier and horse, ludicrously killing each other off for the tiniest affronts. Stupidity is the only thing greater than their self-regard, and this man positively reeks of complacent certainty.

At that moment, Alexander becomes aware of her searching gaze; he stiffens and loses his insouciance. His eyes flick to the horizon. Feeling pleased, Rose turns to her father, who smiles at her and takes her hand in his own. She lifts a dipperful of water from a bucket at her feet and offers it to him.

With the river's high sandy banks shielding the view of the surrounding country, there is little to see as the brigade works its way upriver. It becomes uncomfortably hot, although the bright sun offers a welcome relief from the mosquitoes. Rose leans over the side of the boat, her white fingers trailing in the water, leaving a long, silver ripple. The men's harsh breathing, creak of locks, and the splash of sweeps are the only sounds on the river. She feels bored and lethargic. With a sigh, she settles deeper into the boat.

"You might not want to do that, Miss," Alexander says to her.

"Indeed? Why not?" she replies with what she thinks is just the right degree of haughtiness.

"There are belugas in the river: fierce white whales. Why, they will knock a boat over with one sweep of a giant tail. One might see your finger and think it a tasty tidbit." Rose snatches her hand away; Alexander nods with a grave expression. Unsure if he is making a fool of her, she turns her back on him.

The men row on. Alexander allows a break every two hours, just for the time it takes to smoke a pipe. The Bay men drop their oars, stretch, and sit staring at the river as they puff contentedly;

beside them the Orkneymen and Highlanders sit with their heads hanging, running sweat, aching arms loose in their laps. Although a hard breed, the many weeks at sea as well as the shipwreck have taken their toll.

Around midday, Rose is wondering when they will stop for dinner and have a chance for their private business. Eventually the cook, an Orkneyman — with many years on the Bay, or so he proudly claims to Rose — brings out a canvas sack and removes a stack of dry, brown slabs. He breaks off pieces and hands them around. The oarsmen grab the water ladles and the proffered food, wolfing it. Startled expressions move over many faces and some spit overboard. A host of complaints breaks out.

"Are ye tryin' to poison us?" a man shouts, waving his fist in the cook's face.

"What is it?" Rose asks as a piece is handed to her.

"Pemmican, lass," the subdued cook replies. "Imagine the floorboards of an abattoir mixed with old candle tallow and a few dried berries! Best given to thy worst enemy, but it is the food of the river."

She agrees with him about the taste; the texture is both oily and chalky at the same time. She spits it overboard. The corners of Alexander's mouth twitch.

"It'll come to you all in time," he says. "When you are truly hungry. But you will all be living on it soon enough."

Fortunately, Rose, Lachlan, and Turr are soon invited by the governor to share a shipboard picnic of bread, buffalo tongue, and cheese, for which Rose is extremely grateful.

After dinner they continue rowing and by now Rose's bladder is full to bursting. The oarsmen occasionally stand up and make water over the side, but the needs of the women are forgotten, and she sits on the hard thwart, her knees tight, too embarrassed to mention it. She clenches her hands and focuses her attention on her throbbing bladder, willing it to remain under her control; but with a sudden lurch of the boat, and to her great shame and relief, a warm stream runs down her thighs to combine with the ever-present bilge water at her feet. Her face remains a stony mask she stares forward, the grunting of the men and the creak of the sweeps loud in her ears.

When the sun is low, the boats turn at last toward shore. The long prows slip over the mossy bank as men jump overboard, dragging the boats after them. The passengers, stiff and sore beyond all measure, silently climb out. Some oarsmen can barely move, their women helping them ashore. With an amused glance at the brigade, Alexander grabs his powder horn and Baker carbine from the baggage, and, accompanied by a pair of Indians, moves off along the bank.

The crew starts a fire and unloads provisions, blankets, and oilcloths from the boats. One of the Indian women climbs the steep clay walls, and, attacked by diving swallows, reaches into holes to pull out eggs and young. The bank of the river rises over twenty feet above them and is shadow cool; swarms of mosquitoes materialize, requiring everyone to wrap themselves in blankets and sit close to the smoky fire.

Several shots carry downwind and the colonists huddle closer to each other and wait. The river gurgles and the fire snaps as they stare at the flames in weary silence. The Bay men smoke their pipes and cross their bulging arms and stretch their moccasined feet toward the heat. Laughing among themselves, they trade uncouth yarns while the cook boils water for tea in his great iron pot.

After a long wait, the three men return, carrying several geese. They roughly pluck the birds and pass them over the fire, singeing the remaining feathers that blacken and wither against the white carcasses. They are buried in the fire, and too soon brought back out. Partially cooked and burnt, the carcasses are passed around, and each man cuts away a piece of the fat, dripping flesh with his knife.

Lachlan approaches the captain of the brigade. "Beg pardon, Mr. Turr, but will we not be dining with the governor this evening?"

"I am afraid not, Mr. Cromarty. You see, the governor's private stores are really quite limited. There are also important issues that he and I must discuss this evening regarding the new colony: trivial, administrative issues that are much too dull for entertaining guests at the table. Perhaps when we arrive at Jack River house. The governor is very sorry."

Lachlan returns to sit beside Rose, ignoring her questioning look. A goose carcass is lobbed at him: it tumbles from his hands, falling into the edge of the fire. A neighbour lifts it out, brushes off the ashes and sand, and offers it with a craggy, gap-toothed smile.

He breaks off a leg and hands it to his daughter. They have not eaten in more than eight hours and ignore the sand that crunches in their teeth. The wet, sloppy sound of the ravenous brigade reminds Lachlan of feeding dogs. After they have eaten, they pass a keg of trade liquor around. Turr is insistent that only one tot per man is allowed, against the disappointed protests of several Highlanders, and all of the Indians.

Rose leaves her father resting against a driftwood log and walks down to the river to wash the goose grease from her hands. The cold water does little to clean away the oily film and she rubs them on her dress, which smells of urine. There is no way to bathe in privacy, no way to wash her dress. She has hardly felt so far from even the rudest comforts of civilization. Standing on the edge of the loathsome river with darkness descending in a hellfire of voracious insects, she loses the daylong battle against her tears.

When she at last gathers her composure, she returns to her father to find he has fallen asleep, his blanket having fallen away. His face is grey with a pelt of mosquitoes. She wipes them away, leaving behind thin lines of blood. She pulls up his blanket and covers his face, and it feels as if she is wrapping him in a shroud.

Rolling in her own blanket, Rose lies beside him. There is still an orange glow along the western edge of the river and above her Vega shines brilliant and small. She reaches from her blankets and squinting her eyes, tries to grab it with her thumb and forefinger. Mosquitoes whine about her.

~

The next morning Rose is awakened by a kick. With a groan, she opens her eyes, seeing that most of the camp is up and about, the men loading the boats. Someone must have stepped on her. She pulls her blankets about her shoulders, and shrinks back out of the way. The chill air is damp, and the night's accumulated dew rolls down the oilcloth onto her shoes. Her father is still propped against the log, his eyes bloodshot and heavy. His face glows with red welts.

"Morning, lass," he says. "How do you feel?"

"Sore. I must have slept on a rock." She looks at the bustle around her. "Are we leaving so soon?"

Lachlan nods. The sun has not yet climbed the bank and the river is still veiled, mist climbing out of the valley and glowing in the morning rays high above them. With a painful popping of joints, Rose rises to her feet, depressed at the thought of yet another day jammed into the uncomfortable, crowded boat. She walks to the riverside and bends over; her hair, matted and tangled with dry grass, haloes her face. Her cheek is muddy, forehead spangled by many insect welts. Furious, she splashes her image away.

She realizes that if she is to spend another day in the damned boat, she must be prepared this time. She needs to make water and move her bowels, and requires privacy to do so. Without a word, she walks away down the river.

Evidenced by the fly-crusted piles, others had made good use of the cover of darkness the previous night, something she will have to remember. The river is maddeningly straight and without obstruction, and when the camp is far behind, she comes upon a slab of granite protruding into the river — at last something between her and prying eyes.

When her toilet is finished, she feels better for her cleverness. She pulls her dress over her shoulders and steps out of her shift. Moving into the water she gasps, and her skin feels as if on fire from the cold. Her toes dig into the soft bottom and she wraps her arms about herself. At each step, the river deepens and she rolls onto her back; the twin lines of her thighs stretch out before her, dipping and rising as she kicks. Her belly and breasts are round, pink islands, the nipples tight knots.

As Rose drifts on the cold water, she turns her face to the morning sun, allowing its light and the river's current to wash away her fear and pain. Soon she begins to shiver and becomes aware of the increasing distance between her and camp; effortlessly she rolls onto her belly and swims back.

Rose is a strong swimmer and quickly finds her private spot beside the rock. In the shallows she grinds her dress into the sand, rolling it and squeezing it. When she is satisfied it is clean, she prepares to spread it on the rock, and finds the Half-caste squatting up there like a great toad, a grass stem in his mouth, his rifle resting on his knees. He is not looking at her, just gazing off into the distance. She grabs a large stone from the river's edge and hurls it at him, hitting him just over his left ear. With a *whoof*, he vanishes from sight.

She flings on her wet dress and peers around the rock. He is lying spread-eagled on the beach, blood running from his head, and his right foot waving in the water. Lifting the hem of her dress, she steps over him and runs down the beach to the camp.

The men are very angry, and shout at her.

"It's aboot bloody time ye got here, we bin waiting half the bloody morning!" yells the steersman for one of the boats.

"Get away!" Lachlan says, pushing the man back. He turns to his daughter. "Where have you been, Rose? We have been calling this past hour. Mr. McClure went looking for you. He said it's very dangerous to wander off by yourself."

Rose drops her eyes. "Mr. McClure? I … he was watching me. I hit him with a rock."

They find him propped against the boulder, dazed and holding a handkerchief against his head. The Bay men roar with laughter.

"Better watch out, she's got a mean arm that "un."

"Aye, but only when in *love*."

"Don't know as I want to be loved that way. Me head ain't that hard!"

"Please accept my apologies, Mr. McClure," Rose tells Alexander as his head is bandaged with strips of linen. "I was unaware that your presence was due to concern over my welfare. But you certainly should have announced yourself."

Alexander looks at her, and, to her surprise, begins to blush. "I did not know you were there when I climbed up the rock. The view was as startling to me as it was to you, Miss. I was wondering how to sneak away without being seen when you clipped me with your stone." A faint smile crosses his lips. "Like bloody David and Goliath, begging your pardon."

It is Rose's turn to blush. She reaches up and touches his bandage. "I don't accept that kind of behaviour from any man, Mr. McClure …"

"Call me Alexander, Miss. Now that we are so acquainted."

"All right, Alexander. I hope there are no hard feelings."

"None at all …"

"'Ard feelin's right 'ere," a man says as he walks past, grabbing at his crotch. Several others snicker.

"I beg your pardon?" Rose asks. The colour in her cheeks rises again.

"None at all," Alexander repeats, having missed the insult.

He stands again in the stern of their boat with the men at the oars and Turr sitting in the bow like a gnarled figurehead. As soon as they leave shore, Alexander drops his scull and draws out a bag from beneath his jacket.

"I forgot this," he says to Rose, pulling out some tobacco and a coin that he drops into the river. Seeing her look, he shrugs. "Always a good idea to give thanks at the beginning of a voyage. For good luck."

"I imagine prayer would work better, Mr. McClure."

"Alexander," he replies. "I think it is prayer. What else could you call it?"

Lachlan frowns. "It strikes me a heathen ritual. We observed many such superstitious gestures aboard the *Intrepid*, and I did what I could to put a halt to it. One would expect that Christians would know better."

"Come father, you must not speak like this to Alexander; you are not a schoolmaster here."

"Hush, daughter, *you* will not speak thus to me," Lachlan says to Rose, his voice lowering. He turns towards Alexander. "Excuse me if I seem rather over-pious, Mr. McClure. I suppose I still yearn for a room filled with scholars."

"No offense at all, Mr. Cromarty. We seldom hear the words of God preached in Rupert's Land; there are few priests, and none west of Albany Factory. You will find our religion is apt to be rather slipshod, I'm afraid." As he speaks, Alexander marks the exchange between the Orkneyman and his daughter, and wonders what it means.

The day carries on much the same as the previous, with the unrelenting squeak and splash of the sweeps, the weary grunts of men. Alexander leaning on his scull, smoking his pipe and staring at the river with his eyes half closed as if lost in some distant dream. Sometimes they are at the head of the brigade, sometimes at the rear; often a canoe drifts alongside, Alexander talking with the Indians about hunting and the weather and furs, their conversation drifting between Swampy Cree and English. The Indians are ill at ease; despite the geese they had shot, there has been little sign of any other game. They drag baited hooks and occasionally catch a pike or walleye, but even the fishing is not what it should be. So it is with great excitement when they emerge from the lee of an island to find several large animals fording the river.

"Ituk, Ituk," the Indians shout. Rows of enormous antlers move along the surface of the water, like a raft of floating willows. Black backs and snouts shine wetly; one by one, the animals pull themselves from the river, shake water off in a scintillating corona, and climb the slippery bank. All watching think them magnificent, and in a few moments, the animals vanish onto the tundra, leaving behind a churned-up cutting in the riverbank.

Both canoes pull alongside, and the Indians begin an excited discussion with Alexander. In the end, it is reluctantly decided that after the day's slow start and the necessity for stopping for the ladies, the need of which Rose had communicated to her father, who had passed it to Alexander, to the enormous gratitude of all the women, they cannot afford the time it will take to hunt and butcher, and so they row on. As Alexander reassures them, each day is a new one; each turn of the river, a new hope.

As they leave the coastal lowlands behind, emaciated spruce, cottonwoods, and the occasional jack pine begin crowding the river's edge. They had heard so much about the Northern forests that their first few days of wizened scrub and flat, monotonous muskeg had been a disappointment.

The bank is cut deeper now, and the trees along the upper edge have tumbled into the water. The effect is rather claustrophobic with the high walls and narrowing of the river. Down inside this small arterial cut the breeze is stifled, biting flies and mosquitoes tormenting them. Men's arms run with sweat, and the women dip their scarves in the river.

As the shadows lengthen, they scour the shore for a landing in that great wall of alluvial silt. After a long search, they find a promising beach and pull wearily ashore. The cooking fire is started and tea made, but this time there is no fresh meat. Rose declines the offer of pemmican; she is not that hungry, at least not yet. Supper is quick and subdued. Tobacco smoke swirls as everyone settles in to await the coming of night.

Rose feels a need to stretch her legs. Lachlan insists that he accompany her, and, with a shrug, she turns away and climbs the bank, the eyes of all the brigade upon her. It is a stiff climb, and her legs welcome the chance for movement. Once she has crested the bank, she does not wait for her father — who is grumbling something about precocious sin in daughters — and walks away from the wall of riparian trees onto the open tundra. She faces the westering sun, and yet the greater part of her traces her shadow to the east, back to her homeland.

More water than earth, it is as if the ground itself burns, reflecting the sky's fire in an endless succession of pools and marshes and fens that weave through the spongy muskeg. Every step sinks into the mossy ground. Here and there the odd island of spruce, blasted by wind and frost, struggles for life in the frozen peat. To her the land seems to continue forever, without rise or feature, just carrying on into infinity of green and red and gold and reflecting water.

The sun slips under the night-covers of horizon, and the glowing tundra wraps itself in the diminished shades of twilight. In the nearest pool, she sees the faint stars of Pegasus and looks up to see the Great Square swinging above her. There is no twilight song of birds, no ringing of bells as the cattle return to the barns, hooves clattering on cobbles. It is if the land is drained of all sound, all life.

As when she stood on the shores of Hudson's Bay, she feels again the flood of loneliness. A land so empty and dreary, yet brazen in its bold displays of fierce colour. As if in a fury against its own emptiness.

She hears the squish of his shoes long before he stands beside her. He puts his arm over her shoulders; almost imperceptibly, she shrinks from him.

The two figures stand at the edge of the great barrens, small and alone, like shipwrecked survivors staring in vain for a rescue that never comes, with long shadows reaching into a distant and almost irrelevant past.

Lachlan removes his sweaty cap and waves it at the cloud of mosquitoes enveloping him. He takes a deep breath and looks around. Never had he seen such a country like this, never read a description that could prepare him for it — vaster and more impossible than he could ever imagined. He swings his arm in a futile and empty attempt to encompass it; as he does, he realizes his folly and his arm drops, words dying on his lips.

"It's so empty — a wasteland," Rose suggests in a quiet voice.

"It is not all like this," Lachlan says. "We are on the Northern wilderness. The place called the Forks is different." At that, his mind's eye fills with thoughts of rolling hills with grass knee deep, of broad rivers, and soil black and deep. A land green and warm and rich that puts the very best of Orkney to shame. Good land is the foundation of civilization; poor land the wounded heart of poverty. "I look to dear Orkney and see how many struggle to draw a living from our miserly soils, the want so great because the land is niggardly. Rich land creates a rich people, and we shall be there to see the new beginnings of a wealth scarce known before, and a new civilization. When we arrive you shall see, my daughter; you will behold a light in the heart of a dark country. The thought stirs me so."

"You speak of a lot of new, Father, and yet so far all I have seen is the banality of men, the violence, fear, and toil."

"Ah, but we are not there yet."

"Indeed, but the farther we go, the darker it becomes. I cannot see this light of which you speak. I saw a shadow at the Bay, and the light grows dimmer the farther west we travel. When will we arrive at this dark and promised land, and how shall we see without light when we arrive?"

"Soon, my love, soon, and we shall put our faith in God to provide the light we need. It has always been so, has it not? But let us speak no more of it. I am being consumed alive by these little demons, and I have no wish to be carried away by wolves. Let us return to the fire."

~

The next morning the air is cold and damp, the valley filled with mist. The men return the boats to the endless river. The sweeps take up their dirge, sounding even louder in the cold air.

Soon they pass the confluence of another waterway, seen only as a dark gap in the fog; Alexander identifies it as the mouth of the God's River. Keeping to the nearer shore, they continue up the Hayes, which becomes narrower and shallower. The rhythm of the sweeps increases, the creaking louder, the rasping of breath harsher. Blisters erupt on dripping, knotted palms. But still their progress declines.

After a few hours, the fog burns away, and the river turns fast and stony; the brigade lands. Breakfast is the only break in the day's work. They bring supplies ashore and start a fire. Rose takes her ration of dried buffalo tongue, biscuit, and a mug of weak tea, and, as her father converses with Cecile Turr, she sneaks away to breakfast alone, ignoring Alexander's warnings and Lachlan's order to stay within view of the camp.

As when bedridden, Rose chafes under the constant gaze of others. Not all of the looks given her are respectable or even remotely polite. Many are overtly lustful, and a few of the burly Baymen have even made crude advances when her father's attention was elsewhere.

Through secrecy and deception, she had once made a game of observing others, but now she is the naked one, the object of strangers' desires. She can feel their eyes on her, especially at night, reflected in the evening fire. Ordinarily she would have chosen one — yes, even one of these beasts — to satisfy a curiosity. But that required her to be in charge, to be able to appear and vanish at will. But now she is powerless, dependent, and even worse, vulnerable. Not that she is completely helpless. Rose knows men and what they are capable of, knows that they always show intent long before they act, and so she keeps a dirk under the waist of her shift. More than once she has pulled it out and waved it under shocked eyes.

But this is no bedroom above a tavern or hall, with civilization and all its constraints ready to be summoned at will; here the pillory and gallows do not rule.

Seeing the lack of civilization in those dark eyes, she knows that only a ragged hierarchy and authority protects her from their gnarled hands and ghastly breath. How slim is the veil separating her from them, and she feels it weakening. The farther from York Fort they travel, the more the wilderness creeps aboard the boats while the fear of God and master fades from their hearts. She sees it slipping already: commands are more forceful, responses slower and more reluctant. Wry looks common. How thin must the barrier be by the time they reach the Forks?

She sits on a rock and watches the wild river sliding from the hidden continent to the sea. Although she is utterly weary of the river, from shore it still reflects a wild, secret beauty. She wonders what mysteries it carries; what it has seen. As she dips her feet, she is certain that murder has occurred along its length, and it whispers to her of dire deeds and secrets and fear. It is wild and furious, rumbling and roaring in cataracts and boiling spume. A cold breath rises from the river and mist fills the air, rainbowing in the morning sun.

She wonders how they are going to continue; it seems obvious that further navigation upriver is impossible. Bending, she dips her tin cup into the river; it feels like a religious rite to taste the water, to taste the lifeblood of the secret land that she is destined to make her own.

She senses a presence behind her and whirls, dropping the cup with a clatter on the rocks.

Declan Cormack stands leaning against a tree, watching her, arms crossed against his chest. Like a secret or something precious hides there. His curly dark hair rests on his shoulders and his mouth twists in a grin. His body radiates a conscious attempt at arrogance.

"You startled me," Rose says. She had forgotten about the Highlander who had accompanied them from the Indians' camp. She notes that his peasant clothes have been replaced with Savage leggings and a stained deer-hide shirt. His legs are too short for the barrel girth of the rest of him; whatever else he might be, he is no runner.

"I beg your pardon," Declan replies with his strong, Highland burr in a tone on the edge of rudeness. He moves toward her. "But it be dangerous for anyone to be on their own, much less a lass. If the Savages don't carry you off, fierce beasts surely will."

"I thank you for your concern, Mr. Cormack, but I am sure I will be fine." She moves slowly away from the water, her hand going to her waist.

"I am not sure of that at all, Miss, nor is your father."

"I wish to be alone and think for a while."

"'Tis a crowded life, is it not? I can't remember the last time I spent a few hours alone with my thoughts. There's always someone poking and prying about; it is enough to make a man lose his wits." He crouches down and looks out at the river. "Very pretty, is it not?"

She looks over the water. "Yes. We have nothing so wild where I come from."

"There are many such rivers in the Highlands. The difference is a man knows where it comes from and where it goes. This," — he waves a hand at the river — "is a mystery to me."

He stares in silence for a while, Rose watching him. Everything she sees speaks of peasant: the fingers sausage-thick, the rough clothing, the broad, stumpy body. A man who laboured all day, slept on a straw bed, woke to labour some more. A purposeless existence, she had always thought when viewing peasant life from afar. But watching those blue eyes staring over the river, she sees something new: a fierce yearning and pride rather than the flat gaze of despair and acceptance apparent in the other colonists. As he squats there, it as if she is seeing a part of the earth itself, as if he is made from stone. He appears immutable to her, and she wonders what force could possibly have shifted him from his native lands?

Shaking his head, Declan looks down and spies the lichen on the rock at his feet; he lifts it up to show her. *Tripe de roche,* he says. "Our Savage friends have told me that this is eaten in times of hunger. It will keep starvation at bay, for a little while."

"Do you think we shall ever be in need of such food, Mr. Cormack?"

"Who can know what waits for us?"

"God knows. But what do you hope for?"

Declan looks up the river. "An opportunity for a man to make something of himself," he says.

"So you have the same dream as my father, that farming in the new land will be the start of something unique?"

"Nay. I will not farm."

"Was that not the purpose in coming here? I beg your pardon, but I thought everyone destined for the Forks had been engage to farm the lands."

Declan shakes his head and turns away from her. "I'll not farm," he says. "Digging in the soil with bare hands for what? The lairds throw you aside like a trespassing animal, never mind that your family has crofted that bit of Highland soil since long before this laird were whelped. Your love and sweat goes into the land and even in the best years, it gives back barely enough to pay your rent and feed the bairns and plant for next year. There is more a man can do; there are more things for a man willing to see further. Let small men dig for roots and husband cattle." He turns to her with a smile. "I have other plans."

"I see. And what might they be, my good sir?"

Declan gives her a thoughtful look. "We shall have to see won't we, Miss Cromarty? Yes, we shall see. But it best we headed back, these rogues don't take kindly to stragglers."

"I think you are somewhat of a rogue yourself, sir,"

"Lies, spread by my enemies," Declan says, looking pleased.

Rose hesitates, and accepts the proffered arm. She feels its girth beneath its wrap and knows the man possesses a tremendous strength. "Thank you. On the contrary, one might mistake you for a gentleman, Mr. Cormack," says Rose in a mocking tone.

"There be no call for insulting me," he replies.

As they enter the camp, several people are lounging, smoking their pipes and taking whatever pleasure presents itself before the next leg of the journey. Some stare, including her father and Alexander. A few pointed snickers.

Lachlan lowers his eyes on her; Rose sees the cold, hard light in them. "I thought I had made myself clear about your wandering," he says to her.

She waits for the inevitable punishment, but then with a thrill realizes that without a wall, that lacking their normal social context, he is essentially powerless. He would never cane her in public. The thought makes her giddy.

"Do not fret so, Father. Mr. Cormack felt concerned for my well-being, and insisted I return. There seems to be so much worry over my welfare one would believe this to be a brigade of old aunts!"

Lachlan stiffens. "Oh, indeed? Yet as your caution seems wanting these days I make my desire clearer: as of this moment you are forbidden to leave the camp. I am obliged to you for escorting her, Mr. Cormack." Declan touches his forehead with a finger and walks away.

~

After breakfast, the boats prepare for climbing the rapids. The "toffs" and a few infirm colonists are allowed to stay aboard while the Baymen line them up the cataracts. They fasten stout ropes to the prows of the boats, and the men on shore drag them upstream against the onrushing flow of water, while the rest of the peasants trundle behind them as best that can, burdened with as much gear as they could carry. The banks here are almost vertical and quite treacherous, while the level spots are choked with briars and willows. In some places, the men literally cling to the face of the bank, their feet digging into the soft soil, the ropes flung over their shoulders and threatening to pull them into the tormented river.

Rose thinks the experience exciting; the water roars and hisses about them, splashing the boat's occupants with icy water as the vessel pitches and twists and jerks in the current like a hooked salmon. Declan kneels in the prow — feigning a twisted ankle and

Turr having long since surrendered this damp spot — raising his fists and crowing like a chanticleer, the spray flying against his face.

Progress upstream is slow, but they are closing in on the end of the rapids when a lineman for the lead boat slips and takes down the man following close behind him. They both lose their ropes. The remaining men are suddenly burdened by the increased weight; they hang on valiantly, but are dragged back by the mass of boat, passengers, and stores; backs arch and knotted muscles grip at the cutting lines, quivering legs dig deeper and deeper furrows into the squelching soil. In danger of at last being pulled into the river, they abandon their lines with a shout of warning.

The runaway boat hurls downriver, her passengers slumped and prepared for the worst. Lachlan barely has time to grab his daughter before the collision, the sharp stern puncturing their bow and jamming fast into the planks. Jumping clear, Declan hovers in midair, balances for an agonizing minute, and rolls over the gunwale into the foaming water.

The shock of cold recalls the terror aboard the *Intrepid*. He fights for the surface, his head reeling. His flailing hand finds the gunwale. He yanks himself as far out of the water as possible. The current is too strong. He cannot haul himself back aboard. On shore, the weight of the two boats overwhelms the remaining linemen, and they are surrendered to the river.

Several hands grip Declan, but rock after rock collides against his legs. The river pulls him away, his cold, wet weight too much for those who hold him. Before others can move forward to help, he is knocked from their grasp. His wide eyes are an accusation as he falls below the surface.

The roar of the river mutes to a visceral gurgle and rumble in his ears. Dim shapes of rocks slip past in the tea-coloured water. He rolls along and kicks against the river bottom, trying in vain to find footing, the current repeatedly dislodging him. Disoriented and unable to find the surface, his lungs feel like they will burst.

Lights surround him like luminous smolts. He hears voices; his perception begins to recede and shrink, like a collapsing tunnel. A sob, an ineffectual bubble wobbles to the surface.

As the dim shape of the Highlander drifts past, Alexander reaches out, grabs him by the hair, and wrenches him to the surface; the head breaks free with a heaving inrush of air.

But Declan's weight is enormous and threatens to pull them both away; Alexander shouts at the others for help. They grab onto him as he reaches over with both arms and drags the Highlander aboard. Declan collapses in the bilge, coughing and spluttering.

They are jammed between the runaway boat and a large rock, listing at a sharp angle to the water; spray douses them while water is pouring in through the shattered bow. Soon they will swamp and pitch over.

"What must we do?" Lachlan shouts to Alexander over the thunder of water.

"Everyone into the other boat!" Alexander replies. The women are led forward, and the men help them step over the shuddering gunwale. Soon everyone is trans-shipped except Declan and Alexander, who lifts Declan from the bilge and half-drags him forward. The Highlander's arm dangles at a strange angle. Several hands help pull him across.

Alone, Alexander considers the bales of trade goods and bags of provisions surrounding him. Grabbing a bag of pemmican and his Baker carbine, he jumps off the sinking craft.

With the change in weight, the boats shift and begin rotating. Alexander rushes to the stern, pushing aside the colonists. Just as he picks up the scull, the boats break free again and hurl downstream.

The two vessels are still jammed together, and the offset drag fights with him, trying to turn them sideways to the current. They collide into rock after rock, their prow pushed skyward before sliding over and down and into the next rapid.

"Get that fucking boat off!" Alexander hollers.

Men struggle to obey, but the pressure of the water is too great. An axe works its way forward from hand to hand until it reaches the bow. A man chops at the pointed stern of the offending craft as they bound and leap and twist their way through the rapids. The *chunk-chunk* of his axe and his prayers are swallowed by the thunder of the water; he is veiled in flung spray and mist.

Alexander knows when the man has succeeded when they abruptly swing in line with the current. The abandoned boat strikes a rock broadside and leaps skyward; it twists and rolls, grey belly shining, and falls upside down in the water like a harpooned whale. Packages and bales fly about them.

"Row, you sons of dogs, row for your lives!" Alexander shouts. The men grab the sweeps and run them with a clatter into the locks.

Rowing is nearly impossible with the current and protruding rocks and shallows, and they are constantly knocked off-stride when someone jams his oar or skips it uselessly across the face of a boulder.

A sweep jams, and it rips from the lock and the rower's grasp, hurling across the deck as the boat rushes downstream.

Lachlan flings himself on top of Rose. The oar tears the back of his frock coat as it hurls past. Alexander jumps down just in time as it whips over him. He turns and stares in bewilderment as the oar disappears astern, poised quivering over the surface of the frothing and foaming river.

But they are at the bottom of the rapids, slowly drifting to shore. Men are shouting and weeping; their wives have fallen overboard, vanishing into the river.

Chapter Six

They gather what they can of the spilled gear and retrieve the damaged boat from under the tangled branches of a cottonwood that had fallen into the river. Although a few planks are cracked and sprung, the vessel is still serviceable and Baymen paddle it back to the foot of the rapids and re-stow it with salvaged goods.

Declan's arm is broken and will need attending before he can go any further. Two men set out in a boat to look for the bodies of the missing women, while Alexander and the Indian Iskoyaskweyau — Isqe-sis's husband — minister to the injured. Turr has a small amount of laudanum, and hands a tot to Declan to sip.

Hours pass before the searchers return without seeing a trace of the lost women. The Orkneymen wish to continue searching — at the very least to retrieve the bodies — and the women's husbands are adamant that they will not leave without them.

But their guide is impatient; they have already lost much of the day and have been swept back almost to the campsite of the previous night. The White Mud portage is still ahead, and it will take many hours to get the boats and gear through, which means carrying long past nightfall.

The steersman, from a boat that had successfully climbed the rapids ahead of them, returns along the riverbank, and they hold a council. Many are anxious to carry on, some demand to stay, and the Baymen dismiss it all with a shrug, sitting on the gunwales smoking their pipes.

After much argument, they decide that the boats already above the rapids will carry on upriver, while the rest of them search for the missing women for at least the remainder of the day. They will have to row that much harder the next several days and catch up to the brigade at Swampy or Knee Lake.

There is little time to decide, and Lachlan informs Rose that they will stick with their guide. Declan is unable to make the climb on shore and Cecile Turr is adamant that his heart is not up to such an effort, and God rot it, a gentleman does not scrabble like a goat along cliff faces and mud banks. But some of the passengers from Alexander's boat will not remain behind, and these are allowed to go with the steersman and carry on with the boats waiting upstream.

It is with heavy hearts that those remaining behind watch their compatriots disappear into the willows.

"Damn my eyes, I do not think much of this, Mr. McClure," Lachlan says with a frown. "Dividing the brigade — is this wise?"

Alexander looks down river. He can't agree with the Orkneyman more, but what the hell can he do? A widower sits on the edge of the river with his head in his hands, the other behind him, weeping like a child. He shakes his head, unable to abandon them to grieve themselves into their own graves, nor to force them at gunpoint to follow. There are enough experienced men in the other boats to temporarily lead their part of the brigade. Choice is a luxury they do not have. Not for the first time, he curses the factor for burdening him with the colonists. His heart yearns to be free again: drinking, brawling, and hunting buffalo on the open prairie.

"Their wives are here somewhere, and so we must search, for whatever ease to their hearts such effort will provide," he says to Lachlan. *And to what fate awaits the rest of us? Christ only knows,* he thinks.

They search several miles down the western shore while the boat explores pools and backwaters and the far bank. A blue shawl is found slowly rotating in a whirlpool, but nothing else. Night approaches and Alexander calls off the search.

They sit in the smoke of their fire; no one has much of a mind for eating and not even the indomitable Declan can lift his sprits above the damp misery of the camp. A widower lies rolled in a blanket like a shrouded corpse while another sits staring in silence at the river, as if his gaze could release his woman from its clouded depths.

"I think we can all use a drink," say Turr, retrieving the rum keg. This time all offer their tin cups, and he pours a double ration for the two men waiting by the river.

Rose sits beside her father, her head resting on his shoulder, staring into the fire. She thinks about their hearth in Stromness, the warmth of their cottage on the Ness, overlooking the harbour. Their cat would be on the rug, her purring a gentle counterpoint to the whisper of the peat flames.

The wind along the river picks up, and the trees in the darkness above them begin shushing. A few falling leaves flash across the firelight, golden and flickering like tiny angels.

Alexander lifts his carbine and walks into the darkness. Frowning, Rose turns to her father, but he is fast asleep, his lips slightly parted. His face is closed, heavy with age and weariness. She hopes the dream he walks within is a pleasant one as she pulls the old blanket up and over his shoulders.

Looking around to see that no one is watching her, she follows after her guide. She hears the voice of the river; it has changed for her that day, seeming more menacing. Water can wash away sins and pain, but can also inflict great suffering. She has read of the Mother River of India, the Ganges, and sees the Hayes as also carrying secrets and dread and powers beyond what ordinary men are allowed to comprehend. A holy river washing away the dead, returning them by secret ways to their own country. Maybe they truly are trespassers and the Hayes is cleansing the land of them. She wonders how many other souls lay entombed in her silt, waiting for judgment.

She turns to see how far she has gone; the fire is a distant orange spark surrounded by black forest and a glowing night sky filled with wind-blown stars reflecting in the smooth breast of the Hayes. She hesitates, remembering her father's command.

"Why are you here?" demands a voice from the darkness, startling her.

"To see what might be found," she replies, willing her voice to be strong.

"But it is dangerous."

"If such is the price of knowledge, I am willing to pay."

"Aye, but maybe you have not yet answered for the full toll." But the voice is that of Alexander. "Why do you follow?" he asks.

"For the same reason you once followed me."

"You wish for a glimpse of forbidden beauty?"

"Indeed not. Although in this land, I would give much for even a trifle of loveliness. Pray, where are you? I cannot see anything in this wretched night."

"Over here. Sitting like a foolish squirrel on a log, chattering at passers-by."

As she approaches, she sees the dark form, a shadow against the night, a shine reflecting on his cheek.

"You weep?" she asks softly.

He does not answer, just pulls his knees up and rests his chin upon them. Rose sits beside him — close, but not overly so. She picks up a leaf and twirls it between two fingers. The wind sighs over the surface of the river.

"There is no blame spoken by anyone," she says.

"I am guide and master of this brigade."

"But you are not master of fate. And the One who is would feign have you usurp His role."

Alexander looks at her, but cannot see her clearly. But then the moon escapes from the wind-blown trees, and her silhouette emerges sharp against the silver glow. He feels the heat of her body, the sound of her breath. He frowns, curls his toes in his moccasins, feeling them pop and snap. A sudden urge compels him to reach out and lay his hand on the back of her neck where a few loose hairs dance in the moonlight.

He remembers the first night he saw her: the Indians were raising hell, and she had wandered into the main hall, looking scared and angry and defiant. Her hands gripped one another, as if she were afraid that she would strike someone, perhaps her father, hovering over her as if he were guarding the Royal Jewels. He had brought her out from Scotland, had these dreams of a new land. Like all the rest, he did not understand that the only land is the one you carried inside yourself, carried *in here*. The rest is just geography.

They are always the same, believing that the new must be better than the old. But they bring the old with them, so find it where they arrive, and blame it on the land, the Indians, the Company.

"I see you do not believe me," Rose says. "It is more manly to suffer, no doubt."

"People have died here. And I am responsible."

She moves against him now, her hip pressing against his. He can feel the heat in his face.

"You are responsible for bringing us to the settlement as best as you may. You are our guide. People have died on the river before, and more will do so in the future, but that is not in your hands."

"How do you know this?"

Rose looks out over the water. "I can feel it, Alexander. The river whispers to me; she mourns those spirits that she carries in her bosom. Look there in the water — see the lights of the dead?"

"But those are just reflections … stars …"

"They are just stars, and a man is but a man, and God is … what? There are more things in heaven and earth, Alexander."

"I do not understand."

Rose smiles to herself and takes his hand. "Perhaps I will teach you."

There is a crack of a breaking twig. Alexander whirls, pushing Rose aside, and grabbing his carbine. He cocks the hammer and levels it.

"Who comes? Speak, while you still have a head to do so!"

A shadow moves between them and the distant fire. "Put down your gun, Mr. McClure, afore you hurt yourself. Indeed, I think you have forgotten the ramrod in the barrel. It is myself, Declan."

"Declan? Why are you skulking there?"

"I skulk not. I seek the lady, Miss Cromarty."

"I am here, Mr. Cormack."

The shadow stops. "Miss Cromarty?" he says, surprised. "Your father awakened without your presence to comfort him. He is wroth."

"If it isn't the most confounded nuisance — will you people not leave me be?"

"It is nae safe …"

"She is indeed safe, Highlander, as you can plainly see." Alexander steps forward. He does not lower the gun.

Declan pushes the barrel aside; Alexander sees the flash of polished metal. "Drop the knife! By Christ, I'll blow you to hell!"

"I'll see thee and thy mother there first," Declan says. "But there be nae threat here."

"Then why approach a man in the dark with drawn blade?"

"As I spoke to the lady, it be dangerous in these wild lands."

"For God's sake, Alexander, put away your weapon. He means no harm."

"Harm does not always reveal itself, not at first," Alexander replies, lowering the gun.

"If I bore you ill will, you would already know it, by Christ."

"Oh, God rot you both," Rose says. "I am leaving, and do not either of you follow me!" She jumps off the log and hurries back towards the camp, her dress swishing. Both men watch her run off. They stand in uncomfortable silence, like the proverbial wolverine and lynx, wondering who will strike first and whether it would be worth all the fuss.

"If I might ask, Mr. Cormack," Alexander says at last. "Why are you here? What is your interest in the girl?"

Declan turns towards him. "I could ask the same of you, Half-caste. It is nae proper that Miss Cromarty be alone with you."

Alexander sighs and drops his gun. He sits with a thud on the log. "The girl came to me for what purpose she did not explain. Perhaps it was not I that she sought."

Declan thinks about this a moment. "The girl wanders much. It is a wonder the father allows it."

Alexander lifts his head and looks back towards the fire. "I doubt that is a bird that can be caged, Mr. Cormack. You may as well confine a raven to a dovecote — it will chatter miserably, and drive its companions mad."

"You may be right, Half-caste, but perhaps she wanders because she seeks. Perhaps when she finds what needs drives her, she will be content to roost with the other doves."

"I will defer to your experience, for of women I know little, and like as not have made a fool of myself. Please excuse my foul temper."

"Dinna fash yourself over it. I still think you were at the greater danger, but perhaps I am mistaken? Can you truly use the weapon with effect?'

"I can, if need be."

"So a man might say. May I beg for a demonstration?"

Alexander shakes his head. "The people are at their wit's end and the sound of a gun would have them scattering for holes."

"I see your point. Still, can this musket skill be taught?"

Alexander assures him that the Baker is no mere smoothbore, but that with patience anything might be taught. At this, Declan pulls himself up before Alexander and promises undying love, fealty, and friendship in exchange for training in the use of the gun. Alexander is uncertain whether this ragged and maimed man is presenting an honest offer, according to some strange clan custom, or is attempting ribaldry. He points out that with a broken arm, it will be many days before Declan will be able to hoist a gun.

Declan looks down at his arm hanging in the sling as if he had forgotten it was still there. "My offer still stands," he says, reaching out a hand. Alexander receives it, feeling the man's thick, cool fingers wrap around his own.

At that the Highlander wanders off, and Alexander is left to ponder his choices. But his thoughts keep returning to Rose. He wonders at this and like a badger in a rabbit run, his mind hungrily follows a winding trail of inquiry: *She is different from the rest*, he tells himself. Maybe it is her youth, but more likely her posh life is responsible for the lightness of her step, the way she seems to not even make in impression in the dust. The daughter of a schoolmaster, so want is something she's never known. She has never watched someone die, the way they claw and struggle, the eyes staring, blood foaming at the mouth. The *desire* of the dying to not die; there is nothing quite like it. It would be so much easier for people if they just let go. So much pain for nothing because if you are going to die, you might as well get on with it. Hanging on just to shit yourself doesn't seem like much of a life, even if it is only for a few seconds more. The smart thing is to die — and quickly. What is there to fear?

She is pampered and spoiled like one of the factor's damned roses. Not such a bad thing in Scotland, perhaps, but it won't help her out here. Her father is already doomed, began dying the moment he set foot on the Bay. Is she fated like these women at the bottom of the river, to feed crayfish and worms?

Only the strongest make it. And the most vicious. These peasants that came with her look more beast than human, slouched and gnarled like old spruce. They might survive if they aren't shot or don't freeze or starve.

He looks down the river to the glow of campfire, to where the woman had fled so haughtily, so complacent, her head as high and proud as an old, bull buffalo. *I'm afraid for this girl*, he thinks. *She is so close. She blew in on the winds of a storm, like a goddess, a seed, blown from far-away lands. A Manitou, perhaps, that's what my mother would say. There was anger on her face that night at York Factory, but I saw through that. Fear and a bit of wonder. I can't imagine what it must be like to leave those bare, green Scottish hills they talk about, with their great stone cities and castles. Imagine abandoning all that majesty to get lost in this land.*

He is afraid for her and cannot afford to be. He sees the shadow of hardness in her face. One day she will be like the others if she isn't careful. A pox on her father.

Nothing else must be in my mind than this voyage, he chides himself. *The trees, the bend in the river, the shoals. Too much danger. Damn these colonists, damn them all to hell. I do not know what to say. I do not know the graces. I can shoot the eye out of a flying raven at a hundred yards, can run without rest for hours, swim rivers, find my way home in the darkest night, in the foulest weather. But I cannot say* Good morning *to a woman. What a fool I am. Her wrists move like the neck of a swan. Her eyes trace your exact movements like an owl watching you from across the stillness of a moonlit, frozen lake.*

From the moment I saw her, I loved her.

～

When they prepare to depart the next morning, there is again a chill in the air with the threat of wet weather on the wind. The sky is grey and low, adding to the oppression of the brigade. August has moved into September, and the surface of the river moves with countless yellow leaves, each gust of wind sending a new cohort spinning into the water. Fairy-boats, Rose calls them, and Alexander shivers at the sentimentality of her words.

They hold a hasty conference around the morning fire, presided over by several weeping cottonwoods that rattle and scatter leaves among them. The fire snaps loudly as they speak in lowered tones. Left with few options, they decide to press on. The widowers are in a state miserable to behold, but they cannot stay any longer at the foot of the rapids. Gibson does his best to hide his grief, and even tries to smile once or twice, but the effect is ghastly. Costie remains inconsolable, and Alexander fears there will be trouble when the time comes for them to break camp.

In honour of the dead women, Iskoyaskweyau climbs a large spruce leaning over the water and cuts away all the lower branches. It is a *lopstick*, Alexander explains to them, a prominent pole with a shaggy top used as a landmark and to honor important gentlemen. Along with the marking of the passage of the governor — who seemed remarkably untouched by recent events and hesitated not a moment to carry on with the brigade, leaving Turr behind to mind the dead — all felt it would be a suitable monument for the deceased.

While climbing the tree, Iskoyaskweyau finds a torpid owl in the lower branches; he knocks it on the head and it falls out of the tree in a puff of brown and grey feathers. The cook plucks it, singes it, and tosses it into boiling water. Rose peeks into the kettle, and it so looks like a wrinkled, pink child that she loses all interest in breakfast.

When all is prepared for departure, everyone gathers around the boats; the Indians wait in their canoes a little ways off.

"My word, but it feels damp this morning," Turr comments, staring up at the sky and the clouds gnawing the treetops. "I doubt we shall see the sun today."

Lachlan follows his gaze. "If this were Stromness, I would sur-mise that we are in for some rather ill weather. I hope Mr. Gibson and Mr. Costie are up to it."

"He is nae coming," Gibson says, throwing his bedroll into the boat.

"I beg your pardon?"

"He wishes to stay. He will nae listen to me nor anyone. It is his choice."

"My word, Mr. McClure, surely we cannot allow this?"

Alexander looks down the beach at the man sitting on a log, still staring at the river. He turns to Lachlan: "I have left him what food we can spare, but there is not much we can do. He refuses to leave, and we cannot stay. I can hardly knock him on the head and drag him along."

"I will speak with him," Lachlan says.

Alexander shrugs. "If you wish; I have tried, to no effect. But we must leave presently."

Lachlan walks down the beach to speak with the man; he argues and pleads, to no avail. At last his frustrated shouting carries down the river; all stop and stare. When he returns to the boat, he is red in the face.

"Damned willful fool, won't see reason. He would rather starve than carry on without his wife. I suppose there is a touching nobil-ity in that, but it's a bloody tragedy all the same."

He and Rose join Alexander and Turr in the boats. None of the remaining colonists wishes to ride the rapids again and the Bay men carry the lines. As they are pulled upriver, Rose turns around and sees the tiny figure of Mr. Costie, still sitting and staring at the river. They move around a bend, and he is gone.

Chapter Seven

The two boats follow the rest of the brigade upriver. There is sporadic evidence of them at likely landing places: ashes at the foot of White Mud portage, a torn oilcloth discarded on a beach. A fly-blown pile of quills and guts from a porcupine shot by one of the Indians.

As predicted, the days turn cool with dark masses of thunderclouds threatening the horizon, lightning playing along their foundations. Thunder mutters around them and leaves continue to patter the river. When the skies at last clear, the deep blue of the north is dimmed by a grey-brown haze, and the smell of smoke follows the wind down the river valley. The sun is ringed and dimmed, cut by thin, endless lines of waterfowl fleeing the oncoming winter. All night long, they can hear the train as it heads south; the hurried whistle of duck wings, the honk and yelp of crane and goose. And while all else flees that can, they drag, line, and portage, making their way deeper into the continent, and the Bay now seems a distant memory.

After a long and wearying climb up the Rock Portage, it is late in the day. They drop their burdens onto the muskeg and drag the boats to shore. The evening fire is lit, and the kitchen assembled with a sound of pots banging, and the curses of the cook and his flunky. Alexander sends out the Indians to search for game, and they vanish like a whisper into the bush.

After seeing that camp is well underway, Alexander invites Lachlan and Declan to accompany him inland to scout a cabin he recalled in the area; he discovered it when he passed by the previous spring. It was an outpost of the North West Company — installed with great arrogance as a final attempt to intercept the passage of Indian brigades and their furs to the Bay. Turr declines to accompany them with an impatient wave of his hand, citing a sudden attack of flux, brought on by the incessant harassment of mosquitoes — those damnable, monstrous, bloody-minded little God-cursed beasts of the Devil.

They soon find a small pole shack a little distance back from the river. The lands they have passed through these many weeks is one upholstered in a dense integument of mostly spruce and the occasional pine and tamarack, an unbroken landscape of emaciated trees gnawed by squirrels and afflicted by moulds and disease and perpetually frozen or perpetually flooded earth; but here the forest is neither so dark nor so haggard, the post built in a clearing surrounded by a sward of lovely young paper birch and aspen.

The opening feels like a hallowed space where medicine men gather and contemplate the moon. The north wind blows through the trees, and the ground is alive with the tremors of dry yellow leaves stirred by this cold breath. As the men enter the clearing, all feel subdued as though entering a cathedral. The silence is disturbed only by their footfalls and the hiss of leaves that rise about them, flashing in the sun that has escaped below the purple fringes of wrack. They lift and fall in a choreography of air and space and great secretive distance — a voice to the empty wind. They gather in the lee of the post where they tumble in a column like a Djinn materializing on the threshold.

A raven, dark as night, sits on the ridge of the roof, its black eyes reflecting the sun. At their approach it spreads its wings, hesitates, and flies off, its harsh voice diminishing in the distance.

Alexander has his Baker in his hands, and he pushes the door open with the barrel; the leather hinges are cracked, and the door grates on the floor as he follows the gun inside.

Packrats have destroyed the interior, their moldering nests piled high with trophy mounds of junk. A few old, gnawed furs lie on the floor by the door, and the skin windows and rafters are ghosted with layers of cobwebs that undulate in the sudden breeze from the open door. Lachlan hesitates, and decides to remain on the stoop while Declan follows Alexander inside. The Highlander stops just inside the door, he, too, sensing something amiss.

Looking around the room, Alexander's eyes fall on something bright propped up in a windowsill. His moccasins stir the dust as he walks over and picks up the delicate thing with his thick fingers. It is a small porcelain angel, with cherubic features and a broad, sad smile. Its head cocks to one shoulder, eyes gazing heavenward. It caresses a golden harp.

Turning it over, Alexander feels a lump in his throat. Some Voyageur had carried this treasure thousands of hungry, desperate miles from Montreal; some gift of a loved one perhaps, a woman or a parent sending him off with this tender memento by which to recall them. *But why would a man burden himself with such a delicate trifle?* he wonders. Beyond the fragility of the thing itself, it evoked a fragility of the heart; not an undangerous thing to a Voyageur.

He had seen them several times; they were a colourful people, dressed in capotes tied with worsted sashes and shirts striped in scarlet and open in the front to reveal broad chests. They wore bright sailor's kerchiefs tied around their swarthy necks, and their headdresses were wild and fanciful, sporting all manner of coloured feathers and bullion tassels. They always seemed to be singing, while at work or at rest, puffing their long pipes.

The glaze on the angel is crackled, and a knob on the end of the harp has been broken off. *Wounded, but still capable of loving*, he thinks. Very carefully, he places it back in its spot.

"This is a terrible smell," Lachlan says from the door, holding a handkerchief to his nose.

"Aye," says Declan. "There be vermin here — and more. Look!" He points to a long, rough-hewn table pushed against the far wall, knocked over so the top lies facing them, hiding from view what lies behind it, all but a knot of shaggy black hair visible on the upper edge. They all stare.

"The poor man," Lachlan mutters. Alexander steps forward, but the others do not follow. *There is a story on the other side of that table, and one deserving to be told*, thinks Lachlan, but he has had quite enough of that kind of tale on their journey. A man came here to toil his last day and others might wonder what has become of him, unaware that his bones are lost in some distant tumbled-down hovel to forever stare at a dark and uncomprehending wall until the wood itself rots into the soil around him. Or until others of his kind come and render him with soft words to the earth's breast. He can imagine nothing lonelier.

Alexander stands behind the table for a long time. At last, he looks up and sighs. A final glance around and he leaves the fetid room, herding the others before him. Although it is now cooler outside, the clouds having conquered the sky once more; it feels as if they have emerged from a dark mausoleum into a bright day. Alexander gently pulls the door closed behind him.

He commands the men to gather loose brush and leaves and to pile it about the post. When he is satisfied there is enough, he kneels and stuffs a ball of down stolen from an old bird's nest under some twigs. He strikes sparks from his knife and a flint.

Declan's eyes widen. "No," he whispers. The others do not hear him. A thread of smoke rises from the duff.

Soon the fire is licking at the dry walls of the post and smoke and sparks sail high above them. In silence, they turn their backs on this wilderness pyre and return to the river, each man lost in his own thoughts. When they return to the camp, Rose wonders about the troubled look in her father's eye, but he does not speak of it to her.

~

That night supper is served cheerless and quiet. When all have eaten and feet are offered to the fire and embers to pipes, Declan vanishes. Rose does not consider following; she had come to the conclusion that only a fool took an axe to the rotten bridge that one walked upon and that undermining her father in the opinion of others could prove personally disastrous. Eyes follow her constantly and even her habitual need to flirt is subdued.

Declan wanders into the night, at first with an ear tuned to possible danger, but he, too, comes to a new conclusion, realizing that the true peril in this land is emptiness, the absence of warmth and succor and love. Even the desolate north Atlantic offered fish aplenty, and leviathans, and all manner of birds, and one crewman even swore he had seen a mermaid. But other than the strange deer the brigade had seen swimming the river many days ago, this land seemed barren of warm-blooded life. Scarce ever a bird to be heard or seen, except for the unlovely croaks of ravens and migrating flocks high above the land. He is sure that man in the post had died of aloneness, not violence.

He returns to the clearing, to the still-snapping fire. Sitting in the thin grass, he looks up at a proud moon that shines down into the open space, striking everything in a pale light. The shadows of the trees seem filled with secrets. He bows his head and surrenders his tears.

"*The year of the burning*, they call it," says Alistair Gordon beside the snapping fire. Alexander had asked him why he and his people had made the hard crossing into the unknown, and he looked up to see others watching him. With a cough he rose and walked to the fire and sat close, knowing they would follow like acolytes: as the tale warmed, so would they.

"Strathnaver, Assynt, Caithness, Dornoch, Rogort, Loth, Clyne, Golspie, and Kildonan, all put to the torch. Damn them, damn them to the flames that they had spread so far and wide."

He talks of the destruction of his family's croft, the smell of burning wood and peat and the scorched flesh of his kin, his old aunt too frail to get from her bed and the soldiers, the treacherous, vengeful Irish of the Royal Fusiliers tossing in torches while holding the family at bay with musket and claymore. They had shouted that an old woman lay abed inside the house, and that vile dog of Sutherland, Patrick Sellar, turned to them and said: "Damn her, the old witch. She has lived too long. Let her burn."

Their croft had been burned without warning, his father and mother and two brothers cast out without possessions of any kind. In tears, they stumbled down the road toward the sea, their hearts as hot as the coals of their house. They soon discovered that it was the same everywhere, house after house, village after village burned to the earth to make room for the cursed Cheviots: Grummore and Grumbeg and Archmilidh and Sgall. Achness, Rhifail, Kidsary, Langall, Rossal, Syre, and Ceann-na-coille. Achcaoilnaborgin and Achinlochy. The glens choked with smoke and ash; the glow by night made it seem as if all of Scotland was being consumed in fire.

They had passed the corpses of those dead from starvation and disease and violence; bodies half-consumed by dogs and rats — women, children, the old and sick, piled like fresh-cut turves along the stony path. You could not risk helping anyone who stumbled, anyone who fell.

Sellar had accused Christy MacKay of giving shelter to an old wretch he had previously burned out, and when they found the crone, they dug a hole in the cold earth and flung her in it — still alive — and buried her. They then nailed up 'Christy's house with her inside and set it ablaze. Her cries were heard by many, but none dared come to her aid.

They had seen a man stop on the roadside to bury his poor dead wife. Head bowed, he had said loud enough that many could hear, *Well, Janet, the Countess will never filt you again!* But then the constables rode up and beat him and dragged him away, the unshrouded, fly-covered body left lying in the muddy hole by the roadside.

But when they at last arrived at the lowlands, they found the coasts choked by a miserable mass of once-proud Highlanders seeking shelter and food. And, in the bitterest of avarice, the same lairds who had burned them from their crofts now pressed this desperate pool of labourers into harvesting kelp for almost nothing; the Lady Sutherland had created a nation of slaves.

He yearned to gather a troop of his clansmen to rise up against those who had abused them so cruelly, but the clan chiefs were having none of it. He thought it the vilest betrayal, worst than that of the Sutherlands: you swear your life to a chief and his to yours, and together the clan is unbeatable. The Gunns had rallied against the clearances, to little effect, perhaps, but at least they carried the game to its conclusion. But the Strathnaver chiefs were murdered and bribed and burned out, and the old clans melted away like snow before a warm wind.

The revolution in foreign parts that saw kings and queens lose their heads had struck terror in the lairds and even the merest whisper of discontent was a sure and quick path to the gallows. All knew they waited for any sign of rebellion at which they would push the Highlanders into the sea.

But as long as the people could be sat upon and cowed, they were useful, and so emigration was forbidden. When Lord Selkirk's envoy had offered transit to the New World, Alistair had not hesitated; he had once loved his laird, his chief, and his country, but now he could not wait to see the back of it all. Perhaps now he had a chance to make something of himself. In Rupert's Land, they say a man does not suffer himself to be burned out. And his people will always be suspicious of fire.

The next morning as the brigade heads out into the river, a long pall of smoke rises behind them.

"Quire right," Turr says. "Scoundrels and trespassers all of 'em. They should be burned right out of the country."

This length of the river is a series of falls and tumbling water, and most progress achieved by dragging the boat over many portages and poling through rapids.

After their earlier loss, the colonists are reluctant to remain in the boats through the white water, but often there is no alternative; with no passage on shore, they had to ride it out aboard.

These are now horrible moments for Rose; she sits hunched in the bilge with black hissing water tossing them about, eyes closed and fists clenching the gunwale, a fog of spray dampening her hair and shawl.

Alexander directs them here and there across the surface of the river, and if Rose had opened her eyes, she would have seen the art in this; behind every large stone is an arrow-shaped region of calm backwater, and in this gentle current, the men are able to pull the boat forward with little resistance. Upon reaching the face of the rock, they swing back out into the current and madly pole into the tail end of the next eddy.

In this manner, they are able to climb many miles of rough water without mishap, but the going is exhausting work and provisions are running low; the hunt is poor, the fishing dismal. The daily allotment of pemmican is reduced, which as far as the Orkneymen are concerned is of debatable hardship, but fourteen hours of rowing and poling requires food to sustain itself and their pace upstream slows.

"It is nae what I expected, the emptiness," Declan says to Iskoyaskweyau.

"It is you whites, you *Êmistikôsiw*," Iskoyaskweyau replies, looking at Turr relaxing on a chair with a mug of tea beneath a large spruce. "The Company. They have trapped and hunted out all between the Bay and *Missinipi*." He does not share the universal belief in the canoes, that the sour stink of so many whites announced their coming miles ahead in the river valley, clearing whatever game remained.

"How is that possible? The land is so vast ..."

With that, Iskoyaskweyau tells Declan what life was like for his grandfather, and his father, who lived and hunted throughout the north before the *Êmistikôsiw* came inland, when York Fort was a wigwam on the Bay. In those days, his people brought furs to York Fort while the *Êmistikôsiw* hid in their wood house, like children.

He tells him of growing up along the coast, hunting inland. The families came together every summer for feasting and storytelling, but during the hard, lean winters, the families dispersed to hunt on their own. Game was never plentiful in the lands haunted by the ancestors of the Swampy Cree, even before the foreigners arrived at the Bay, and certainly there was never enough in one spot to support a whole village through the winter. So they loaded up the women and the dogs and dispersed throughout the forest, each family claiming several hundred miles of hunting territory for their own use. Sometimes even then there would not be enough game, and whole families would starve.

Iskoyaskweyau lowers his voice and looks around. That's when bad things would happen, sometimes. Cannibalism was always a danger in the winter, he told a shocked and delighted Declan, and was a terror to the *Ayisiniwok*. After the dreadful feast, the cannibal was said to be possessed and would henceforth always crave human flesh, and no one would trust him. It was the duty of the man's family to kill him, as soon as possible. The killings that night at York Factory were because the woman and her children had eaten one of her cousins this past winter, and the people were terrified of her. Many times she and her whelps were seen walking at night among the tipis, the moon reflecting on their long knives. It was her husband's duty to kill them, and the people had long insisted, but he loved his family, so until that night had refused. After he had performed his rightful duty, this man had himself become possessed and pistolled himself. To the people, the killings were a cause for celebration.

But since the *Êmistikôsiw* had left the Bay and marched inland, that kind of evil had occurred with increased and alarming frequency; the food was not to be found where it once was and the old ways were no longer working. Men preyed upon men the way they once preyed on moose or the *ituk*.

And now more and more *Êmistikôsiw* come from across the great water, come down the rivers. Canadians, too, and the game and his people were being crowded out. Forts sprung up like smallpox sores along every waterway, and you couldn't throw a turd without hitting one. But the *Êmistikôsiw* said they were just passing by. Some left, some stayed, some married Indian women. The land is great and can provide for all, or so they had once believed. But the *Êmistikôsiw* destroy as they pass, and the land is now empty.

"Even the bears and wolves shit ashes these days," Iskoyaskweyau says.

"That is bad. I know what it is like to have land stolen."

"And yet you come to take ours." Iskoyaskweyau smiles at him.

Declan shakes his head. "I come to take nothing. I only pass through this grand country, to see what I might, to learn what I can. But if you are so beset, why dinna you fight?"

"Some fight, some kill the Whites. But the *Ayisiniwok*, my people, are few and scattered. Much disease and death. And we battle with our enemies, the Stone Indians. We cannot fight the *Êmistikôsiw*, too."

Listening to Iskoyaskweyau speak, Declan has an image of a people done a terrible injustice. He knows that his kind had brought

Christianity to the Savages, and he deeply believed that whatever may befall a man in life such was nothing compared to his fate in death. And yet for all that, he has an uneasy feeling that it is his own that are in the wrong, a patently foolish notion. But what if the lands are not quite so empty and free as he had been led to believe? He hears of this suffering of Iskoyaskweyau's people, but what of others? Are there more savage kingdoms farther along the river? Are they all as accepting as these poor, bedraggled forest creatures of the overlordship of the whites? After all the lurid, brutal stories, he has heard regarding the North American Savage, he is surprised to find such a meek, complacent group of half-starved curs as he had seen on the Bay.

He knows he has a lot to learn from these people. While it rankles his pride somewhat, he will take knowledge wherever he might find it. His arm mends nicely, but until it is fully healed, he is vulnerable, a feeling of which he does not think highly. And he has come to the quick understanding that in this land that skill, not rank or title, is power, and he will learn from a deaf rabbit if he has to.

He smiles at Iskoyaskweyau. The Indian has taken somewhat of a shine to him, an advantage the Highlander is polishing like a blade. He is learning to hunt and fish and walk easily through the forest. Although they really were Indians of the coast and feel unhappy when hemmed in by the miles of forest, Iskoyaskweyau's people have great skill in the wilderness. Though they think him a great, clumsy, ignorant buffoon, they seem pleased that he has taken it upon himself to learn what they are willing to teach, in the manner in which an elder craftsman might be pleased when a small child picks up a hammer and bangs away at a piece of scrap wood.

As those will who have a close conversation with death, they have a profound sense of humour and laugh at him a great deal, and just as often curse him roundly for making noise when they are hunting. From Declan's limited position, it seems obvious that there is nothing to hunt, and so what is all the fuss about, but the Indians inevitably tire of his shadow, and they vanish, leaving him to break his foolish neck or find his own way back to camp, according to the whims of the *Manitou* or fate, or some damned man-eating Frenchman.

The first time this happened, he had been bent over and querying them about a plant when they looked at each other, and, without a word, disappeared in a manner that would have done credit to the wind.

Declan had waited for them to answer and when he stood up and looked about, he realized his abandonment. He felt terrified, but held his composure and sat where dropped, like discarded trash, until they returned to pick him up on their back trail. He was cold and very hungry when they found him, clapping him on the back and laughing at his discomfiture, telling him he was lucky to still have his head as they were certain it was a bedded moose they heard beside the trail, so much noise he had made sitting on a pile of dried leaves.

After that, he always took great care in noting their back trail and returned to the camp on his own.

"Why you follow us, hey?" they ask as Declan prepares to accompany them yet again. It is a morning pregnant with fog; the fire is cold and it is so quiet that the loud snoring in the camp seems almost offensive in that otherwise pure, heavy, white silence. Beads of dew cluster to so many surrounding cobwebs, it is as if the little beasts have spent the night attempting to trap them.

"Why you not stay here like the others," Pisiw demands. "Stay with the women and children. That's what you *Êmistikôsiw* do, is it not? This is not your country; you will die out there." He steps up, and, holding a handful of arrows, taps them on the Highlander's chest. "Why you not stay at camp and fuck a woman. Or maybe you fuck man instead? *Êmistikôsiw* damned good at that. Out there — he points to the forest — out there is only the *Machi Manitou* waiting for you."

Declan is much larger than Pisiw, but has no doubt the smaller man would cut his throat before he could even unsheathe his own blade, so he simply shrugs and raises a finger and wags it slowly in front of the man's face.

"Piss on you," he says. The Indian follows the finger a moment, and then meets Declan's eyes. They stand chest to chest while Iskoyaskweyau squats on the ground nearby.

"Why are you waiting?" he says. "Kill him or tongue his asshole, but be done and let us go."

Pisiw smiles, nodding. "You may be piece of shit *Êmistikôsiw*, but you are friend, hey? You may follow us, but shut the fuck up. No words." With that, he makes a slashing motion across his neck.

Declan knows he is in danger of being lost or killed by the impatient Indians, but he is young and strong and a Highlander, and anyway, the walking is a welcome respite from the cramped boats.

But if Declan expects the Indian's magnanimity, he is shocked the day that Iskoyaskweyau offers the Highlander his wife. After Alexander rather hesitatingly explains that this is a common politeness among the Indians, Declan does not hesitate to accept the man's offer.

The Indians invite him into their wigwam — a low hut made from willow branches bent over in a dome shape and covered with hides. He spends much time in the company of the Cromartys, making his interest in Rose plain to both of them, an interest the father is clearly warming to. But that evening, he offers an excuse to Rose is that he is planning a hunt and will remain with the Indians far into the night. He is surprised at how easily the lie falls from his lips.

Many soft furs carpet the wigwam floor, with everyone including the three dogs crowded inside. The small space reeks of the Indian's unwashed bodies and smoke from the little fire makes his eyes water. But he pays the strong air no mind; it had been worse aboard the cramped frigate on the journey from Orkney.

Iskoyaskweyau rolls over and falls asleep at once, while Isqe-sis sidles over and lies beside him. The other two people talk quietly among themselves for a while, the child occasionally peeking over his furs and staring wide-eyed at Declan, who responds with faces that make the boy duck in a fit of giggles. Eventually all is quiet, but for the lamentations of an owl in the trees somewhere high above them.

He sees her staring at him in the dark, her face shadowed, her eyes kindling in the coals of the fire. Her hair is of a great length and as she undoes it, it seems to cascade everywhere, covering her furs, her head and down her shoulders to her hips. She seems as if painted in ebony.

As she pulls off her clothing and moves on top of him, her determination and strength astonishes him; his experience is with a more passive kind of woman. Her knotty hair swings down over him, drags across his face and covers her hands that rest upon his breast. Her thin knees pinch him, and he gasps. He still cannot see her face, but can feel her enmity giving energy to her lust. He steadies her with his hands at her waist, willing her to go slower, knowing that it has been too long and he cannot hold himself back. Indeed his climax is almost immediate, though she continues rocking until he feels himself fall out of her with a wet and ineffectual *pop*.

She continues to move atop him until her head swings and her hair flares like the spreading of a raven's wings as she collapses onto his chest.

Lying like an infant at his breast, her breath comes in short gasps. He can feel her heart against him. Soon — altogether too soon — she pulls away, leaving his body cold. She wraps herself in a fur and lies down behind her husband, Declan watching her. He feels rather forlorn, but for what reason he cannot tell. Wrapping himself in his own fur, he hears the sound of a loon on the river and imagines the creature is laughing at him.

—

At the sound of a distant howl, Rose wakes with a start. The fire is quiet embers. Shadowed humps and nasally whistles are the only evidence of the brigade. The moon is low, the night already old.

The wolf howls again, more distant this time. *Travelling on the wind*, Rose thinks, and shivers at the thought of that gloriously wild creature gliding through the forest, crying aloud its yearnings.

Her father is rolled in his blanket beside her, snoring gently. Her leg aches and she stretches, feeling the lovely tingle and heat as blood courses down her limbs.

At the memory of the departed day, her heart quickens. Sitting in front of Alexander, she had been palpably aware of his presence: the smoke from his pipe, the occasional shouts to the men. Whenever he is occupied, she steals furtive looks at him, admiring the expanse of his shoulders, and strong arc of his back as he pulls on a hawser. Her gaze had slipped lower before she realized what she was doing, and with red face quickly turned away. Her father had given her a quizzical look.

Since their meeting on the log beside the river, thoughts of him had occupied her; she wonders what it would be like to run her hands through that long, yellow hair, what that beard would feel like brushing her chin.

They had flirted with each other in the subtlest ways possible: a brief glance, a smile was all it took to convey enormous meaning. But with the people so close — and especially her father, who would be outraged if he knew — it felt even more delicious.

The Highlander Declan had chosen to approach her formally, through her father, and Lachlan seemed intrigued by this. She had no opinion of the man one way or another, happy to play her game of old, even though the stakes and chance of being found out are much higher. The idea of her with the Half-breed would set all Rupert's Land aflame.

But for all Declan's peasant pretence to social formality, it is Alexander's rough wildness that calls to her, his ability to absolutely experience the moment, almost like an animal, his mind not burdened by rules and convention. Her desire had always been so.

Tearing her mind from him, Rose follows time's back trail, breadcrumbs of memory leading to her careless youth in the Orkneys, to her young friends Isobel and Agnes. Like Rose, they refused the attentions of the local boys, waiting instead for one of the men from the ships that berthed at Stromness to take a fancy to them, and remove them from what they saw as a dull and provincial backwater of the kingdom.

Lachlan had been appalled by their intransigence. "Life is not literature, my dears," he preached from around his cigar, standing in their tiny drawing room with his hands in his waistcoat pockets and watching Rose and her friends with a mixture of annoyance at their ridiculousness and admiration for their optimistic stubbornness.

But Rose saw little around her that she thought worthy of her time or consideration; the men of her station she considered spoiled, effeminate, and filled with an unwarranted pomposity. There were a few crofter's sons she briefly considered and though her father's disapproval was enough to make her give these lads a second look, there was only so far she was willing to challenge him.

If truth be told, there was really not much to any of them, either. So she waited. And as her father's concern for her increased, her own melted away, and she entered womanhood carrying on her secret games in the town, loving lightly and without concern. Although the thought disturbed many of Lachlan's nights, the idea never occurred to her that she was well on her way to spinsterhood.

Yet now, for the first time in a long while she finds herself truly drawn to a man and wonders what to do about it. She looks at the face of her father, a widower for most of her life. His concern is deep and true, and yet what did he have to teach her about the ways of love? His own is as dry and mummified as a dead bird carcass long trapped inside a chimney.

The obvious occurs to her with a sudden shock. But dare she? What is the limit to her courage? She had long ago decided to follow her own path, despite all the world against her. For many weeks she had been subservient and dependent, but at the thought of rebellion her old spirit rouses to flame.

Carefully, she lifts the blanket away from her body; she shivers again as the night air finds her skin. She wishes she could keep the blanket about her, but it is entangled with her father's.

Wrapping her arms about her, she steps away from the cocoon of warmth. Her bare toes sink into the cold, damp sand. Alexander usually slept upriver from the brigade; he had a small tent that he pitched against the night, a luxury that raised the ire of many of his followers. She hurries toward this dark shape.

As she approaches, she stumbles on an unseen branch and it breaks with a sharp crack, cutting her. She freezes, listening with pounding heart, expecting the whole camp to be wakened. The tent is very quiet.

Rose has no idea what to do next; she realizes that she had no plan from the start, and wonders what ridiculous notion has drawn her into this position. The man she had tried to approach in the dark is heavily armed and knows nothing of her intent or identity; her people may have been frightened by the sounds of furtive steps.

"Mr. McClure," she says, scarcely audible over the pounding of her heart. There is no response.

"Mr. McClure," she says again, a little louder, agonized. "Alexander."

"Miss Cromarty?" whispers an incredulous voice from the tent.

"Yes, it is I. May I come in?" The tent flap opens, and she can see little inside, but the highlight of a rifle barrel is unmistakable.

"Come inside, and be quick."

Needing little encouragement, she pushes past him. She does not know what to say, and they sit together in embarrassed darkness. Soon his hand runs up the side of her arm, and she takes it to her mouth and kisses between his fingers. Without a word, they come together, and explore each other in the dark, their bodies moving it seems of their own volition, without thought or knowledge.

Before the wraith of dawn shows the horizon, she wraps herself in her blanket beside her father. Lachlan at once awakens and pulls himself to her and folds her in his arms, his brow furrowing at the unfamiliar, wild scent clinging to his daughter.

The next morning, he is particularly attentive to her, aware of something new and yet familiar about her, something he is not privy to. For a brief moment, he is terrified that she might have caught some kind of flux, but the way laughter bubbles out of her puts that fear to rest. Her spirits are obviously high, and when he catches her humming something lovely to herself and asks her to name the melody, she cannot — or will not — humour him.

~

Rose shivers as she sits beside Lachlan in the boat. Mistaking this, he reaches below the thwart and pulls out a blanket that he wraps around her shoulders. She takes it with a small smile. Her shiver had not been from the cold. She had been surreptitiously watching Alexander, her eyes following the lovely curve of his hand as it grasped his scull, edging the boat here and there with skilled movements.

That same hand had caressed her in the darkness of the tent, anguished desire in its wake. She could see the red welt on his forearm, the place she had bitten him when he had stifled her cry, the warm salt taste of his blood on her lips. The memory had caused her body to betray itself to her father.

Each stroke of the oarsmen moves them across the river in a gentle rhythm, their bodies rocking as hips moved before heads. The motion feels soothing and safe, and she suddenly realizes that Alexander had moved on top of her with the same slow cadence. After all his years on the river, the motion has become one with the man, an ineffable part of his nature. It is in how he walks, how he swings his gun, how he makes love. Perhaps it echoes his very heartbeat.

"A lovely morning," Lachlan informs her.

"Indeed," she replies. "It is warmer than it has been for a long while."

"Yes, the sun is low as befits the season, but the weather is uncommonly civil. Perhaps it is a harbinger? I shall speak to Mr. McClure about it when we stop for our breakfast."

"I imagine he if anyone would know all about heat and premonitions, Father. I too would like to know what he believes the future holds in this regard. There has been too little of it, and I wonder at its sudden, unforeseen arrival. Should I trust it or will it quickly flit away on the heels of storm?"

"You are poetic this morning, I see. Or perhaps the more correct word is philosophical?"

She smiles at him again. "I do feel passionate. I have had unusual dreams of late, dark phantasms that make my tongue waggle nonsense."

"Passion is it? Well, I think we could all use a little passion. And it is not to wonder that your dreams are disturbed; there has been much gloomy talk and murmuring among the brigade; a good dose of passion might set everyone to rights."

Rose does not respond, but looks up again at Alexander. For a moment, their eyes touch. That fleeting contact carries much, and she feels a surge of delightful fear, thinking that others must see and be aware of their thoughts and emotions. But she must have a care. Her play with her father is one thing, but it is harder for the eye to deceive. Words may hang a man, but it is the glance, the gaze, that truly condemns. She has a sense of recklessness, like riding a horse too hard and fast, on the edge of being thrown.

"Mr. McClure?" she calls, pleased to see him jump.

"Yes, Miss?"

"Do you think that passion arises at night? In dreams?"

"I beg your pardon?"

"Is night the wellspring of men's dreams and desires?"

"Now, Rose, don't go bothering Mr. McClure with your rubbish," her father says. Alexander turns away and coughs.

Rose opens her mouth to rejoin him, considers the wisdom in this, and then dismisses them both from her thoughts. The thwart board digs into her and she squirms, doing her best to smooth her muddy skirts. She thinks of her Bible and hurriedly puts that also out of her mind; with a sigh, the ever-present boredom blankets her yet again.

The deep wilderness and dark river have long lost their novelty and each day seems much like the interminable last, with neither the landscape nor anything else changing. The rhythm of the oars, the taciturn quiet of her companions, the slap of water repeat themselves endlessly, and she has a feeling of traversing a long dark tunnel.

The shock of the accident at the rapids has worn off and she catches herself almost wishing for more mishap, anything to interrupt the tedium of staring at a changeless nothing.

When her father first told her about his plans, Rose had been quite excited about the prospect: wild lands, fierce Aboriginals, iron men. Perhaps here she would find the dash that was missing from her life. But as she watched, the dark trees lining the riverbank move slowly past, she feels quite dissatisfied with the experience so far.

The trees seem like a wall to her, behind which lay unknown secrets and half-imagined threats. She feels no more a part of this land now than when they first saw the shores of Hudson's Bay.

It occurs to her that the water on which they travel flows into that great Bay, which itself communes with the North Atlantic, that frigid sea bearing her beloved Orkney. In a sense, they had not really left; not until they abandon the river will they really know the land they had come to claim as their own.

The thought frightens her. The journey so far has been far more brutal than she could ever have imagined, weighted with unimaginable suffering and squalor. The few books that had been published by men who had adventured in Rupert's Land talk about courage and adventure, not about death and filth and fear and this deep, gnawing hunger.

Alexander shouts to the leading boat, and like a naughty child her mind returns to the forbidden. He had at first been very gentle with her, like she was a flower he was fearful of treading upon, like she was made of delicate petals needing to be opened with the most delicate of touches. She soon learned him that this orchid was a snapdragon, her teeth leaving marks on his shoulders and neck, nails furrowing his back like a lash. She sees how artfully he has covered his throat with a red sash and smiles again, squeezing her hands.

He had been surprised by her, Rose is certain. She knows what is expected of a woman, how the game is played. But she is no virgin. That honour she had long ago bequeathed to a cousin who often visited her and her father when released from University. A pale, gangly sort with a topknot of red hair and an unquenchable ardor. He collected maidenheads as other men collected anecdotes, and was constantly being called out. He was no great shot with a pistol, and more than once found himself carried from the field of honor with a father's ball as a token of the experience. But she had found him irresistible and gratefully surrendered to his advances.

"Better to offer the thing to a stranger or a cad, so that one can focus on more important matters with one's husband," she had told her friend, Agnes. "All that weeping and blood cannot but distract your dear man from his duty, and I will not bear anyone who finds such things to be his taste." She had welcomed Alexander with far more than he had a right to expect.

But he was more of an enigma. Her cousin was only one of many lovers, and she knew the feel of experience on her and in her, and Alexander's rush was urgent and hastily done. His lack of finesse was quite distinct from the skilful manner with which he played his scull. In other men, this frequent ineptitude merely amused her, but with Alexander, it evoked tenderness; she knew the lack was one only of practice, of opportunity, and felt glad that he had not made a habit of bedding Savage women. She could teach him much, and yet careful as always to have him believe that it was she who was the student.

Pipe smoke and small conversation swirls about her. The water bucket rattles as someone removes the ladle. A short, harsh laugh. Squeezing her father's hand, she returns his smile and rests her head on his shoulder.

Chapter Eight

The mood as they divide the loads is one without enthusiasm. Robinson, Oxford, Knee, and Swampy Lakes are behind them, and they prepare to enter the sluggish and marshy length of the Echimamish River. Although this length of the passage from York Factory to the Forks flows with them rather than against, the weeks-long journey has taken its toll on their bodies and spirits. And they still have not found the rest of the brigade. It seems that Semple decided to not wait for them at any of the portages, but pressed ahead as if the Devil's whips were lashing his back. Alexander wonders if there has been some troubling news; that rumours he has heard, now old, did not bode well for the settlement.

He shares the great man's desire for haste, but for different reasons, and he has not the governor's authority to be able to drive them as he would; he is a simple guide, no more; the true captain of their journey has long ago abandoned them at the foot of a rapids, to follow or else seek their fate as they may. Turr was ostensibly in charge, but the man is too without spirit to occupy more than the stool behind the throne, whispering intrigues and advice in his master's ear. He had not yet taken his sceptre, preferring to let the burden of command, the daily details of managing a host of ill-equipped and ill-suited passengers and crew to fall on other's shoulders. Alexander wanted to give the laggard a good shaking, or more.

The mood that morning had been particularly difficult. Squabbles had broken out, and men argued over trifles. The complaints seem endless: not enough food, not enough shelter. He tells them repeatedly that this brigade is like any other, that hardship and hunger are part of travelling in Rupert's Land. But the colonists are unmollified: hardship had been their lot for all their short lives, and they needed no Half-caste to teach them about fortitude. Stoicism was one thing, but needless suffering was another, so they blamed him, the Company, the Indians, and the governor for their troubles.

He is aware that all the prating, the discontent, is more than hunger or tragedy or even their guide's unmistakable uncertainty. Many of the people have been together since Orkney, and living so closely they have established a feel for each other, an undercurrent of understanding forged in hardship and uncertainty. Most days what needed to be done had been done, with no argument and little discussion. He had been amazed at how quickly these unprepossessing people had adapted to the rhythm of life on the river.

But something had changed. He does not believe that anyone as yet realizes what is occurring between him and Rose; no one has seen her enter his tent at night. But all depend upon each other for their very survival, and their tight and inflexible society may be incapable of accommodating the subtle shift that has taken place.

He is a strong believer in the power of things that cannot be seen, and is afraid they are all aware at some obscure level that their bond has been betrayed, that an illness has crept into their lives.

They would likely kill him if they knew. And Rose would be cast out, which in this wilderness would be much of the same. It disturbs him greatly that she makes sport of their love, teasing him before his men, and even her father, with obscure, dangerous references.

She watches him far too much, and he has taken to avoiding her glance, deeply though it pains him. What he wishes most is to be able to speak freely, to laugh and sing and announce his love for her to others, and to his *Manitou*, Jesus.

Their nights together are wonders within themselves, when for a moment they can cast off most inhibitions, although they must remain mute. So they let their hands and lips and bodies speak what may not be spoken. And while the ecstasy of these moments is beyond anything he has known, there is always a part of his mind listening, watching, and waiting for the sound of footsteps outside his tent, and the inevitable calling out. The rope would quickly follow: soft and pliable in the beginning, hard as iron at the end.

Rather than quench his fire, the danger stokes it, his heart presumably feeding its desire while it may. It is possible the girl feels something similar that would account for her foolish behaviour and this unnecessary risking of hers. It may be that she needs the fire more than he, the flames building in her breast to eventually consume them both. He has never heard of a desire like theirs; the drunken debaucheries the men brag they share with the Home Guard women are debased liaisons that pale in comparison.

Occasionally he had sated himself there, but always the thing was one of lust, and always he would slink away in shame, like a cur. He did not know where this grief came from, as such liaison was acceptable and even typical among his mother's people.

He suspected the priest's thundering blandishments had distorted his thinking; he had heard the man condemned any such practice since Alexander was a boy. He had even caught Alexander fouling himself and had beaten him with a stick until the blood had flowed freely down his back. His father had threatened murder if he ever laid a hand on the boy again, but Alexander could always feel the priest's malignant eye on him. All his life he feared the hellfire that he had been threatened with, his almost inevitable lot not only for his behaviour, but also for his unclean, Savage blood.

What he feels for Rose is unlike anything he has experienced with a woman, and he cannot believe that it is not a gift from God itself. He yearns to speak of it but cannot, and the need drives him mad.

As Alexander had predicted, the weather turned to the north and brought with it clouds and almost constant rain. The factor had not supplied the colonists with adequate tents, assuring them that he in fact had none, and that the tradition of using the York boat sails as an awning against the weather must suffice. After all, if it was good enough for Company men, it was bloody well good enough for a rabble of Highlanders and Orkney peasants.

So the sails are removed from the boat and crude communal tents made to shelter them from the worst of the onslaught. There is little dry wood, and they huddle beneath the tarps shivering and stinking and eating cold pemmican. Everyone is wet through, and even the blankets are mouldy and soaked.

The Indians seem much better off; they have brought several stout hides with them and each night after landing the women scour the bank looking for saplings for poles. They cut a lattice of spruce branches for a floor, covered by an oilcloth. They erect the poles, and drape several hides over this frame. They leave a gap in the covering for access, closed off by a tattered *okimow*. Inside, a small fire warms the cozy space.

But there is hardly room for the entire brigade in a small skin hut, and the only ones invited inside are Alexander and Declan; the rest do their best to keep out of the rain, maddened by the warm light that escapes beneath the edge of the Indian's comfortable, dry shelter.

It is better in the day — for the men — for although completely exposed to the weather, the hard work warms them and, as they row, their coats and shirts steam with their heat.

It is inevitable that sickness appears. Sniffles and coughs and fever. Even the Indians are not immune. The child develops some type of bowel ailment, and one evening squats and ejects a noxious yellow stream from between his flaming buttocks. Isqe-sis grabs him and bends him over her knee. She takes the blunt side of her knife — the one she had been using to fillet a fish — and scrapes away the feces from his buttocks. After releasing him, she wipes the blade on the moss and rinses her hands in the cooking water. Everyone watches in silence. The evening meal goes untouched by any but the Indians.

With the advent of sickness, the pace of their traveling decreases still further. Alexander is furious at them; they do not seem to comprehend that they are on the run from the winter that he knows is waiting just over the horizon. If things seem difficult now, they simply would not survive if they do not leave the North country within a few weeks. September is already old. But no matter how he curses, no matter how he exhorts them, the pace of the brigade declines even further.

"What disturbs you so, my love?" Rose asks, nestling under his arm and resting her hand on his breast. Their lovemaking had been half-hearted and unsuccessful and he had given up, lying down beside her while beads of sweat cooled his hot, brown skin. Rose enjoys the colour of him, seeing it as exotic and lovely. Men she had known always bore an unhealthy yellow or white pallor where the skin was covered, and red where it was not.

He grunts and rolls over on his belly. She traces a choreography of history with her fingers on his back: scorings of the lash, puckered lips of a knife wound that became severely infected: results of a drunken brawl, the point to which he could never recall. The small, white moon where a sharp willow had pierced his shoulder when he had slipped on a riverbank.

The scars whisper to her, telling of a hard life in the wild: pain, rage, repression; violent death always a moment away. But if the body shows its trials in its ragged integument, the aroma it gives is pure and sweet and healthy, unsoiled by time or human failing. It reminds her of fresh-mowed hay mingling with the blowing salt of the sea. He has been wounded, surely, but his scent reassures her, his soul remaining as honest as the day he was breeched. She moves her hands down and entwines her fingers in his own. He turns his head and looks at her, but her eyes are in shadow. The candle gutters, throwing wild shapes against the tent wall. He lifts her hand to his lips.

"It is this voyage, I suppose," he says at last, in answer to her question. "When journeying I always know where I am going and how — the road is clear. But the future is full of doubt, and I cannot see where it leads. All seems hidden to me."

"Is your mind clear? Do you know whither you would go?"

Alexander smiles at her. "I thought I did, but then you arrived in my bed."

Rose turns away. "Please do not say thus, Alexander. You cannot blame me for your loss of vision. Such a burden would be too much to bear."

"I do not blame you, Rose, but my purpose no longer seems as sure as it did, that is all."

"Pray, what was your purpose?"

"A good question. It once seemed to me to simply live free was enough, but as time passed, more was expected. Have you noticed this? Everyone wants you in their fold, to follow their path; you belong to me, you belong to us. Yet to chose a path requires one to abandon another perhaps equally worthy."

"I do not understand; please speak plainly to me."

"You are of one house and nation, of course you would not understand. I am of two fathers, each demanding absolute fealty. I am both Cree and Scots, and, in secret, these families despise each other."

"But you are more Scots, are you not?"

"My mother was Cree. And so lies half of my heart."

"So honour both."

"I would, but others seem baffled by such ambiguity; it is choose one or none. Your country fought America — what would you do if your father was American and your mother British? Where would your allegiance be then?

"That would be a difficult choice."

"So it would. Especially when one is doomed to defeat by the other."

Rose is about to reply when the sudden, distant yell startles both of them. Alexander jumps up, throwing on his trousers.

"Stay here," he whispers, checking the flint on his carbine. He leaves her sitting there, wide-eyed and trembling. Several men have climbed from their sleeping blankets and they all stand staring at a fire burning a little distance upriver. There is a flash as a musket fires into the night sky.

"Bloody hell," mutters Turr, running his hand through his thin hair. He turns toward Alexander. "We have a problem," he says.

"'Tis the Indians, sir," adds one of the Baymen. "And a few of them Highlanders. They's scarpered with some of the rum." They all watch as a keg moves around the circle.

"That does not look good to me," says Lachlan, suddenly appearing. "And where is Rose? Hellfire and damnation, she was not with me when I woke up!"

An Indian grabs the keg from a Highlander and pulls it to his mouth. They begin fighting, the rest of the Highlanders standing in a dark group a little ways off from the Indians, grinning and swaying slightly.

Turr straightens his back. "Well, as you are responsible for the company's supplies, Mr. McClure, I believe it falls upon you to retrieve the liquor, at once." Another shot is let off.

Alexander considers this. "No, I do not think so. It would be worth my life. And I need not remind you that discipline in the brigade is your responsibility, Mr. Turr. But it is best that we arm ourselves."

Lachlan puts his hand on Alexander's shoulder. "Explain to me, what is this? What is happening?"

"It is the liquor; a madness comes over them. I've seen it ravage the Indians almost as badly as the smallpox. Worse maybe."

"So they really are Savages ..." says Lachlan.

"Do not say that. Their ways may seem strange to you, but that is your ignorance. I lived many years with the Ayisiniwok, and the evil always came with the traders and their drink. Do not say that!"

Several of the Baymen quietly retrieve their guns from the boats and crouch down, resting their weapons on their knees and watching the revellers.

Quietly, while attention focuses on the fire, Rose leaves Alexander's tent and moves unnoticed into the crowd of watchers. The Indian women are also drunk, and Rose sees Isqe-sis stumble toward her husband, grabbing at the keg. Iskoyaskweyau strikes her across the side of the head, and she falls hands-first into the fire. Shrieking, she rolls away while her husband yells at her, kicking her in the side.

Over the last few weeks, Rose and Isqe-sis had become close. She had learned that talk while travelling is frowned upon, but once ashore and the work of setting camp and cooking is completed, conversation, flirting, and much banter is the order. The two of them had passed many evenings deep in conversation. She had been shocked and deeply disturbed to discover that the Indians knew all about her trysts with Alexander, and that they gave it no thought whatsoever.

She also learned that the Indians did not share European ideals of love, and the women offered themselves to all, seemingly without regard or discrimination. They laboured like farm beasts while their men sat around drinking their horrid tea, gambling, prating about their bravery, and abusing them. She thought it monstrous, but Alexander had often cautioned her not to interfere with nor judge the Indians' ways.

"Rose!" Lachlan shouts as he sees Rose burst from the crowd and runs toward the fire. Several men hurry after her. When they reach the fire, Iskoyaskweyau is kicking his wife in the head, still yelling, spittle spraying from his mouth. Rose shoves him hard in the back and he trips over Isqe-sis, almost falling. His moccasin strikes a burning log, and sparks and fire roar about him. He twists in the flames, a knife appearing in his hands. He lunges at Rose as Lachlan jumps in front of her, and it sinks deep into his side; with a grunt, the Orkneyman falls to his knees. Declan sweeps up a great branch from the beach and brings it down on Iskoyaskweyau's head.

When Lachlan awakes it is morning; a canvas has been stretched over him, and he can hear the chatter of rain on the dripping cloth. A fire burns nearby, and smoke fills the small space. Someone has placed a wet cloth over his forehead. Alexander and Rose sit next to the fire and behind them he sees the dark shape of Iskoyaskweyau, his head wrapped in a bandage. Lachlan struggles to sit up.

"No, Father, you must lie quiet."

"That Savage …"

"You are safe, Mr. Cromarty," Alexander says. "The drink has left him."

"His soul to the Devil! And what say you now about these Savages that you defended not a day ago?"

Alexander looks uncomfortable. "What I have always said. It is the drink that makes them mad."

"Get him out of here!"

"I cannot. He is here to minister to you."

"Eh?"

"Yes. Iskoyaskweyau is the best healer that I know. I asked him to see to your wound."

"I'll not have that damned Savage touching me. Be gone, you loathsome creature!"

"Then you will die. Look!" Alexander pulls away the pad of linen pressed against Lachlan's side. Lachlan's shirt and the pad is soaked in blood; from a long cut protrudes a tongue of liver. The cloth sticks to it when pulled away.

"Without his treatment, you will die. With his treatment you may still die." Rose chokes. "We have no physic here, nor surgeon."

"And what assurances do I have that he will not simply finish what he failed at last night?" Lachlan says, his strength leaving him.

"A rope around his neck."

A silence falls. Iskoyaskweyau moves beside Lachlan and as he kneels, mutters apologies. It was the drink, he says. It sets fire to him, takes over his spirit. He meant no harm to his friend's friend. He is shamed. He has lost his wife and his friend is angry with him.

"What does he mean he has lost his wife?"

Alexander sighs. "Isqe-sis died in the night."

Lachlan rolls over. He cannot believe what he is hearing — the same man who almost killed him is going to heal him. And everyone thinks this is a capital idea, despite the fact that this Savage murdered his wife not many hours ago. What an ugly, insane brutal country this is. What had he been thinking to bring his daughter here?

"It is not how you think it is," Alexander says as if reading his mind. "This is a different world than the one you know. It seems cruel, but women — women do not have the same value as in your country. But families are strong, and the men faithful and loyal. The missionaries try to change the attitudes, but it is tradition. A man may kill his wife, if he so decides. He must apologize to her family, and they may take revenge, but it is their way. We cannot interfere."

"And this is acceptable to you?" Rose says turning to him, her mouth a tight line.

"I did not say so. I am just describing what is. It is always best to accept what one cannot change."

"Like Isqe-sis's death?"

"Like Isqe-sis's death. Like Iskoyaskweyau's drunkenness. Like the presence of the traders who bring drink to the Indians. Like the disease brought by the Whites that killed my mother, and many of her people. I have told you before that there are many ways to die here."

Rose shakes her head, but does not argue. It seems to her that while there were indeed many evils in the world, the responsibility of the civilized person is to not accept them, but to move against them wherever they might be found. *Is that not what raises us above the Savage level, that we aspire to be more than the mean situation we might find ourselves in?*

She looks at the Indian sitting beside her father. She hates his foul presence, that he will be Lachlan's physician. As she watches, he gets up and mumbles something to Alexander and leaves the shelter.

"What did he say?"

"He will make a sweat lodge for your father."

~

"What shall we do with her," one of the Baymen asks Turr, indicating Isqe-sis's body.

"Damned if I know. As husband, she is his responsibility. Leave it to the Savage to decide what to do."

"It's making the men upset."

"So I see. Damn my eyes, there's always something, isn't there? You there, Mr. McClure!"

"Yes, Mr. Turr?"

"Speak to the Savage, will you? He must do something with this body."

"What would you have him do, sir?"

"She must be buried or disposed of in the river or something. The men are quite upset about what has happened, and I wouldn't be surprised if our noble provider over there found himself hanging from one of these trees before nightfall."

"Many Highlanders were also involved last night. Sir. It would do well to remember that."

Turr takes him by the arm and leads him away. When they are out of earshot, Turr leans towards him. "There is trouble festering here, Mr. McClure. I fear that this brigade is on the verge of rebellion. And it is not just the colonists; even our own men are as surly as I have ever seen."

Alexander looks over the camp. "You are right, Mr. Turr, I have not encountered such malaise, nor such wretched ill luck on any similar brigade. It should not happen this way. I am not sure — we are behind our time, but it is more than that. I no longer trust our journey."

"Oh, indeed?" says Turr, giving him a surprised look. "And what is the source of this misgiving? Is it the regrettable losses we have sustained? Or is there more? Perhaps the ferrying of Selkirk's trespassers into your lands sits poorly with you?"

Alexander stares at him. "I have nothing against these people, Mr. Turr."

"Then you are unique among your kind. It was your tribe who threatened the settlement last year, if I recall."

"I believe that was Nor'westers, sir," Alexander replies, keeping the edge from his voice with effort. "And Half-breeds. But I ask you to speak plain; do you believe me intent on sabotaging this brigade?"

"Hardly. But what a man thinks, and the choices he makes can oft be at odds with what lies hidden within his heart, hidden even to himself. I wonder if you are not so tormented with your current charge?"

"You may rest assured that there is no such conflict. The welfare of the brigade is my only concern at the moment. Though I wonder if it is not against God's will that we do this; perhaps He disapproves of Lord Selkirk's grand plan?"

"Who can know? But I am glad to hear of your allegiance; in times such as these all must choose sides: Scots, English, Savage, and Half-breed alike will be called to make a stand. The fate of the Company, and therefore England in Rupert's Land, hangs in the balance, and it will surely be war. Mark my words."

"I mark them, but it already *is* war, Mr. Turr. Word has long since caught my ear that the settlement has been burned out, the Nor'westers threatening death against any who return."

Turr stares at him. "My God, you are sure of it? The settlement has been dispersed?"

"I am not, but it would hardly be surprising giving the mood of the land."

"But the governor may be walking into a trap. We must inform him!"

"We cannot go any faster than we are now. I have been driving the people as hard as I might, to little effect. And now we have a wounded man to consider."

"There must be some way …"

"I will speak to Iskoyaskweyau. We can send him with a letter. I doubt the governor is far ahead of us."

~

Iskoyaskweyau tends the fire as Alexander pushes the door cloth aside.

"You look terrible, my friend," he says.

"I am a fool. Look at what the *Machi Manitou* in me has done." He rests his head in his hands.

"Yes, you are indeed a fool, Iskoyaskweyau. A coward who has done great harm, and for this you must make amends. Why do you cringe in here? There are things that must be done; you must complete the journey that you started last night."

"What do you mean?"

"Your poor wife lies outside like carrion for the dogs to pick at and you sulk in here like a child. You must attend to her."

"I had forgotten that in my grief."

Both men leave the lodge. Iskoyaskweyau begins peeling birch bark to weave into a coffin. He will lace them together with hemp and cover it with several soft sleeping-furs.

He and Alexander lift the body and place it near the river. Iskoyaskweyau kneels beside Isqe-sis and smears her swollen and burnt face with vermilion. All of her possessions are arranged at her feet. Iskoyaskweyau takes a small printed sheet of paper from out of his jacket, an English wood cut of a fisherman with a creel bulging with fish. He places the prized talisman on Isqe-sis's breast.

When they are finished, Alexander looks down at her. Her broken jaw is grotesquely swollen, her hair rolls partially burnt. He wishes for something pretty to accompany her, but there is nothing at hand. Not even a flower. But then he sees Iskoyaskweyau's silver earrings, and he points to one.

"Leave that with her," he says. Iskoyaskweyau nods and places it in her hand.

Alexander stands up. "Everyone, gather around, please," he says to the watching colonists. "Mr. Turr, perhaps you might say a few words?"

The brigade shuffles up, with several black looks to Iskoyaskweyau.

Turr rubs his jaw. "The twenty-third psalm, I suppose? Has anyone a Bible?" There is an embarrassed silence. "I see. Well, I shall do my best." He clears his throat. Everyone except Iskoyaskweyau lower their heads. The Indian sits on the ground beside his wife, and looks out over the river

"We are gathered here to mourn the passing of this poor woman. Her life was like that of most of her kind: full of savagery and hardship and brutally cut short. Such is the lot of those who live without the grace of our Heavenly Father ..." Rose walks over and places her hand on his arm and speaks into his ear. "Are you sure?" he says, looking startled. Rose nods.

Frowning, he addresses the company again. "I have just been informed that our sister here has been baptized, and was in fact a Christian. Praise ..." At that moment, a crow discovers an owl hidden in a nearby spruce and begins a frightful racket. Several other crows immediately gather, perching on nearby trees.

"Our Lord,"

Caw-caw-caw

"That He found this ..."

Ca- caw-caw

"Child in the ..."

Caw-caw-caw

"... wilderness ..." Turr's face turns a bright scarlet, but still he perseveres.

Caw-caw-caw "... and in his ..." *caw-caw-caw* "... mercy ..." *caw-caw-caw* ...

Declan takes two long steps, and before Alexander can react, the Highlander grabs his carbine and fires into the trees. The suddenness of the report makes everyone jump, and the crows burst protesting into the forest. The report chases itself with an echoing crash down the river valley. Declan hands the carbine back to Alexander.

"Thank you," Turr says. "Where was I? Oh, yes. And so we thank our merciful Lord that he has shown his light to this poor sinner, that she might indeed be part of His holy harvest. We pray that he forgive her evil and Savage ways. Amen."

"Amen," they all chorus.

"Where shall we bury her?" someone asks.

"We shall not," Alexander replies. "Iskoyaskweyau shall stay behind to build her a coffin. He will carry her into the forest, where she will be placed in a burial mound. This is their way."

Muttering breaks out among the men. One of the Highlanders approaches. He stands in front of Turr, feeling the weight of his fellows behind him. He is a small, round man with a yellow face and a greasy horseshoe of bluish-grey hair about his temples. His eyes are the colour of ashes. As he stands in front of the officer, he spreads his legs a little.

"Mr. Turr, we canna allow this; if she were Christian, she be deserving of Christian law. It is not right that man be left free."

"Since when did you care what these people do to each other, Mr. Burgess?" says Turr, cocking an eyebrow.

"I never liked those bastards, Mr. Turr, and there be a good man lying in there with his guts hanging out. That savage should be stretching hemp."

"Oh, indeed? But Mr. Cromarty has not yet succumbed to his wounds, and there are circumstances that you have not considered. Like where the Indian came by the liquor in the first place. We all know the Savage does not tolerate drink, which is the reason I limit the distribution of spirits. But someone pilfered a keg last night, with tragic consequences. I would like to know who that person is."

"The Savage ..."

"Does not go near the boat. Ever. No, it was one of you, a verminous scoundrel who has not the balls to step forward and take responsibility." He glares at Burgess, who stares right back. "She is the Savage's wife and will be dealt with according to their custom. I will hear no more of it!"

⁓

Lying in the steaming heat of the sweat lodge, Lachlan spends the day drifting in and out of sleep. When he at last fully awakens, he cannot tell what time it is, the only light coming from the coals of the fire. The smoke burns his eyes, although he can see the lodge is empty. His side feels as if on fire and perspiration beads his face and forehead. He yearns for his daughter to be with him, but is too weak to call for her. A twig snaps in the fire.

He remembers that day in Stromness, the day his life changed. It was cool and raining, the spring grass growing in the cracks of the cobbles and the rain-polished stone houses. The air was filled with the rich smells of peat and kelp fires wrapped in the muddy aroma drifting down from the tidal flats of Hamla Voe.

Sitting at his window, he had the shutters open, listening to the rain and staring at the Whitehouse Rock lighthouse across Stromness harbour. He had been composing that afternoon's Greek lesson when the sight of the harbour distracted him. He often looked down at the comings and goings in the harbour, at the lovely ships and the green islets of inner and outer Holm bejewelled with countless white seabirds. Like a scholar, he often wished he was elsewhere, yearned to walk across those heath-covered rocks, stealing eggs and frying them on a peat fire overlooking the great barques, sloops, whalers, and frigates crowding the harbour.

The sound of footsteps echo in the narrow, winding street, and he saw the figure of the father approach, his black cassock swinging. Tall and gangly, the priest often reminded Lachlan of a black stork. But he could tell by the man's quick steps that there would be no smoking in front of the fire that day, as they often did, musing on the finer points of philosophy and Greek poetry.

"Good morning, Lachlan," the priest said, spotting him in the window. "You seem like one contemplating truancy, if I am to judge the wistful manner in which you stare out your window."

"You are correct, Father, for there are times when I feel it would be worth a beating just to flee from here and run wild upon yon hills."

"And the beating well deserved, the misdemeanor being worth thrice the price," the priest responded, but Lachlan noticed that he did not smile.

~

"So what do I owe the pleasure of this visit? May I offer you some tea?"

"No, thank you, my son, I cannot stay long." They sat in Lachlan's office, a small damp cave wherein as the master of the school he meted punishment to students, convened with the schoolmistress, and composed his lessons. A massive oak desk dominated the room, with a Bible resting on one corner and a cane on the other, the twin pillars by which he impressed his authority upon the student population. There was barely room left for the two of them. Lachlan leaned back in his chair and lit his pipe.

The priest sat upright on his own chair, his dark head almost brushing the low ceiling. He watched Lachlan with eyes that were large and sad, in a face that carried the marks of a life spent toiling in the service of others, fighting a battle that could not seem to be won. His hands were very large with long fingers and knobby knuckles, and he rested them on his threadbare cassock.

"Will you not smoke, Father Louttit?"

"I doubt I will enjoy a smoke with you in here again, my friend. The Society has decided to close the school."

Lachlan stopped mid-puff, crossed his hands on his stomach, and stared out the window for several minutes. At last, he turned back to the priest. "Can you tell me why, Father?"

"Listen," he replies.

"I hear nothing."

"Exactly, my son. Subscriptions have fallen drastically this past year."

"But Father, 'tis the noon meal ..."

"Forty percent, they tell me. You must know how things are in the village, Lachlan. Many can find no employment. Poverty is rampant, and some of these men returning by ships have brought disease. There are whispers of plague returning, and many people are leaving Stromness, at least those who can afford the school's fees."

"This is not very good news, Father."

"Indeed, but the Society for Christian Knowledge is not heartless." The priest looked at him with a wry smile. "You are an accomplished headmaster, and the Society recognizes this and wishes to keep you on, but in a slightly different capacity."

So the priest told him about Red River and the New Colony, and the Society's belief that knowledge must follow into the wilderness to keep the settlers from falling backwards into darkness. Lachlan would begin the very first school at Red River.

He was at first shocked at the suggestion; he had never been away from Scotland in his entire life, and now they wanted to send him, at the age of thirty-nine, to a tiny settlement deep in the heart of what surely was a dark and savage land.

He had at first refused, but the priest told him to think about it. "I suggest you make good use of the next seven days and decide what is truly best for you and your daughter. It is a challenge, I agree, but not one beyond your capacities. I will return in a week for your answer. Until then, God keep you."

He and Rose did just that, spending their evenings around the fire talking about the possibilities for them, both in Orkney and in the new colony. Lachlan was concerned that his daughter had not yet been courted, and that her prospects would be greatly lessened if they were to settle in remote Selkirk's Grant, which was where the new colony was located. They spoke with people who had family and friends working with the Hudson's Bay Company, but these were individuals planning to return to Orkney after their usual seven-year contract at the Bay. No one knew of anyone who had surrendered their life on the islands and moved permanently to Red River.

"Be thou careful, schoolmaster. I's heard of some troubles out West," a neighbour told him.

"Trouble? What kind of trouble?"

"Ah dinna ken, ah only knows at I's heard, from the boys off the boats from the Bay. Settlers stuck in Prince William Fort for the whole winter; trouble with the Indians or something. Best watch out for thy lass."

When he mentioned this to Rose, she just shrugged. "Here, there, life is not easy no matter where we are, Father. There are troubles in Mainland, too."

He had to agree with her. Just the previous day, a storm had blown through Mainland; it was a fierce sou'wester, and, channelled by the mountains of Hoy, had wreaked terrible damage to the barley crop used by many crofters to pay their annual rent to the lairds. As if life for the poor was not difficult enough.

He had walked on Brinkie's Brae, the heather-capped ridge looming over Stromness. The hills were vacant but for the occasional flock of sheep stark against the emerald hills and a cool, fresh wind blowing in from the sea. Lachlan had a deep love for these empty, barren places, but as he bent and dug his fingers into the thin soil, he was reminded of the precariousness of life in the Orkneys. The island could not feed itself if the frost came too early or a summer storm destroyed the crop.

Remnants of ancient feudal systems still held sway, and most farmers still struggled to grow enough to feed themselves and satisfy the lairds. Lord Dundas, William Watt, James Riddoch William Graham, and William Honeyman all grew fat while their tenants starved.

Year after year spreading dung and kelp over the fields, sowing and praying that the crop will come. Sometimes it did.

Thin rocky soil; jealous soil. A turnip garden behind a damp stone house where an entire family lived with their animals. No windows, a smoky peat fire, muddy floor. Hunger always sleeping in their doorway. Walking barefoot in the mud, stepping unheeding in the cow's dung. Filthy children rolling among the animals, ignorant and barely civilized through no fault of their own, left behind by a world where nations are born under such banners as "Liberté, Egalité, Fraternité," and "All Men Are Created Equal."

Just then, a deep boom had echoed from the harbour. On Stanger's Brae, overlooking the entrance to the harbour, sat a cannon captured from an American privateer. It was fired to herald the arrival of the Hudson's Bay Company fleet. Climbing onto the crest of Brinkie's Brae, Lachlan looked down at a flotilla of three Company ships approaching the harbour. The clouds to the west broke and slanting sunlight shone through their billowing white sails. The sight took his breath away.

Oh, God, is this a sign that you have sent me? Shall I pull up from this harsh, miserly, beautiful place and start a new life in Rupert's Land, where the soil is not thin and rocky, but deep and loamy, where a man can work his hands and grow something to be proud of, something that will last forever?

There was no further sign, and even if there had been one, he would have dismissed it as coincidence. The clouds swallowed the sun again, and the ships reefed their sails and pulled into Stromness harbour.

~

Iskoyaskweyau pushes aside the bearskin that serves as a door to the sweat lodge. He dribbles some water from a skin flask onto the fire, and steam rolls toward the roof of the habitation, looking in that dim light like thunderclouds. He kneels a moment in silence beside the fire, as if praying. After a time, he approaches Lachlan, who, alarmed, tries to sit up on his elbows, but the bolt of pain that screeches up his side knocks him onto his back. He lays staring at the roof, panting, lightning bolts flickering across his blurred vision. He doesn't notice Iskoyaskweyau remove his bandage or pull out his long knife.

There is a tugging and an even sharper pain at his wound. "Oh, dear Christ …" he gasps, tears filling his eyes. The swimming shape of the Indian looms over him, and something soft and wet presses into his mouth. He begins chewing, the taste of his own flesh revolting him. He tries to spit it out, but Iskoyaskweyau shakes his head, and thrusts it back between Lachlan's lips. Gagging, Lachlan swallows. The Indian lifts his head and gives him a sip of water.

Laying the Orkneyman back down, Iskoyaskweyau reaches into his bag and pulls out some short willow twigs. Using his knife, he shaves one, and, with his teeth, peels off the thin white inner bark. He chews this a moment, and then leans over and spits into

Lachlan's wound. He does this several times, and the Orkneyman can feel the cooling saliva running down his side.

Chew, spit, chew spit. It seems to Lachlan the most absurd farce imaginable, and he yearns for the strength to strike the big, dumb brute. Soon most of the twigs are chewed, and Iskoyaskweyau wipes his mouth with the back of his hand.

"Soon you feel better," he says to Lachlan, ordering him to chew a bit of the bark himself, but to swallow, not spit. As Lachlan does so, he is surprised to feel the pain in his side diminish slightly. He contemplates the significance of this when he feels a pattering across his breast. Looking down he sees that Iskoyaskweyau has tossed some tiny bones on top of him, bones from some kind of bird. With that, the Indian picks up his drum.

He begins to chant a deep and melodic entreaty to his God to save this poor fool of a White man who is so far from his home and is in need of help and guidance and healing. The drum beats are slow and thoughtful, laying a deep, deep foundation to the man's sad song. Lachlan suspects the song to be a dirge.

The chanting carries on long into the night, Iskoyaskweyau's eyes distant and unseeing, his body covered in sweat, glowing in the light of the coals.

Chapter Nine

The rain stops some time before dawn, although every branch, every leaf tip, still drips. As the morning light broadens, they look out into a narrow cut in the forest thick with fog; the light grows to a dull grey, but stubbornly refuses to brighten any further. The snapping of the campfire sounds loud and disturbing in that silent, thick air. Every footstep, every muffled cough seems to draw attention to itself. All is silent except for the murmur of the river.

Alexander stands on the shore, moccasined foot resting on the gunwale of the boat, his carbine across his knee, smoking his pipe, and staring at the water. He is wondering whether they should attempt the next set of rapids that morning, or portage. They are nearing Jack River House and he is anxious to press on, but there is a real danger of missing the landing in the fog.

The length of the Echimamish River between the Nelson River and Robinson Lake is a twisting labyrinth of shallow reaches and swift waters, trapped-out beaver ponds and dams and spooky, burned swamps. Through this torturous region, they drag the boat more than paddle, running an endless succession of shoals.

All are obliged to walk, carrying as much gear as they are capable of. The boats are dragged through the portage, a rocking motion of heave, lurch forward, heave again, and with each effort advancing perhaps a yard or so, the wooden keel pushing aside the mud or rolling over hewn lengths of logs, the men sliding in the greasy holes left by the boots of the man in front. Now and then someone will slip and fall, and their progress lurches to a halt.

Behind the cursing and mud-splattered crew, the colonists stumble, their backs bent beneath their burdens and harried beyond belief by a fog of mosquitoes, horseflies, deerflies, and blackflies.

In the middle of one such portage, Alexander calls for a rest, and, with relief, the crew stops pulling; like the flowers of desert plants after a passing rainstorm, a host of pipes emerge and after a fire is struck the crew leans against the boat, puffing clouds of smoke.

Their leathers caked in black mud and sweat running in their eyes and dripping from their matted beards, they look like a troupe of circus bears as they spit and grunt and stare with their tiny blue eyes at the sky.

The portage runs through a great burn, and blackened stumps and jumbled lifeless poles surround them. The tangle is unbelievably thick, with visibility so limited they can scarce see a hundred yards in either direction. Beneath them is a soggy carpet of mud and ash, with just the beginnings of new green showing through. A year later, the land still reeks of smoke and charred wood.

A chickadee flutters to the top of a burnt spire and calls out *tee-dee-tee-dee* before arcing away in a flutter of tiny wings. Rose watches the bird for a moment, and then drops her little pack in the mud and straightens her back. Neither she nor Lachlan is expected to carry anything, but she cannot walk beside her people with their burdens without making an effort herself. Her dress clings to her back, and as the fresh air moves against it, goosebumps rise on her arms. She pushes her dripping hair from her face. The shadows of the forest are long, and the insects dancing overhead catch the last rays of the setting sun, turning them into early stars.

Rose's hair reminds Alexander of the autumn leaves he had seen that year he had travelled with his father to Montreal; mountain after mountain blazing a brilliant scarlet as if the frost had turned to fire. In the gloom, her hair shines with a deeper glow, like the embers of a fire. He sees her father approach, and he frowns. Although well-tended and his wound is healing fast, there is still something very much wrong with the man.

After the stabbing, Rose had not come to Alexander for many nights. This did not surprise him, as her father needed nursing and close care. But when he finally heard those footsteps outside his tent, he felt very pleased and welcomed her with feverish long-denied kisses. But later, she simply lay beside him, his arm around her and no more. She did not speak to him. After a few long, quiet hours, she had left his tent without a word or backward glance. The next night she did not return, nor the next.

A howl distant yet sharp and clear, breaks the evening peace. Rose looks sharply at Alexander.

"Wolves," he says around his pipe. "There are many along the river. I often see their tracks on the river's edge and hear them at night."

"Surely they are a danger? Must we flee this place at once?" Nearby colonists look concerned, but several of the Baymen grin.

"Ah dinna think we need be afeard o' no wolves, lass," one of them says. He is a large and hairy man, with round red cheeks and missing his left eye — from falling drunk on a poplar sapling. He wears no patch and the brown, shrivelled lid sags over the dark slit. The other is a bright as the sky, and his rusty beard is stained dark with tobacco about his lips. "Savages an' Nor'westers an' Country Born cut'roats like our Mr. McClure are what thee need to beware of."

"You are saying, sir, that the wolves are not a threat?"

"Ah dinna say no such thing. Thy wolf is a cunning brute, with blazing red eyes and jaws that will crush a moose's hind leg like a willer twig. Even the Indian be scared to death o' him. They'll come into village at night and carry off the young. Nothing the Savage can do about it either. Arrows just bounce off the thick hides."

"Then why are you all just sitting here?" says Rose, her voice rising.

"Do not mind them," Alexander interjects. "These are merely tales told to frighten children."

Rose turns on the man. "So you think I am a child, sir? That it is right to mock me?"

"Nay lass, nay," says the man laughing, bending over and whacking his knee. "An' I beg thee pardon. But thee want to be careful who thee listen to. I'll be damned if McClure were not raised by wolves himself, or so they say."

"And you think that it is tolerable that I should be so misused by this fool?" Rose asks, turning on Alexander.

"Just a bit of fun," he says. "No harm intended."

"Indeed, well, I do not intend to remain here and bear the brunt of this man's mischief. You are an uncouth scallywag, sir. Good day." She stomps off as best she can in the slippery mud.

Alexander stares after her, oblivious to the laughter of his men.

"She got a temper, that lass," a soft voice says beside him. He turns and looks into Declan's face.

"Excuse me?"

"And not much of a sense of humour. She will peel a lad like an apple if he gets on the wrong side of her, and once peeled, I have no doubt she be finished with him."

"Yes."

"Forgive me for interrupting, Mr. McClure," says Lachlan hobbling up. "But I was wondering if I might have a word with you,"

"Certainly."

"Why don't you join us, Mr. Cormack?"

"Aye."

"Lead the way to yon hillock, Mr. McClure."

"That would be ill-advised, sir. You are not yet healed."

"Take me. I must see!"

Alexander finds the easiest route to a rocky outcrop that they had seen from the portage. Lachlan is puffing by the time they reach the crest, his face cadaverous and leaning heavily on Declan's arm. They now have a good view of the country for many miles: a solid and featureless pelt of black, burned spires that runs from horizon to horizon, split by the undulating silver ribbon of the river. Thick clouds pass above their heads, so close that it seemed that they could lift a finger and pierce that grey cover, leaving a ragged tear.

"Where are we, Mr. McClure?" Lachlan asks, his voice unsteady.

"You should sit down, sir."

Lachlan shakes his head. "It is but a passing weakness. You were saying …?"

"We are almost at the confluence with the Nelson River. See there? It's hard to tell with the haze. We have run most of the portages now, and I daresay it will be easier and quicker going."

"And after that?"

"Well, Jack River House. South along the eastern shores of the Big Water — *Missinipi* — until the Red River and then a day's paddle to the Forks."

"That does not sound encouraging. We still have much distance yet to travel?"

"We have."

"I doubt I shall see the end of that journey."

Alexander looks at him, searching his face. "No, I do not think you shall."

"Dinna speak thus," says Declan.

"No, he is correct, Mr. Cormack. But it is a damned shame, you know. I had such great hopes for this new life, for this empty country. To be part of a great beginning."

"Beginning of what, Mr. Cromarty?"

"Oh, I don't know. A new nation perhaps? Civilizing the wilderness and all that."

"I hear this often. But what if the country you call wilderness is in fact the home of many people?"

"I do not understand."

"My people — and many others — live at the Forks. We live on the river for a time and hunt the buffalo. We hunt and we fish and we trap furs. We plough little, but this rich land you describe provides in many ways, and we do not go hungry."

Lachlan looks down at the camp below them. "But what does this forebode? Are these lands free or not? I was told the Red River Valley was bereft of all humanity, a rich land begging for the plough."

"I am sorry, but you have been told a lie."

At that, Alexander crouches on the rock, leaning against his rifle; Declan takes Lachlan's arm. Alexander stares out into the distance. He shakes his head.

What does it forebode? he wonders. *A good question, and it is a shame that only now this poor, doomed fellow bothers to ask it. It is indeed a rich land, but one occupied by Indians and the Half-breeds and the Country Born, not to mention the Canadian Nor'westers. People whom Selkirk and his ilk did not consider worthy of consulting; being less than human in the eyes of Scottish and British toffs. To them the land is indeed empty, counting the current inhabitants as they do the buffalo and the coyote.*

With this prejudice, they deposited at the Forks a weary and ramshackle band of colonists — interlopers and trespassers who proved themselves as helpless as children in their new promised land, and who would have starved that first year if the inhabitants had not taken pity on them and lead them to safety at Pembina.

We were fools to offer such kindness. Year followed year with the same result, caring for people who would otherwise perish, not wishing them success, but not ready to turn our backs on them and witness so many innocents die. Now Selkirk's arrogant fool Macdonell has set himself

up like Caesar with his pemmican proclamation, stealing food from
those who had always willingly fed his miserable band of trespassers.

But trespass is one thing, usurping a man's livelihood is quite another.
Selkirk did not count on the North West Company, and their jealousy
of their ancient trade routes. By attacking them at their very heart, he
has guaranteed war, and it is a very long way from the Bay to the Forks.

He had always traded with the Company of Adventurers, as did
his father before him, but in his deepest heart was more in tune
with the Nor'westers, those who befriended the Indians and did not
try to supplant them. Almost all of those living in the valleys of the
Red River and Assiniboine were Canadian and Cree mixed-blood,
and although his father came from Glasgow, it is his mother and
her people with whom he feels the closest affiliation. The Country
Born are often in conflict with the Half-breeds, but in this case,
they are allied. The time is fast approaching when he will be forced
to choose between these heritages.

"Dinna fash thyself, Mr. Cormack," says Declan in a soothing
tone. "I'm sure all will be well." He takes Alexander by the arm and
pulls him away, whispers in his ear. "What mischief is this? You
must not upset the old man."

"He has a right to know," says Alexander, pulling away. "What
does the coming of your people mean?" he says to Lachlan. "It
might mean many things. And war not the least likely. With
Macdonell acting like a pirate, passing shitty laws and stealing food
and supplies needed for the Nor'Westers and Half-breeds alike,
many say that Lord Selkirk has much larger designs, and is in fact
in league with the Company. A few more people living at the Forks
doesn't count for a hangman's fart, but a plot of colonization and
trade breaking will mean war."

"But … this is intolerable!"

Alexander's voice softens. "Aye, but here we all are, trapped in
Selkirk's nasty web. This will play itself out as it will, and we pawns
must act our little roles to the end. Mark my words, there are greater

stakes than our own at play here. Mine is to bring you to the settlement. It is your people's role to arrive there, prepared for what awaits them. It is yours perhaps to die along the way."

Lachlan collapses on the cold rock, staring out at the land with a blank expression. Alexander is watching a flock of geese pass overhead when he feels the Orkneyman fall against his legs.

Mosquitoes bite, and men and women scratch at the glowing lumps, smearing blood on their faces. Slaps are delivered and curses are muttered around a snapping fire, a waning gibbous moon latticing them with the shadows of fire-blasted cottonwood branches. Occasionally a branch will pop, sending embers tumbling skyward, to be swallowed by the silver moonlight. As the night ages, one by one, shadows leave the small comfort of the fire to retreat to bedrolls and windbreaks. In the darkness, a branch falls from a spruce snag leaning over the river and hits the water with a loud splash, and several heads swivel. The river chuckles and someone spits into the fire, the wad sizzling. A few dead leaves skitter past them, blown by a cool breeze.

It is dark inside Alexander's tent, the nearby fire casting flowing, ballooning shapes against the glowing canvas walls. Several mosquitoes hang upside down in the apex of the tent, graceful legs arching against the bright cloth. The tent flap pushes aside, and they puff into the air with a hardly discernible whine.

"I've brought you some water."

"Please sit beside me." Lachlan looks cadaverous yellow in the canvas glow, as if his laggard body needed to catch up with an already departed spirit. Burning with fever, he has kicked off his coverings and lies naked. Once on the verge of being what he called "portly," he now appears as knotted branches draped in a loose skin blanket, dark hollows collecting on him like pools of spilled ink. His voice is a rasping struggle for breath. The bright smell of rot thickens the air.

"Come kiss me," he whispers. "I'm afraid my voice fails me."

Rose takes a hand that feels as light and dry as a wad of old leaves. She kisses the knuckles, feeling the arm joints pop and click as she lifts it to her lips.

"I feel it is time to finish what I may," he says, eyes hardly open, visible only by a glint of reflected firelight below the dark lashes.

"Do not speak thus, Father, you ..."

Lachlan shakes his head. "I can see almighty God more clearly than I can yourself, my beloved daughter. It is time. Our Father has come for me." Rose bursts into tears, gripping the hand so hard it turns white.

"Nay, do not fret. I only ask that you forgive me."

"Forgive? What is there to forgive?" she asks, between her tears.

"There is much to forgive, lass. But what now troubles me is where I have brought you — you once said this is a dark and promised land, and, in my eyes, it is darkening by the moment. Soon all light shall be extinguished, and I will spend my allotted time in purgatory. I ask for your forgiveness, for I have brought you here and here is where I must leave you. I had hoped for so much better."

Tears flow from his eyes as he begins to choke. Rose props his head and gently rolls him onto his side with no more effort than turning over a baby. She gives him a sip of water from her skin.

"Of course I forgive you, Father," she says in an old voice.

"Nay, not yet," he replies in a wheeze scarce louder than the mosquitoes ghosting about them. "I have one more thing to request of you before I depart."

"Whatever you wish, Father. My soul belongs to God, but my heart is yours."

"I wish you to marry the Highlander, Declan."

Rose's eyes widen and she slumps back, dropping the hand. "You cannot mean this. I — I have no feeling for the man."

He turns his head towards her, tears again squeezing from the slitted eyes. "You must do this," he says. "Else I fear my stay in purgatory will have no end; my punishment for failing you so. And I may not rest, not without there is someone to care for you."

"Oh, Father, how can you speak like this? This is so, so cruel."

"It may indeed be cruel, as life so often is. But it is the lesser cruelty, I hope. I have always done what I can for you, my love. Many times I have failed, but my intent was always noble, and so lies the gilded road to hell. I believe you can spare me such a fate, if you do this thing I ask."

Grabbing his crisp, empty hand again, she clutches it to her face, tears flowing without reservation now, her body shaking. "I am yours. I will do as you ask."

Lachlan smiles ever so faintly. "Please forgive me," he says.

The noise carries from Alexander's tent, and those huddled around the fire stir. Lachlan has been retired inside, and they all wish for some kind of music or song, anything to mask the sound of impending death. Death they well knew, a familiarity carried with them all their days, but death next to a warm hearth and death in unknown wilderness were different things entirely to the Orkney heart: here there was no priest to bless and protect from evil, and they imagined all kinds of demons and wraiths haunting the shadows of the scabbed and burnt trees, ready to snatch the man's soul as soon as it was released. Several of the women began a soft, muttered prayer together. Those who have already retired lie staring up at the sky or a flapping oilcloth, listening to the comforting words.

Alexander spreads out in the bottom of the boat, smoking his pipe and watching the stars. The prow had been pulled up onto the bank, but the floating stern bobs on the river. Ripples slap the side of the hull:

Plip.

Plip.

Plip.

The night feels breathless.

He takes a long pull of trade rum from a skin bag slung at his waist. During the previous night, he had secreted the liquor from Turr's guarded stores. As it fills his mouth, he revels in the swirling heat. The strong vapours rise into his nose, and he shoves a finger along the base of it to stifle an imminent sneeze, his eyes watering from the fumes.

He might have been raised a Christian by his father, but his mother had told him that the world of the spirit might not be as simple as the one the priest described, the one with all the rules and proscriptions and well-defined characters. The Christian would say that angels now gathered to take the Orkneyman's soul, but he was uncertain what his mother would have told him; something equally difficult to understand, if not more so.

As he lies pondering, he sees a snail creep along the gunwale. Backlit by the rising moon, its silhouette is sharp, and he can see the creature's tiny eyestalks wave about as it scans the night. He takes another long swig of the rum.

Alexander marvels at the creature, at its slow yet persistent manner of travel, scanning the world as it goes. He wonders if it sees the stars as he does, whether the spirit of this humble creature also does homage to that which it does not understand, and yet stares at with awe.

The eye stalks pull back as he pokes at it with a calloused finger. They wave about for a moment and then the creature continues on its quest. It feels damp cold as it moves onto his finger. He lifts it toward him, and, at that movement, the snail pulls into its shell and he grabs at it to keep it from falling into the bottom of the boat.

He stares at the thing, rotating it in his fingers. *It has pulled into itself, only the base of the foot visible at the entrance to the chamber. So might a man retreat from what it does not know, assuming the worst. Perhaps that is the way with all things small and vulnerable.*

A moan carries over the water. He looks towards his tent where the girl nurses her dying father. He empties the skin into his mouth, the heat flowing through him.

What was I thinking ... like snails without their shells: lost and utterly naked. Not a soul among them that who does not wish for the kind of shelter this little creature carries. But myself and my men are

the best they can do, and I can tell by their looks and wonder and fear
that it isn't nearly enough.

The man dying in the tent cannot live without his shell.

While he lies watching the riverbank, he sees the Indians' encampment far downstream; Iskoyaskweyau had delivered his message to Semple's brigade and returned to them in his much faster canoe. Alexander wishes his friend had carried on and retreated to the Bay. Custom forbids hunting for one year as mourning for the dead, and he will be little more than another mouth to feed: indeed, a hated mouth. Although the Indians can be very dangerous when roused, so can the Whites, and his presence is sure to cause trouble.

At that moment Alexander perceives, or thinks he perceives, something moving along the riverbank. He stiffens and tries to focus; sounds sharpen in his ears. Gurgle of a protruding root, the slurp of the water on the bank, the conversation around the fire. Whistles of men snoring.

The shadow is in the deeper shadow of the bank and is invisible. But Alexander has no doubt that something is there. He sits up and reaches for his rifle; very carefully, he cocks the hammer, his other hand covering it to muffle the click. Crouching, he rests the barrel on the gunwale and peers along its length. The moonlight reflects across the top of the metal, highlighting the forward sight.

He swings this star across the shadows. The sight wobbles. He takes a deep breath, willing his heavy arms to respond. The site moves in and out of focus. He hawks and spits, trying to clear his mind. The creature lurking along the bank moves again, although stubbornly refuses to expose itself.

It waits there a very long time and Alexander loses count of his breaths. He rubs his eyes with a hand. He suspects the thing's intent is predatory, drawn by the sounds of suffering. The scent of fire and men would be signals of danger, and Alexander wonders whether the animal's hunger will be sufficient to force it beyond its fear.

He feels a pang as he contemplates the narrowness of the animal's purpose and hopes that it will reconsider the danger and leave as silently as it came. He places the sight on a spot where he believes the thing's heart to be and waits. One more step and its spirit will join the Orkneyman's that night.

Another murmur from the tent and the shadow moves closer. The flash of the gunpowder in the lock blinds Alexander and the thunder of the carbine shears the night, rolling and tumbling down the river.

Throughout the camp men leap up, pushing their womenfolk down to huddle as best they can in their bedrolls, to bury into the sand and disappear. Men run back and forth along the beach, tripping and shouting and cursing, grabbing at weapons while the women cry out. If it was indeed the Indian attack that all of the colonists — and even a few of the Baymen — fear, they would have been slaughtered.

By the time they grab their weapons, powder, and shot, and have their guns loaded, their enemies would have already been departing downriver, their victim's wet scalps hanging from the prows of their canoes.

Alexander shouts at them, but the uproar drowns him out. Cursing, he steps out of the boat and catches a foot on a thwart, catapulting overboard.

At that sound, all guns swivel towards him and let go in an awful fusillade. Smoke boils from the bank and a dozen balls whistle harmlessly over the river to smack into unseen boles on the opposite side. A few disturbed leaves fall.

Choking, Alexander stumbles to shore as the men begin a hasty reload. Fortunately for their guide, he is close enough to the fire to be recognized. Carrying a burning length of driftwood down the bank, they search for the dead wolf. There is nothing to be seen, just a churned-up hole in the bank from Alexander's ball.

"Ah, well, lad, shooting in the dark be no easy feat, moon or no," one of the Baymen says. Everyone is staring at him now; all can smell the strong aroma of rum.

Alexander runs his fingers through the river muck, shaking his head. He is about to reply when a wail breaks from his tent; the shock of the firing guns had given the Orkneyman to God.

~

The brigade stands at the water's edge, their heads bowed. Someone had produced a Bible — one noticeably absent from Isqe-sis's brief service — and Turr is reading from the twenty-third psalm. The shallow grave is along the bank in wet soil, mounded and already gathering leaves to itself. Two peeled aspen poles had been tied into a rough cross and pushed into the mud at the end of the grave. The temperature had dropped that night, and a few snowflakes swirl around them, frost already forming on the newly disturbed soil. The Baymen wrap their hide jackets tighter against the cold, though the frock coats of the gentlemen snap in the wind and Turr has a difficult time preventing his teeth from chattering while he reads. Flakes of snow wet the thin pages and he wipes it away, peering closely at the tiny print as he recites the verse. His voice carries in a flat drone, scarce heard over the wind in the surrounding trees. When he finishes, the *amen* lifts from the valley, to be picked up by the wind and carried into the wilderness.

After the service, a smoky fire of wet willow and spruce is lit, and the men huddle around it, warming themselves with a pipe and a mug of steaming tea. As he sips, Alexander notices an unsettling quietness about the men, that many will not meet his eye. His spirit feels heavy, thinking that they hold him responsible for the disasters that have afflicted the brigade. Searching his heart, he knows he cannot blame them. If there had been another to whom he could transfer his authority, he would gladly do so, but he is alone with his flawed leadership and no one can relieve him of his burden. Whether anyone likes it or not, these people are stuck with him. Once again, he curses the factor who has saddled him with this responsibility.

Pulling off his wool glove, he lifts his dudheen out of his jacket. After tamping down the tobacco with his thumb, he lifts a twig from the fire and thrusts the burning end into the bowl. Drawing deeply, the aromatic smoke fills his mouth and he closes his eyes. *There is nothing like a smoke in the morning*, he thinks. *A smoke and a mug can go a long way to setting a man right.*

He opens his eyes and sees Rose sitting on the bole of a huge cottonwood whose roots had been eroded free by the spring melt, and had toppled into the river. The root ball stands above her in its fine tracery, and she seems haloed like a madonna. Her head hangs low and her shoulders slouch, her hands clasped together on her skirt. A tattered shawl drifts about her in the wind.

Alexander walks over to a boat and removes a blanket. He drapes it over her shoulders. Without acknowledging him, she clutches at the cloth, pulling it tight around her. She appears so small and diminished that if one were to wrap the blanket but a little tighter, she would vanish from the world. No doubt, that is just what she wants. He aches to cover those small red hands with his own.

Yet for all her misery, the worst is yet to come, for when the brigade departs this little beach she will have to leave her father to the river. He turns away from her. "Ho, get those boats loaded," he shouts. "Mr. Ramsay, Mr. Farquhar, as quickly as you may, please."

At that command, the men rouse themselves from the fire, tapping out pipes against their boots, and throwing the remains of their tea into the fire. They drop the mugs into a crate as they line past the cook's station. Gear is gathered and oilcloths and bedding are rolled up.

As Alexander watches them, he suddenly realizes that the Indians are absent.

"Mr. Thompson, I do not see Iskoyaskweyau or his people. Do you know of their whereabouts?" Keith Thompson is a short, broad Highlander who barely meets the chin of most men, and he knows it. He compensates for this lack of growth by drinking more and fighting more than most of his peers, and by growing a tall, matted cap of red hair that he refuses to comb down, the result being that from a distance his head appears as if capped by a red skep. He seemed to believe that in any intercourse with a man, he would invariably come out the worst of it, and so he avoided contact when possible and whenever not, carried himself as if ready to lunge. One never felt comfortable approaching the strange little man.

He does not look up from stuffing his bag. "Gone," he says.

Alexander raises an eyebrow. "What do you mean, gone?"

Thompson turns and spits. "Like I said, mon. They's gone."

"Indeed? And where have they gone to?"

"Ah canna say. The heathen left in the night."

Alexander looks around. "Who else knows about this?" They all stop working and stare at him.

"There was a private discussion o' sorts last night. Seems they dinna like the topic. Left in a right bloody hurry."

"What kind of *discussion* was this, Mr. Thompson?"

"We dinna like at happened to Mr. Cromarty. We thought we would bring it to the murdering Savage's attention. Seemed he dinna want to hear what we had to say."

"So you ran him out? Mr. Turr, are you aware of what occurred last night?"

Turr shakes his head. "First I've heard of it, although I cannot say as I am surprised. And I shall not mourn his absence. The Savage has been little use, and source of much grief since we left York Factory."

"The Devil take it! Every hand is needed and now we are short. Did any of you fools consider why the Indians were engaged in the first place?"

"We dinna see them providing aught," Thompson says, reaching for the knife at his belt. "And I'll no' have a Half-caste bastard calling me a fool, by Christ." The men begin gathering.

"Do not chafe with them, young Alexander," Turr says in a low voice. "There is mischief afoot, and naught to do at the moment. You dare not rouse them against you."

"It is beyond the pale, Mr. Turr. Mr. Cromarty did not die from the wound he received from the Indian."

"Perhaps not, but you must be shy of their tempers. Let Macdonell deal with them when we reach the settlement. To harrow up further ill feelings can only lead to disaster for us all."

They are aware that the brigade has split yet further, this time between those who carry the authority of the Company, and her sullen employees and charges. There are two against a dozen or so unhappy men, and they have few illusions as to how things would pan out if it came to it. "Unity, sir, I beg you to seek unity."

"I am sensible to your plea," Alexander replies slowly, as if deciding as he speaks. "Although I have no idea how it might be achieved. I would gladly leave this rabble to Macdonell, but what of it? We have lost men, and those who were to provision us. As you know our foodstuffs are very low, and there has been no game."

"I am aware of these things, but I have no doubt you will find a way. You have shown yourself of remarkable wit so far, and in the most trying of circumstances."

"I thank you for your praise, as ill-befitting as it seems to me."

At that moment, Declan walks up, and, before Alexander can intervene, whacks Thompson across the head with an enormous pine branch. Bag, knife, and the little man fly across the beach, landing in a heap at the water's edge. His long red hair flags in the water like garish seaweed. Declan turns and faces the others with legs spread, his cudgel slowly circling in their faces.

"Anyone else have aught to say?"

"My word!" says Turr. They all stand in shocked silence.

"I thought not," Declan says.

Alexander puts a hand on his shoulder. "Enough. Come, you men. I meant no offence to Mr. Thompson or any of you. I retract my comment. Why do you all stand gaping? Mr. Ramsey, will you please ensure that Mr. Thompson is still alive? The rest of you, get those boats loaded, and make haste!"

Slowly, the men turn away and begin ordering the brigade for departure.

"Thank you, Declan," Alexander says. "Although likely not necessary, I'm glad you have my back, friend."

"Perhaps thee is right, but I am quite finished with this traitorous lot. The Devil can take them. Besides which, there are times when authority needs a little muscle to assert itself, is this not true?" He winks at Alexander. On the beach, Ramsey props up Thompson. He looks at Declan with a scowl, holding a rag to his wound. Alexander shakes his head.

⁓

They push the boats back into the channel of the river and the current sweeps them away from the beach. Alexander takes his place in the stern and the men begin pulling at the sweeps. A bite of foam appears at their prow as they continue their relentless journey into the heart of the land.

When they reach the first turn in the river, Alexander watches Rose closely; a tear appears on her cheek, but she says nothing, just sits with her hands gripping one another on her lap. Declan sits beside her, lost in thought. He reaches out to places an awkward hand on her shoulder, hesitates, and drops his arm helplessly. They turn the bend and the abandoned camp is lost to sight.

Back on the beach, the coals of the fire burns down. The snow has abated and only a few flakes vanish with a hiss into the embers. A thin and grey swirl of smoke drifts away, hovering over the cold grave a moment before lifting out of the river valley. Carried by the breeze, it weaves through the thick stand of dark timber, passing the stiff and bloodied body of a naked man swaying beneath a giant cottonwood. A raven calls in the forest.

Chapter Ten

Aside from the night noises of the brigade, the faint snores and wheezing, all about them is silent — no sigh of wind, nor call of night-birds. Not an insect stirs in the cold.

She had never known such depth of silence before, a brooding weight and presence, and as the darkness and night deepens, her mood changes, and, within that void, she wonders if she has at last comprehended the voice of God. It seems to her fitting, one that the Almighty would choose. The Savage may run and scatter at a thunderclap, but this silence is immeasurably deeper, and you could easily lose yourself in it, walk naked into its emptiness.

The feeling is on the periphery of her senses, and, as an experience, it is hard to hold. For the silence lies over a vast wilderness, and the teeth of the land always draws attention to itself, blinding the viewer to the profundity behind the threatening mask.

She knows of no grand myth of the land to grab hold of, to steady her, to give her direction. All she can claim is an inchoate yet growing fear of the unknown. Primitive and corrupt, these routes of trade seem to her threads of spider silk traversing the unlit, empty space of a stone crypt.

Declan had accompanied Alexander on a hunt, and they had not returned. She feels their absence, as well as that of her father, and the silence grows still further, her ears pounding. She struggles to hold back her tears; in her solitude, she can ill afford any weakening of her will. She knows that if she were to let go, if only for a moment, she would plummet into a hole from which she might never ascend.

She yearns to sink into someone, to be able to let go knowing there is soul keeping a strong line on her, allowing her to trace her return when her grief is spent. And if she has not the strength to find her way out of her labyrinth, he will enter in and retrieve her. But all she has is the silence.

She shares an oilcloth tarp with an Orkney family and although they have comforted her as best they might, they had fallen asleep long ago, and she is alone. Alone in the wilderness and it is her own doing. It is chiefly because of this that she bites down so on her grief. Her heart had been against the journey from the very beginning, but seeing her father's joy at the prospect, she had withheld her reservations, not wishing to bring ill luck upon them or dampen their spirits. There was a part of her that indeed rejoiced at the prospect of a new life and adventure in the great lands to the west, but beneath it all was a mistrust and foreboding. Now God had decided to punish her for her wantonness by taking her father.

Unrestrained, her mind wanders, peeking into holes, caverns of old and dusty memories. Moonlight on a sash, a lover's breath on her naked breast. Her father bent over his books, preparing the week's lessons. The mongrel their cart had run over, crushing the life out of it. Flashes of moments, all lit with the energy of life, emotions, and powerful thoughts. Slowly these pieces come together, coalescing on a memory of one dark night and a cobbled street shining in the wet.

She and her father were coming home late from a visit to an acquaintance from his school. They commonly spent their evenings going round to his colleagues, side by side almost in the manner of a married couple. Lachlan was very social and conscious of their position within the city's small establishment, and often entertained or visited among the learned elite.

That night they had taken the curricle due to the threat of foul weather, and, despite her father's protests, she insisted on walking back. He could either abandon the carriage to accompany her on foot, and therefore be forced to walk back and recover it, or he could proceed home ahead of her, and she would catch up with him shortly. It was no great distance.

But Lachlan had consumed much wine that night and was in no mood to compromise. After cursing that he was damned that he would walk both ways, so she could bloody well walk by herself; with any luck it would begin raining and a good lesson it would be. He shook the reigns and headed off.

It *had* rained earlier, though the weather remained warm. The wet cobbles of the road shone on the moonlight, and after the *clop* of the horse's hooves had faded in the distance, Rose was finally able to relax. The after-dinner discussion had dragged on for her, the men discussing something called *phenomenology*; arcane and pedantic talk that she did her best to shut out, focusing instead on the cuckoo clock, waiting for the silly bird to show itself. The lady of the house prattled on about a woman's duty, asking why was such a pretty young lady not married? This kind of drivel was much worse than the *dialectic*, and Rose ignored her as much as she was politely able, willing that feathered fool to show its painted, crowing head.

When the visit was over, it felt a relief to be outside and embrace the night. She carried a parasol with her in case the rain returned, and she swung it as she walked along the narrow road. The village of Stromness sloped toward the harbour, and she could see between the buildings the fog-shrouded lights of the many ships anchored there; she wondered if a future lover or husband waited on one of those ships, looking out at the town with a yearning hope and desire.

As she walked toward the water, the fog began drifting in. Above her, the moon sailed bright, illuminating the ghostly tentacles that crept toward her between the buildings. The air chilled and became damp, and she lifted her knitted shawl over her head.

She was walking in a narrow lane when she heard a sound — nothing identifiable, just the sudden awareness that she was no longer alone. A light glowed in the window of the house beside her, and, curious despite herself, she crept closer and peeked inside. The curtains were sheer, parted slightly at the middle. It was someone's drawing room, a well-to-do family judging by the dark, ornate furniture and the artwork that covered the walls. At first she thought the room empty despite the warm peat fire in the hearth. The choreography of light in the room bewildered the eyes with lumpy shadows that moved and rolled with the draft moving through the chimney. She was about to turn away when something caught her eye.

On the floor, a little distance from the fire, sat a man and a woman. He was dressed in white breeches and blouse, which was unbuttoned at the neck exposing a mat of thick hair. His back was toward the fire, and he was barefoot. The woman faced away from the window, her long black hair lay like ink rolling down her white muslin gown. The two of them sat together in a golden chiaroscuro, and, as Rose watched, the man leaned forward and kissed the woman on the neck.

Rose stepped back from the window, her face hot. She looked around; the foggy streets seemed deserted but for the distant sound of a man singing, down towards the waterfront: *Kae and k-nockit, kae and k-nockit, kae and k-nockit corn; the only meat we ivver get, is kae and k-nockit corn.*

She knew that she must keep on walking, but the fog seemed to surround her in a delicious anonymity.

Almost against her will, she turned back towards the window. They were sitting closer now and the man's thick hand was on the woman's shoulder. Gently he slipped the gown to the side, a pale shoulder emerging. He bent down and kissed along its length. His other hand worked its way into her cascading hair, wrapping it around his fist; he jerked her head back and lowered his mouth to her proffered throat. Rose could clearly see the welts he left as he bit across her skin; the sounds the woman made were sharp and breathy. The man helped her lift her gown over her head and laid her down on her back. He guided the woman's hand into his trousers; she rocked her arm back and forth awhile, until he got up and removed a candle and holder from the mantle and lit it in the fireplace.

Returning to the woman, he reached down and produced a knife; Rose gasped. She saw him plunge the knife into her, cutting sharply along her chest. The lacing of the woman's corset parted and it fell to the sides, exposing her breasts. She lay with her face turned to the fire, her dark neck rotated in an exquisite contrapposto, her breasts rising and falling with her breath. The man lowered his mouth to them, his lips seeking, rough hands moving over her.

He lifted the burning candle and tipped it over the woman, tracing a line across her breasts. As each drop landed, the woman gave a little jump, and Rose jerked in sympathy, imagining the hot wax on the soft flesh. Her own breath was raspy, and, with each exhalation, a faint mist briefly clouded the window glass.

A sudden noise in the lane and she whirled around; a large emaciated dog emerged from the fog, following the edge of the walkway with its nose. It almost collided with her before it realized she was there, seemingly as surprise by her presence as she was by its own. Its hackles lifted, teeth shining against dark fur.

Rose raised her parasol over her shoulder, the dog's eye's following it. A whimper came from behind the window. Lowering the parasol, Rose extended a hand. Very carefully, the dog extended its muzzle to sniff. She reached a finger forward and caressed it. Slowly, very slowly her hand moved forward until it lay upon the dog's hard skull. She began fondling its ears and the animal's tail dropped. She squatted, moving her hand along its back, feeling the jut of bones beneath the soft fur. Her hand became wet with its coat of dew.

A last lick at her hand, the animal turned and disappeared into the moonlit fog.

Slowly Rose stood up, felt drops of sweat chill on her forehead, uncertain of whether they were the result of the fear at the encounter with the dog — or something else. Another noise came from behind the glass. She wanted to leave that haunted lane, but something had awoken within her and it cried out in frustration. The sounds from the room reached into her and drew her back to her place, and she saw that the pair were completely naked now. Holding himself up by his arms and gleaming with firelight sweat, the man lay between her raised knees, rocking, the woman's dark head nodding back and forth. His face lifted towards the window, and his eyes met Rose's own.

She leapt back from the window and ran all the way home. Her father was just leaving the stable to search for her. He was very angry and whipped her with his crop. Afterwards she undressed except for her shift and crawled into her bed; her buttocks ached from the beating and she squirmed with a mixture of anger and shame and delight, the tears drying on her cheeks. Something inside her grasped at the blows she had received, and she could not take her mind from that fog-shrouded window.

Her hand moved by its own accord, and she watched, spellbound as it lifted up the light cloth and worked into the place, finding it warm and wet and receiving to her touch. Her body convulsed. And again. Wave following wave flowed through her while the slatted moonlight from the window crept across her swinging hand.

The next day she felt great shame about the whole business. The ways of a man with a woman were still secret to her — as were the ways of a woman with herself.

Although she swore she would never sully herself in that manner again, she found herself needing a quiet moment alone to compose herself quite frequently. She assured her father that it was just passing weakness, and when he inquired just what kind of weakness would send a young, healthy woman abed several times a day, she could not answer.

She also began going on long commons by herself, especially in the evening, which Lachlan quickly put a stop to; it was unseeming for a young woman to walk the streets at night, and if she needed so much exercise, she could go by day, with him along, by God.

But when the chance presented itself, she would sneak out of their cottage by night and make her stealthy way back to the lane. Often she would find the young lovers in front of their fire, the curtain slightly ajar as it had been that first night, and she would lean against the damp stone, watching; sometimes her hand would even do its marvellous dance, and she would feel as if she had joined them. She was certain they knew of her presence by the window, and that knowledge and the possibility of discovery made her feel even more wicked.

But one night when she took her spot at the window, she found the wizened face of a harridan glaring out at her, and, with a curse, the old woman thrust the curtains closed. The next time she arrived to find the gossamer replaced with heavy wool. She never returned to that lane.

As she lies in the darkness of a land thousands of miles away from her warm bed in Stromness, she again pursues the solace that she had once found, seeking pleasure through her grief and tears, desperate to shut out the awesome silence. As her fingers find that comforting place, she thinks of the two young lovers, and for the briefest of moments is no longer alone.

Chapter Eleven

The wind that had blown from the north for the last several days turns about and carries from the opposite riverbank, bringing with it the tattered remnants of a summer that still lingers in more southerly parts of the continent. The low clouds that had seemed to drift about their very ears lift and dissipate, leaving behind a sky as blue and luminous as the inside of a sunlit robin's egg.

Rose is surprised to see the sun so strong and high; the weather had been so cold she had forgotten that the season was not far advanced, and the harvest moon had not yet waxed to its full. The warm air seems to blow new life into her, and she breathes deeply of it.

The weather seems to have a similar effect on her colleagues: the squabbling and division that had bedeviled the brigade is replaced by crude humour and the occasional hummed song. But, despite the lifting of the mood, her mind stubbornly drifts back to Lachlan, and the two women, and the husband left sitting forlornly by the water. She knows she will never take a river for granted again.

For those that had been left in the river's embrace to wait until the coming of Jesus with his fiery sword, she had great pity and sorrow. Especially her father — that was a wound so large and bright she forbids herself to approach it, entombing it until the day she feels safe enough to surrender to that unquenchable misery.

Turning toward the water, she leans over the gunwale, peering into the river. Her own eyes look back at her, dimmed by grief and loss. A goose feather rotates across her reflection, blown by the warm breeze; the water split by its small wake comes together after its passing and the eyes return with the same pain, the same confusion. She looks up, resting her head on her crossed arms.

Far overhead, a raven passes over them, watching the tiny almond-shaped vessels crawling up the silver band winding its crooked way across the dark forest. The raven cocks its wings and drifts in lazy, slowly descending circles, curious about the light flashing from the swinging oars. The river enters another, much broader river, and the boats move straight out from the smaller river's mouth, a wide *V* spreading behind them. A flurry of activity on board and twin poles are raised; they hoist sails and ship sweeps, and surge along in the freshening breeze. The surface of the water is corrugated by wind and sun, and the sound of singing voices rises from it like smoke.

> There were twa bonnie maidens, and three bonnie maidens,
> Cam ower the Minch, and cam ower the main,
> Wi the wind for their way and the corrie for their hame,
> And they're dearly welcome to Skye again.
>
> Come alang, come alang, wi your boatie and your song,
> To my Hey! bonnie maidens, my twa bonnie maids!

The nicht, it is dark, and the redcoat is gane,
And you're dearly welcome to Skye again.

There is Flora, my honey, sae neat and sae bonnie,
And ane that is tall, and handsome withall.
Put the ane for my Queen and the ither for my King
And they're dearly welcome to Skye again.

There's a wind on the tree, and a ship on the sea,
To my Hey! bonnie maidens, my twa bonnie maids!
By the sea mullet's nest I will watch o'er the main,
And you're dearly welcome to Skye again.

Alexander leans on his scull with a grin, listening to the singing of the Highlanders. The men are pouring their hearts into it,
though one can imagine by the restlessness of their hands that they
miss a tankard to go with their song.

The blue water of the Nelson River is stirred into a fine chop, and
the heavy boats seem to scud effortlessly along the surface, driven by
the press of canvas. It is rare when they can make use of the sails, and
the men sprawl in the bottom of the boats in grateful contentment.

Rose sits in her usual spot against the starboard gunwale, staring out across the water. A few hairs have escaped from beneath
her shawl, the fine red strands twisting in the wind, reflecting the
afternoon sun. As Alexander watches, he feels an impulse to reach
for those lovely hairs, to have their softness in his hand. Her cheek
glows with light from the glittering water, and he craves to again
run his fingers over that warm, yielding flesh. Terrified that he will
do something foolish, he folds his arms over his chest, the scull
jammed in an armpit.

He turns to check on the following boat. They are falling behind,
her young and inexperienced steersman unsure of how the rig works,
the sails twisting and spilling air. *They will catch up eventually*, he

thinks. He suppresses an impulse to slow down, remembering that it is the responsibility of those behind to keep his pace, not the other way around. Turning back, he notices the empty places in the boat, and they sadden him, but his grief is tempered by the long roll of loss that he carries in his memory; death is but a freak snowstorm or a damaged canoe or a charging buffalo away, and the living can ill afford more than a passing nod for those taken. Life takes one's full concentration, and time is not to be squandered by worrying about what might have been. It is all in God's hands, anyway.

To the south of them is Jack River House, the last Company post before the Red River settlement, and he fancies he spies a thin line of smoke rising from a distant point. The sight gladdens him, for tonight they will eat fresh meat and have their fill of drink, and the colonists will at last have walls between them and the forest. It matters little to *him*: as something that had spent too long in a cage, he could not long stay inside. He would get edgy and seek a door, or the light of a window. He was never far from one. When staying at York Fort, he preferred to sleep in the courtyard, or alongside the great river. Even when summer thunderstorms marched up the valley, washing over him with light and noise and rain, he would lie back in the warm moss, the water flowing over his face and into his beard. The Indians peering out from their tipis would sometimes see him, lit by lightning, and mutter to themselves, cursing him for a devil.

"Mr. McClure, what is that I see there?" asks Turr, interrupting his reverie. "It appears to be smoke."

"I am uncertain. I had first thought that it was Jack River House, but we are still too far north. We shall proceed carefully, but I suspect it is a camp of trading Indians."

"What is Jack River House?" someone asks.

"It is our last post before entering *Missinipi*, the Big Water. As you know, we follow the eastern shore of the lake until the mouth of the Red River. From there, it is but a day's easy journey to the settlement. Tonight you shall all eat your fill and sleep behind closed doors." A cheer went up from the boat.

"Why, it sounds like we are almost there," says one of the Orkneywoman with a wide smile.

Alexander shakes his head. "It is not called the Big Water for nothing. It is a great ocean in the heart of Rupert's Land and it will take many long days to reach the southern end, and that with favourable weather; there may be terrible storms waiting on *Missinipi*, and we cannot take anything for granted, most of all time." The woman's smile vanishes and she lowers her eyes. Her shoulders slump as she recedes into herself.

"That does not sound very promising," offers Rose in a quiet voice, looking at the filthy, haggard wretch with as much sympathy as she could find in a dry heart.

Alexander's nervous laughter dies on his lips when he realizes that she is serious: that their journey had taken much from them and the possibility of more danger and adventure might prove more than they could bear. As for Rose, she had been as stoic as any man, and Alexander has been unaware of the price she has paid for this. He had seen the limits of the father, why would he expect the daughter to be so different? He does not reply, cursing himself for his loose tongue. They sit in silence, having lost their good humour, and the sunlight no longer feels so warm.

~

The brigade creeps farther south, and, as they near a headland, Alexander realizes the smoke they had seen from the mouth of the Hayes is indeed not from Jack River House, but from an Indian encampment along the shore of the river. As they approach, they see many canoes pulled onto the beach, and Alexander orders the sail dropped and the sweeps put out. He steers them away, but it is too late. While they watch, three canoes put out with four Indians in each; two more appear from the opposite shore. They all have black scalps dangling from their prows.

The canoes are much faster than the York boats and Alexander orders the first three lines of rowers to ship their sweeps, the last line he leaves to give them steerageway.

One the Baymen reaches for a fuke.

"Leave it," Alexander mutters alongside his hand. "Make no sudden actions, any of you, for your life's sake!"

The canoes quickly draw alongside them; the Indians all have the short-barrelled muskets they prefer, resting across their knees, and Alexander does not wonder if they are primed. Their faces are painted in ebony and white, and they have partridge fathers hanging from their long, black hair. Charms of bone and silver drape about their necks. Their eyes sweep the occupants of the boat. Seemingly recognizing him, one of them addresses Alexander in a unique tongue.

"Who are they?" Turr asks. "And what do they want?"

"They are stone Indians. *Asinepoets*. Their chief wishes to speak with us."

"Tell them we have no time. Tell them to go away."

Alexander stares at him. "To do so would be an intolerable insult, and an invite to battle. We have no choice but to accept the invitation."

"The pox on them. I will be damned before I stick my neck into that trap!"

"We have no choice," Alexander repeats.

"I do not agree. We outnumber them three to one."

"And the women?"

"Ah, yes, I forgot. Blast and damned, this is not good … what the deuce is that fool doing?" he says as the other boat — the one having difficulties with their sail — shoots past.

"Hola!" Alexander shouts at their rapidly retreating stern. "Ship your sails. Come about!" The Indians had not yet engaged in chase, but he doubts they will remain still if the boat carries on much farther. It takes those aboard an uncomfortably long time to get things organized, and when they finally work their way back, they accidentally collide with Alexander's boat. There is a great deal of jostling and cursing, and Alexander cannot imagine what the Indians think, but is sure he sees laughter in their dark eyes.

After arranging themselves into a semblance of order, they follow the Indians to shore. A large crowd watches as they approach, wrapped in white capotes and hides and many carrying fukes. The forest stands behind them like a dark wall, and several women and children melt into the shadows of the trees. The sun is lowering over the western shore of the river and the light reaches between the dark spruce, illuminating the shaggy grey mosses hanging there, glowing motes of dust and insects woven into the interlaced space. Shadows move there, glimpses of people or ghosts slipping from bole to bole, only half realized.

"Why the unease?" whispers Rose. "Do the Savages truly pose a mortal threat?"

"Proportionately, no," Turr replies under his breath. "Any number of misfortunes might befall a man in life, though a tommyhawk between the eyes or an arrow through the ribs is in fact most uncommon."

"This is not what I would have expected. After all I have read and what I have since experienced, I am struck by the violent passions of the Aborigines."

"They are rather too busy making war amongst themselves, my dear, to bother with us. Besides which, they have become rather dependent upon our trade."

"Might I suppose by that you mean our liquor?" says Alexander.

"No, sir, you may not. And I must insist that while I despise that aspect of trade as much as yourself, it has long been out of the Company's hands. If one must seek fault for the deplorable liquor habit of the Savage, one must look south and east. Do you think a *Canadiene* worries about such things? The scoundrels will approach the Savage's tents while the beaver skins are still warm, and upon offering the Indians rum, acquire all available peltries on the spot. The Company resisted until the Indians would no longer trade unless liquor was part of the bargain."

"Hardly a moral position, sir."

"Perhaps not, but there is precious little morality in this land."

"In my short time here, I have seen what drink does to them," adds Rose. "And I am shocked that than any god-fearing soul would dare trade in the vile stuff. He will have much to answer for when he is called before God."

"I agree, I agree, miss … but in answer to your question, in truth most Company men are lost by drowning and untreated hernias."

"Indeed, sir? You amaze me."

"Oh, yes, the men carry packs that weigh close on to two hundred pounds through the portages, and at a sprightly gait. If mishap should befall him, there is not a physician available for many hundreds of miles."

~

After a quick debate, it is decided that the Company representative and leader of the brigade shall leave them and meet the chief; the rest are commanded to wait in the boats.

As Alexander steps ashore, Turr grabs his arm.

"You are going unarmed?" he whispers, not taking his eyes off the Indians waiting for them.

Alexander shrugs. "One shot is hardly much use. Besides which, I know of no reason to be concerned … leastwise not yet," he adds in an undertone.

"I suppose not, but damn it, man, this is extraordinary. Walking into a camp of these devils with naught but superior wits and a king's reputation behind us."

"I'm not so sure about superior wit, Mr. Turr; if we were so clever we should not be in this scrape, nor do I think the name of a distant monarch will hold much currency here, but we shall see, by and by."

"What about the brigade?"

"I beg you make your thoughts clearer, we have no time."

"Forgive me, but perhaps we will prepare them for an untoward outcome of this parley? Perchance we encounter mischief, they should be armed and prepared to fight."

"I suppose so, but I am doubtful in my mind," Alexander replies. "I fear an ill-considered reaction on the part of a man left behind; one witless fool with a tender trigger finger and we shall all have our throats cut."

"But we cannot leave these women undefended, possibly to await death, or worse."

Alexander's frown deepens. He steps closer to the nearest boat, lowering his voice. "Mr. Ramsay, get those muskets loaded and armed. Pass one to every man who can hold one without shooting himself. Load, prime but do not cock! If I see but one taut hammer when I return I shall personally shove the gun down that man's throat. Be quick but discreet."

"Wise, sir. Very wise."

"Foolish, bloody foolish, Mr. Ramsay, but there is nothing for it. Are you content, Mr. Turr?"

"As much as possible, given the circumstances."

"Then let us go. Lead on," he says, waving his hand to the four Indians who are waiting on the beach, watching them.

They follow their hosts into camp. The smell of wood smoke is heavy in the air and they walk past a rack of willow branches upon which long strips of moose meat are drying.

"Someone, at least, has had luck on the hunt," Turr observes.

The Indians lead them to a tipi, and one of them lifts the hide covering the entrance. He points inside with his musket.

"My word, I don't like this ..."

"Steady, Mr. Turr. I do not know what is in train here, but pray for smoke."

"Smoke?"

"Tobacco. If they intend mischief there will be no pipe offered." The Indian gestures again with his gun while the others move closer, surrounding them. Looking hard at the man holding up the hide, Alexander ducks his head and steps inside, Turr close on his heels.

Several Indians sit in a semicircle about a central fire, wrapped in capotes and buffalo skins. Smoke drifts upwards toward the smoke hole, glowing in the sunlight that shines through the yellow hide. It is hard to see clearly in the thick haze, though the murmurings that they had heard outside stop as they too sit cross-legged in front of the fire.

"Welcome," says an Indian in the Stony language, of which Alexander is no expert. Squinting, he cannot make out the face opposite him because of the smoke. After a moment, he nods in reply.

"You must be hungry. Please eat with us." Chunks of moose meat impaled on twigs are pulled from the coals and handed to the two men. So that was what he had been smelling without knowing it. His stomach contracts; the aroma is delicious.

"We thank you for your hospitality," Alexander replies cautiously, taking the proffered food. The Indians sitting next to him do not look up from the fire.

"You have journeyed a long way?" says the voice.

"Yes, from York Fort on the Bay."

"A fair distance. You are trading?"

"Yes."

"That is good. Trade is good. But why do you bring women? Are you trading women now?"

Alexander hesitates. "They are the wives of some of our men."

Soft laughter carries from beyond the fire. "That is very unusual is it not, for a White man to bring his wife with him? I have never seen this before. The Indian takes his wife with him, but the White traders leave her behind, is this not so?" Alexander bites into the food without answering the question. There is a long silence, and he can feel Turr's agitation beside him.

"You have many guns my warriors say," the voice begins again. "Guns and much gear."

"We have what we need."

"All men have needs. But it seems to us that Whites need much more than Indians."

"A man must decide what he needs and does not need."

"Truly, and so you will decide thus."

"What are they saying, Mr. McClure?" Turr interrupts.

"Who is this rude idiot?" says the voice. "Tell him to shut up."

"Do not speak!" Alexander says to Turr. Perspiration slicks his forehead. He knows that a parley is occurring, couched in nuance, and he struggles to understand the meaning behind the chief's speech.

"A raven spoke to me in a dream."

"Raven is wise."

"But foolish."

"But his foolishness always has a purpose, whether we understand it or not."

"This is so. In my dream, raven carried a brigade to me, on his back, telling me the *Manitou* has given it to me for my glory and greatness. But he said to be careful and use the gift wisely, for it is dangerous."

"His words are indeed mysterious."

"Not so mysterious. The brigade promised me has arrived."

"I beg your pardon, but we are not the brigade promised. We are men travelling through this land seeking naught but trade and beaver furs. Do you have furs to trade?"

The laughter again. "Indeed, we will trade with you. We will trade you half of your gear and supplies for your lives. Raven warned me I must be cautious, and so I will wisely only take half, leaving the rest to whatever fate the *Manitou* has in mind for you. Now this is very fair, for I could easily take everything you have, including your scalps."

"Truly, but then the king will be very angry with you, and his soldiers in the red coats that you so fear would seek for you, and you would be destroyed."

The voice changes, becoming harsher. "I am Ikmukdeza, and I do not fear the red-coated king's men. If they come into my territory, it is they who will be destroyed, and I will have their scalps on the prow of my canoe!"

"I have not heard that your people are so warlike."

"I am Ikmukdeza! I do as I wish and take what I will. My people follow me because they know of my strength and courage. All will soon know of me."

"I must consult with my comrade, so that we may consider your generous offer."

"As you wish," a dim hand waves at him.

Alexander turns to Turr. 'We have arrived at the pinch of the game. I have had dealings with the *Asinepoet*, and they are a good people who would not countenance such treatment of guests and strangers. I believe this chief is no more than a common highwayman. He is ransoming us for one half of everything we have — the trade liquor, supplies for the settlements, guns, powder, and shot."

"One half? But that's impossible. The guns!"

"There is nothing we can do. With the settlers in the brigade we cannot afford a confrontation, although myself I would dearly love to get my hands on this arrogant bastard's neck."

"So what must we do?"

"Agree to their terms. Hand over half of everything, and then get the hell out of here."

Turr closes his eyes. "When London gets word of this, I shall be roasted alive. I shall be ruined."

"It shall be hard all around. Those supplies are needed for the settlement." He takes a deep breath and turns back to the smoky fire. "I have spoken with my friend and we agree to your terms." Several of the Indians nod and smile.

"Very wise. Then let us pass the pipe of peace." With that, a long-stemmed pipe wrapped in strips of hide and decorated with dangling feathers is lit and handed to him. For the first time since he had come ashore, Alexander relaxes, and he draws deeply on the pipe.

They pass it around several times, and then Alexander stands up. "I must prepare the brigade to distribute our gifts to you. But I have not seen you clearly, and I would like to truly meet the great Ikmukdeza, so that I will know him the next time that our paths cross."

There is no reply, just the snapping of the fire and swirl of smoke. All eyes turn towards him. After a long silence, the chief gets to his feet. He is a man of about twenty-five, of no great height, with broad shoulders. Smallpox scars corrugate his face, and the remnant of his left ear is no more than a tiny flag. Elaborately carved trade silver pierces his nose and ears. A breastplate of mussel shells with red and blue quillwork decorate his chest, and a lithograph of King George hangs from his neck on a beaded chain. Feathers are tied to his black hair, which drapes untied down his back. His eyes are challenging and there is a hard edge to his mouth.

"Truly, I will remember you," Alexander says, with just the slightest menace in his voice. Ikmukdeza smiles slightly and bows. Alexander pushes aside the door hide and steps out, Turr almost crawling between his legs in his haste to follow.

~

"Get that last boat unloaded, Mr. Irving, if you please." Several bales had already been moved to shore when the young steersman, hurrying to obey, trips over a poorly stowed mast and falls in the water. He thrashes about, choking.

"Mr. Ramsay, could you please lend a hand to our young Mr. Irving? I do not wish to pen a letter to his widow telling her that he drowned in four feet of water and not but two paces from shore."

"Aye, sir," Ramsay replies with a grin, walking into the river and lifting the young man by his collar. "There ye go, lad, just stand up. That's right." Irving's feet find the river bottom, and he stands up, water streaming from him as he coughs and hacks. Ramsay slaps him hard on the back and the off-balance Irving trips again, his arms cartwheeling and knocking the man sitting in the boat beside him. The man's musket fires, and, in response, a fusillade erupts from shore, answered by several following shots from the boats.

"Hold!" Alexander shouts. The gun smoke drifts away, revealing two Indians lying on the strand, one holding his stomach and feebly attempting to crawl away. Several others stare at him, frozen in the act of reloading. In the river behind him, Irving's body, pierced by many balls, begins to float away.

No one moves. Those in the boats and standing in the river stare down their barrels at the Indians, while those on shore respond in kind. The brigade is vastly outnumbered, but far better armed than most of the Indians with their miserably inaccurate trade muskets. But if it came to it, the final outcome would undoubtedly be a bloodbath. The Indian crawling up the strand stops with a shudder and a few feeble kicks of his legs.

Alexander knows that they stand on the edge of a blade, and that someone will very soon do something stupid, yearning for something, anything to break the awful tension. He slowly lowers his carbine into the bow of a boat. He raises both his empty hands palms out toward shore. "Mr. Ramsey, get the men into the boats, quickly but slowly, he says," speaking over his shoulder in low tones. "Tell them to lower their weapons."

"But sir!"

"Do as I say!"

"And what about poor Mr. Irving, dead in the river, filled with the Savage's shot?"

"Put him into the boat and make haste."

Alexander has not taken his eyes off the warrior closest to him, willing him not to shoot; the Indian is very young — hardly more than a boy — and sweat runs down his brown cheek. The muzzle of his fuke wavers with his trembling, and fear calls from his eyes.

Alexander turns and looks at the body of Irving as it is dragged into the boat, then at the two prostrate Indians. "Accident," he says in Stony language with a shrug. "We will leave now, no more shooting."

The young Indian takes a deep breath and lowers his weapon. One by one, the rest of his companions do the same.

"I want to kill those fucking bastards," Ramsey hisses into Alexander's ear.

Alexander nods and answers, "The women, Mr. Ramsey. If we are ready let us get the hell out of here."

He turns to step into his boat and almost collides with Rose, who has not moved since the shooting. She is staring wide-eyed at the dead Indians leaking blood into the sand.

"Miss Cromarty, quickly now." Taking her by the arm, Alexander eases her aboard. The sweeps are put out, and the boats back away from the beach with the sound of creaking oars; Alexander turns them into the stream of the river. His back to the shore, he says in a low voice: "What are they doing, Mr. Ramsey?"

Ramsey looks up from where he is sitting with his head in his hands. His cheek is wet with tears. "The buggers ain't doing naught, sir, just staring."

"If any Indian raises his musket, kill him; if any Indian makes for a canoe, kill him. Any man aboard with an empty gun, reload, now!" Raising his voice, he hails the other boat. "Mr. Hollar, make for the further shore; we must travel as many pipes as possible before nightfall."

Chapter Twelve

As the brigade approaches, there is little to see but a jumble of low cabins scattered amongst grey rocks and wizened spruce, shadowed by a particularly squalid encampment of Home Guard. The smoke from the chimneys does not rise and dissipate in the cold air, but sinks and clings to the immediate environs so that the place seems wreathed in fog. An unseen dog barks as the brigade drifts toward shore.

"It is a — a simple affair is it not?" says Rose with a cocked eyebrow, regarding the crude peeled-poplar buildings and discarded refuse littering the site. Several Indians are sprawled on the ground, succumbed to disease or liquor.

"Shabby or no, it will be a blessed relief to warm my toes before a proper fire, by God," says Turr, looking for evidence of the governor. Several York boats are stowed in the shadows of the spruce, but none belong to the rest of the brigade; they have missed them yet again.

Their boats touch the shore at the same instance, the foremost rowers jumping overboard and pulling them onto the rocks. With muted relief, the colonists tumble out, clustering together and whispering amongst each other and staring at the unfamiliar surroundings. Grabbing his carbine, Alexander leads the way to the trading house.

At this time of year, the house would normally be almost empty except for a few permanent laborers and Company staff. But, as they walk, Alexander notices many people about, including a line of very wretched individuals sitting outside the trading house. Obviously Europeans, they stare at the ground or off into space, eyes empty and lifeless. A few women rest their heads on the shoulders of their men, who lean against the rough wall with their feet pulled up and knees bent, red hands resting on the dirt. Their frock coats, bonnets, and dresses are torn, dirty, and threadbare. A fly wanders across the face of one of the women and she makes no attempt to brush it off. As they pass, none of them speak or acknowledge the newcomers.

They push inside the trading house where a clerk, engrossed in his ledger, looks up and scowls.

"Jesus, Mary, and Joseph, not another lot! God in heaven, we shall be sunk."

~

From behind a boulder, Rose shadows the figures on the beach. She hates sneaking about this way, becoming the mute shadow that most men want and expect of women, but she needs to know and suspects them of hiding the truth from her and the other colonists. Things had not come to pass as expected — that part was clear to everyone in the brigade. But she is certain that anything revealed to them would be altered for her presumed benefit. And she would rot before she allowed that. Her father had always been straightforward with her, but she knows she cannot expect that from any other man. She is on her own and needs information — she needs the truth.

Holding her breath, Rose moves closer, her bare feet chilled by the smooth, cold rock beneath her. She sidles up to a knot of cottonwoods and a few leaves rustle beneath her, then skitter away in a gust. The bark is rough against her hands, like stubble on an old man's cheek. The men's voices are small but clear against the chilly night. She feels power in her secrecy, and blesses the darkness.

Utterly dark it truly is, the moon discouraged to a pale wash by thin cloud. Duck wings whistle overhead and out on the water a loon laments the cold. The night carries the smell of burning tobacco and wood smoke. From the Home Guard camp carries the sound of a crying child. The three men sit on the granite of the water's edge, wrapped in buffalo hides and smoking their dudheens. The water laps at their feet.

Although instinctively seated close to each other against the cold, they are invisible except when someone draws on his pipe and the outlines of his face are for a moment defined by the dim, orange glow.

Alexander stares up at the faint stars overhead, not seeing any particular pattern or mythology, just a scattering of improbable motes that give shape and often guidance in the pathless night. The veiled moon is nearly full, low on the horizon, and barely revealing a sawtooth line of treetops.

Turr pulls his cloak tighter, staring into the darkness and shivering.

"Well, well, well," he mutters, for probably the tenth time. "So your rumours have proven correct, Mr. McClure. The settlement has been put to the torch and the colonists scattered. An act of war if ever there was one, methinks."

"War, indeed," replies the factor, Samuel Lynch. "And none too soon. No more border skirmishes, no more insufferable diplomatic rows with the damned Nor'westers. The Company will now be forced to raise the issue of her monopoly at Whitehall. Lord Selkirk's damned enterprise has set a stoat loose in the hen coop and now that the gamekeeper is aware, its hide shall soon hang from his gibbet."

"I wonder if the foreign secretary will see it that way," muses Turr. "I've long appealed for a military wing of the Company to protect our interest from Canadian and American invaders. But after three major wars in thirty years and preoccupied with Bonaparte's rampages in Europe, Parliament has been unwilling to consider further military intervention in North America, especially by a private force of arms beyond their control."

In the distance, a wolf howls, followed by an orchestra of answering calls. The wind picks up, searching for weakness in the men's wrappings. Unconsciously they move closer to each other, the tempo of their puffing increasing. The river before them murmurs.

Lynch rubs his hands together as if in anticipation. Or perhaps simply to warm them. "Recent events will force them to reconsider," he replies. "The colonists were driven north and east in July, although many that arrived here have since returned with a Mr. Colin Robertson. I understand he is to be the new governor of Assiniboia as Macdonell has been seized and taken away in disgrace to Montreal by the Nor'westers. The rest of the settlers await transport back home, but I daresay they will wait long. I do not foresee any such opportunity until the brigades pass in the spring; that is if any of the wretches are still alive by then. Damn and blast, it shall be a hard winter with so many beggars to feed. The pox on them."

Samuel Lynch is small and mean, with a despotic disposition and ill patience for those who disagree with his opinions. The bastard son of an Anglican priest, he had not been many years at the post, but since arriving had made for himself a reputation that went far and wide through Rupert's Land, one far surpassing the relative size and importance of Jack River House. A harsh and unforgiving master, meting out punishments exceeding his authority and more in line with what is considered the norm in a taut Royal Navy man-of-war.

Although he reserves flogging for the Indians, banishment and withholding of pay and provision is common punishment for Europeans. He even had a crude pillory built, which provided great sport for the Home Guard, although many thought it barbaric, not least because they were most likely to find themselves locked within its embrace. A visiting Company official passing inland had been horrified by the spectacle of a White trader taunted and stoned by Savage children, and had ordered the pillory dismantled. But after word arrived that this man had drowned in a rapid, it was quickly resurrected.

Even if such violence is rare in the Company, in the surrounding wilderness, murder is weighed only in the cost of corresponding shot and weight of powder, and such trifles as a miscreant being sent without food or stoned in a pillory passes without much comment among the brigades. While Lynch is proud of his reputation, which runs from Pembina to Great Slave Lake, he would be disappointed to learn that it is not his Christian discipline that gives him fame, but a Ferdinand Hoffman grand piano imported from Vienna to London and then to York Factory at incredible Company expense — recorded in company records under *trade bayonets, ten gross.* An entire York boat and crew was dedicated to smuggling it inland where it now stands in the factor's personal residence, the only Hoffman in the continent, and the only grand piano west of Montreal.

He had a passion for the concerti of Brahms and Hayden, and it was not unusual in the evenings to hear the sweet voice of the piano offering a melodic counterpoint to the dirges of wolves and loons. But his playing is the only evidence of a sensitive nature to be found in the factor, and he rages against this unwelcome burden placed upon him by events far beyond his power, foreseeing greater troubles ahead.

"Too long has this damned rabble run free and loose," he says in a rising voice. "Usurping trade and assaulting the king's subjects and servants. The Free Half-breeds of Red River they call themselves; they even have raised their own filthy flag. But now they have crossed the line in the sand and with God's good grace, their freedom shall be brief and their necks destined for a rope."

A wall of darkness rises from the northern horizon, and soon the pallid moon is fully veiled. The wind dies as the silence of the forest deepens. Even the river seems hushed. Alexander pulls a pewter flask from beneath his buffalo hide and takes a deep pull. The smell of rum swirls about them. He hawks and spits into the darkness.

"A fine solution, no doubt, Mr. Lynch, but one cannot hang every rebel in the west. Did not the English attempt as much in the American colonies? For myself, I have not seen a a rope cure any ill, much less one so sticky as this. A corpse may be satisfying but what a martyr carries in his heart is rarely dispensed with so easily."

You are a shit, Lynch, Alexander thinks, clearing his throat and spitting into the river. *And a fucking pompous bore, in the bargain. If that scrub Selkirk had made his intentions plain and not sent that lunatic Miles Macdonell as his thug, things need not have taken this deadly turn.*

All the Half-breeds desire is to live their lives as did their fathers, trapping, growing a few crops, running the buffalo. Sing and dance and fuck and drink and fight. A wonderful, free life all in all, and one much to be envied. All they ask is to be let alone. They have peace with the Indians and the Nor'westers, living at the Forks as they have for generations. One would think the land great enough for all, but Selkirk and his miserable band of trespassers mean to toss the Half-breeds from their lands and trample them underfoot, like weeds. As if the disease and liquor the king's traders have brought with them aren't enough, now there is undeclared war on the peoples of the land. But this time they have misjudged, by God; this time they do not know the anger they have roused, the heat that burns in the hearts of all who live and journey between the Athabasca and Fort William.

These interloper colonists, these Orkneymen and women, these Scots, have been tempted to disaster like a wolf to a poisoned carcass. Oh, my poor darling Rose, what misfortunes await you at Red River?

"And what about these people, Mr. Lynch?" he cries, the alcohol beginning to take him. "They have been carted halfway across the earth, carried into a strange and lonely country, only to be burned out and perhaps abandoned, perhaps shipped back. It is criminal, I say."

"So you go on," replies the factor in offended tones. "But I have never seen a Half-breed that did not love a fight and quarrel, and it is beyond the pale to suggest that the Company, the lawful and only possessor of these lands, should negotiate for that which is already its right and has so been for more than a century. Does the landlord negotiate with the thief that breaks in and steals his silver? A knock on the head is what they deserve, by God."

Choking back his anger, Alexander stands up, tapping his dudheen out on his boot. A sudden flash of sparks falls to the ground. He hears the rustle of branches and freezes.

"Mr. McClure …" Turr begins.

"Hush," he says. Crouching, he slinks into the darkness. A sudden scuffle and crackle of twigs.

"Hold, damn you. Hold I say! God damn your eyes!" Rose has bitten his arm, hard. A blow and a cry.

"Devil take it! What is afoot?" Turr shouts.

"Bring a light! I have caught a footpad."

Lynch hurries off and returns with a torch and several men.

"Miss Cromarty!" Turr says, aghast.

"Rose!" Alexander drops her onto the stone. Her eyes glare up at him. He looks down at her, confused, his head spinning. Dark blood runs down his arm. "Why come you there?"

Rose scurries to her feet, and shoots a piercing glance at them before running into the darkness.

~

Later that night he hears the sound of moccasins on deep moss, and the flap of his tent is lifted.

"I did not think you would ever come again."

"I told you earlier of my intent," says Rose.

"Indeed, but constancy has not been your strongest suit this little while."

"My father is dead, Alexander."

"I know this …"

"And yet you question why my mind has been elsewhere?"

"Pray lower your voice or you will be found out. Or is that your wish?"

"My wish? I will tell you what I wish, Alexander. I wish we had never left my country. I wish that my father would yet be alive. I wish that we could turn around this very moment and leave this accursed land. I wish that that monstrous Savage had never laid upon my father with his wicked shank. But all wishing is in vain, is it not? It seems all my wishing is to end in bitterness."

"I cannot help but note my absence from your list of impossible wishes." She does not respond. "Answer me!"

"I have not heard a question."

"Why have you neglected me for so many weeks and days? Why are you so cold?"

"I do not know what you are talking about."

But she did know. Her anger at the Indian who killed her father had wrapped itself around her heart, squeezing the warmth from it. All that she had seen since arriving at the Bay told her that the wild people of the land were hardly better than animals — worse, in that animals do not turn upon those of their own kind, do not kill those with whom they mate. Only the lowliest, most basest of creatures, like spiders and the mantis did so.

She has come to hate everything about the country, the land the air, the water, the people. By simple association, her feelings for Alexander had drained away with her father's blood, along the fuller of the Savage's knife. She may have loved him once upon a time, but believes she cannot do so any more than she can love the land itself. As far as she can tell, they are one of a kind.

"So now you are reduced to a lie. Has it really come to this?" Alexander says.

"Pray, do not speak to me of lies! What I have overheard this evening confirms my worst fears. Why did you never speak to me of this?"

"I did not know. You must believe this; events have moved faster than the brigade and what was once a suspicion has been shown to be fact. You cannot hold me accountable for Selkirk's mischief."

"You all seem in league against my people. But it ends now. I will reveal what I know to the party. Choices must be made."

"Just so, and I imagine the heroic Declan has a cruel part to play in these choices?"

"Now it is you who must lower their voice. Declan has nothing to say in this."

"Perhaps not, but he will answer yet, by God!"

She places a hand on Alexander's arm, willing it to be warm. "This has little to do with Declan; pray do not lash out at an innocent as succour for our own foolishness. You and I are of different kind, Alexander, we serve a different purpose in life."

"You crossed an ocean to meet with this land. How can you say I am out of reach?"

"The gap between us is greater than any sea, my love, and it has only lengthened with time and circumstance. We knew it must be so from the beginning, else we would not have been so circumspect."

"My love, my love, what noise you make, like the nattering of an owl."

"I must go."

"I love you; do not leave."

"I have already gone, as you well know. Good night, Alexander."

~

It is very late — near dawn, or at least whatever dawn can pierce the heavy sky. Alexander helps himself to a keg of trade liquor and disdaining the comfort of a closed door, borrows an unwatched canoe and pushes himself into the water.

He is carried back downriver a fair distance until caught in an eddy, where he is drawn to the bank, swirls against a boulder, and then swings out into the stream where he again is turned and drifts back toward shore. Around and around he swings, in a slowly looping ellipse. Lying in the bottom of the canoe, he is mindful of the fragile material between himself and the icy river, and can feel the cold of the water seep through the robe. He stares at the unseen sky, taking frequent gulps from his keg. Soon large flakes of snow begin to fall, and he can feel their cold wet bite against his upturned face.

If anyone were to pass by, an Indian on a hunt perhaps, they would think they have spotted a bier floating a corpse over the grey water. But despite the hours he spends pondering, he is no nearer to a decision, and the liquor does little to calm the torment of his heart.

Since that night in his tent so long ago, she had not returned to him, nor did he expect her; the thought of her warming the Highlander's bed compelled him to damn them both, although this fire left behind the ashes of a loneliness of the like he had never known before. It was if the two that he loved beyond all others had climbed into a boat and pushed off, abandoning him to the little island where they had all three lived together for a long while.

He would lie awake at night listening for footsteps that never approached. Often he would get up and pace about the camp, shooting suspicious glances at the place where he suspected she slept with Declan. He paced to and fro, reminding himself of the woman who had feasted on human flesh and was doomed to stalk the nights in the Home Guard's camp.

It is true that he hungers for a sweet flesh. He was utterly inexperienced before Rose, and, having feasted upon her, cannot not imagine sustaining himself without her. He thinks he will surely go mad. He returns to Jack River House later in the morning, slipping and stumbling on the skiff of wet snow frosting the stone shore.

Turr approaches him with a frown. "What the devil is wrong with you, eh?" he says, grabbing him by the arm.

"It is nothing."

"Nothing? I dare say it is something. See here, sir, you are like a man possessed, provoking the factor like that."

"Piss off!"

"Upon my word, I never!" Alexander reaches for his knife and the thin man scurries away.

Seeing this, Declan walks over. "There seems to be a great palsy upon you, my friend. What is it? What evil has taken you?"

Alexander laughs at this, a high, shrill laugh. "A palsy is it? Indeed, I suppose it is, one of love and friendship and cruelty and shit, all baked in the foulest pudding. Such are my dinners of late, and my blood is poor and black on account of it."

"I am concerned to hear of it," Declan replies, surprised.

"But enough of me, how is the arm, old friend?"

"It troubles me naught."

"Good, good, I am glad to hear of it. We must then challenge your shooting skills."

Declan's brow furrows and he drags a hand across his beard. "If you think it best. What have you in mind?"

"A target, a challenging target — I have it!" He picks up a small, round piece of driftwood lying on the rocks. "I shall stand against a tree and you shall, you shall shoot the piece from atop my head."

By now several people have heard Alexander's raised voice, and many faces turn toward them.

"What is this? You mock me, my friend," says Declan in a wounded tone.

"I do not. Raise your weapon."

Rose hurries up. "Please, Alexander, do not do this," she says in a quiet voice, placing her hand on his arm. "The people …"

"Unhand me, woman, and stand aside." He backs against a spruce, unsuccessfully attempting to balance the wood on his head.

"There, I am ready. I beg you to shoot."

Declan does not move.

"Are you deaf, my friend, or merely simple? I am ready, I tell you. Shoot! Damn your eyes, why do you look at me thus? All of you, why do you stare?" he begins shouting. "Asses and fools. Staring like besotted sheep, ripe for the slaughter, still stupidly trusting in the shepherd. Bah, you waste my time." He points a shaking finger at Declan. "I shall cut you a willow bow and arrow and with that, that you shall practise your marksmanship." He turns to walk away, and strikes his head on a low branch, collapsing to the ground.

~

The booming of a great horned owl drifts from the spruce behind Jack River House as Alexander slips out of the cabin. He throws his pack over his shoulder and straightens his octopus bag, reassured by its weight. Checking the prime of his Baker carbine by pipe glow, he heads toward the river, the snow glowing pale in the dark and crunching beneath his moccasins. A dark-stained bandage wraps his head, and his uncovered pate is chilled by the caress of a frosty early dawn.

Reaching the shoreline, he follows the sound of water lapping on birchbark, and soon comes upon a canoe waiting under a bluff of naked cottonwoods. He grunts at the dark form of a man seated in the stern, throwing his gear behind the empty place in the bow. He pushes the canoe from shore, icy water flowing into his moccasins. Heaving himself aboard, he grabs a paddle. There is a swirl in the dark, and the canoe turns into the current.

Smoke drifts from the post, tugging at him, but he turns his back on the past, and, digging the blade into the water, moves himself into the broad face of the river. In a few moments, he disappears into the gloaming, leaving behind the sound of cold water lapping against grey stone.

Book Two

Chapter Thirteen

After so many countless days following the confining river, *Missinipi* appears like a vast ocean to the colonists. Wind carries without abatement along its choppy surface, often threatening to swamp the low boats. Their sailing rigs are primitive and can only be hoisted when the wind is aft; a head wind means beating into the waves by rowing, drastically slowing their progress and soaking the passengers. They travel south, close to the eastern shore, but outside of musket range, following the distant grey buzz of naked cottonwoods.

When Rose first saw the lake, she thought for a moment that they had somehow become turned around and had arrived back at Hudson's Bay. She could not imagine a body of water so vast that was not an ocean. Only after tasting it did she believe it was, after all, a lake. As the days passed and still the lake carried on, she dipped her finger again and again to reassure a doubting mind the absence of salt.

But aside from the welcome novelty of a grand vista to accompany the ongoing dirge of sweeps and heavy breathing, of stand-sit-row, stand-sit-row, life continues on as much as it had. The decline of the days quickens as they pursue the sun in its daily retreat southward. Lack of surrounding forest means the wind blows freely over them, bringing with it the smell of ice. They unpack extra blankets, and all those not rowing pass the days swaddled against the cold breath of the lake.

After the affair with Ikmukdeza, their loads are much lighter now, although their pace is hardly improved. The York boat was designed for tons of gear, not speed, but a greater effect is the spirit of the group; they had seen what became of their Orkney precursors. Long had they abandoned their hope for a new and bright beginning, but now even survival seemed in doubt. Lost in a land vaster than any comprehension, they could only move forward, but all dreaded their destination.

They pull the boats ashore as they have every night, but the sense of exposure is unsettling to all. In the forest, what was unseen had caused anxiety, now their own visibility creates unease among them. Like most comfortable people, Rose had never fully appreciated the role of a wall in the human sense of well-being, but now is convinced that humanity cannot survive without it. Without shelter, man must surely perish, through fear if not exposure. They keep their fire small and assign a formal watch, with armed men assigned responsibility for their collective safety.

If the news of the rout at Fort Douglas was received with an apparent stoicism by the colonists, the Bay men see themselves as employees of the Company and warring is not why they hired on. Their protests were loud, and a few insisted they return to the Bay — a demand wholeheartedly supported by the colonists — but Turr had forestalled them, telling them that any man who returned now would be thrown out of the Company, and the Orkney folk could swim back to Scotland.

During the long, cold days when all she could do was sit and think while the oarsmen laboured, Rose raised her father from the dead, imagining him beside her on the thwart, and not Declan's great bulk. As the boats descended the addled water of the lake, she recalled her old life in Orkney with an additional sense of loss and loneliness. Almost as much as her father, she missed the women with whom she had once read, painted, and discussed her deepest dreams and fears. Over the passing years, this cohort had diminished, as one by one they married and disappeared over the Atlantic or into their husband's houses. At society functions, she would sometimes catch up with them, but the marital bed had changed them for the worst in her opinion, their discussions now limited to the failings of servants and the paucity of adequate wet nurses. They had turned into feminine proxies for Lachlan as they chided her lack of husband, making her feel like a cabbage that had been left too long in the garden and was beginning to rot on the stem.

There was no role for her other than someone's companion and bedmate. Painting watercolours, reading (within reason), entertaining, philosophical discussion, and perhaps a little writing was all that was permitted of a highbred woman. Little of it she found appealing, and had spent much of her time alone, riding her quiet mare through the green meads and rocky valleys of Orkney or reading in her father's library. This constraint also motivated her secret forays. But she now saw this as a lack of wisdom and adaptability, and ultimately responsible for the fact that she was now alone.

The end of the Great Lake appears as a wide fen of stunted willows and extensive tracks of cattails where the mouths of the Red River flow into the lake. As the brigade noses into one of those mouths, they are cut off from the surrounded landscape by tall rushes as thoroughly as in the deepest northern forest. They cannot see more than a few dozen yards ahead in the meandering channel. After the expansive vistas of the lake, the way feels claustrophobic, and their tension rises as several Baymen check the prime of their guns.

Rose sits on her familiar thwart, Mary Isbister's arm over her shoulders. After the loss of her father's protection, the women in the brigade had surrounded Rose like defensive wagons, but rape had remained a constant threat. She looks up at the hissing and rattling cattails on their tall stems, their brown knobs waving in a breeze that cannot be felt down on the water. A redwinged black-bird perches on one, staring down at her and swaying to and fro on its narrow stalk. The rest of its kin have long ago departed for the Gulf of Mexico, but, like Rose, it is in the wrong place at the wrong time. It burbles forth a lovely descending melody as if welcoming Rose to her new land. The sweep's creak and the men's raspy breathing suddenly becomes loud in the narrowing channel, and the dark bird lets go of its perch and swoops over them with flashing red epaulets, vanishing into the rushes. Rose wishes it well over the deadly winter to come.

Declan sits to the other side of her, staring around at the impen-etrable wall of reeds, fingering a borrowed musket. Mary glances at the Highlander with distaste, her arm tightening around Rose. While the Isbister family watched and protected her, Declan had made his intent toward her known in the brigade, both as additional comfort to her, and to forestall any who might see her as free for the taking. As far as the brigade is concerned, she is effectively Declan's property, and all have noticed his continued practice with the musket.

Mary Isbister has little use for Declan and is inclined to send him packing with a curse and a tossed pot, but Rose recognizes her vul-nerability, and knowing her father's final hope for her, encourages his advances. She is aware there is no room for an unwed spinster in the land of her father's dreams. Especially one on the verge of dis-solution. All that she has cared for has been taken: country, family, lover. Her mind is an soaring edifice of sticks, and, with each jar, each tragedy, each witnessed death and loss, it feels as if one or more has been yanked out, the whole thing in danger of tumbling around her. She holds herself rigid, willing with all her inner strength to maintain composure, the terror of collapse and exposure the one tiny candle that warmed her spirit, kept her taking the next breath.

She feels that if she relaxed but a moment, her house would collapse and she would be reduced to a gibbering idiot.

She feels the Devil tugging at her mind, wishing to destroy whatever humanity she still holds within her. Often as they had rode up a swell, Rose had held her breath, hands gripping one another as she willed a sense of permanence and stability in a rolling, pernicious world. At such times Mary had watched her, aware of some great struggle within, but wary of speaking, afraid that any request of her, even speech, might prove too great a disturbance. So she held Rose's hand, wishing for her strength to flow into the grieving girl.

"Lord, you are cold," Mary says to her, wrapping her in a blanket. Rose smiles faintly at her.

"It is nothing," she says.

"Oh, it is something, all right. The falling damps … sure you will get a chill. Come sit closer to me. Be a dear and move over, Margaret. That's a girl." With a sigh, Rose relaxes against her friend, her face gaunt and tired. She rests her head on the bony shoulder as the thin arm wraps around her, imagining Alexander's embrace protecting her from a hard world.

It is more than the series of shocks she has been subject to: so much has been removed, so much upon which she has shelved her idea of herself, that there seems precious little of her left. And what to replace it with? There is nothing around her that she can see capable of supplanting that which she has lost. She is in an unknown land at the brink of war; hungry, cold, and frightened, and bidden to a man for whom she has little feeling. What is there to replace the world of security, predictability, and dashing risk-taking that she had known for so long? Even if return to Orkney was possible, nothing remained there for her; what few kin she has are scattered throughout the Empire. It might have been possible to ally herself with one of Lachlan's friends, but that would mean entering a parasitic relationship, one likely to devolve to little more than prostitution.

Even if she had been willing to consider such an arrangement, there seems no way to return to York Factory, or arrange for passage back to Stromness. On the entire journey, they passed no brigades heading east. In this country, the only people she can lay claim to are these ragged and rugged individuals she accompanied across the Atlantic. But now she is a supplicant, and so had determined to leave behind her status and become one of them. Over the ensuing weeks even Cecile Turr forgets who and what she used to be.

~

The brigade proceeds a short distance into the marsh before pulling up onto a muddy bank. The landing is small, a greasy strip bounded by water and thick reeds. Several men stamp around in a circle, flattening the grasses to make room for the people to disembark. Declan and a few armed Highlanders fan out, instantly disappearing, though leaving a clear track through the rushes.

After the death of her father, no one challenges Rose's forays away from the camp. As soon as the evening meal is complete, she leaves her companions and follows a deer trail back to the shore of the lake. The sun has long since set, and only the last vestiges of twilight remain on the land. But, as daylight departs, eyes adapt and the land and water become luminous. Declan finds her sitting alone under a wizened jack pine murmuring with the cold breeze off the lake. She sits quietly on a pile of needle duff, a blanket wrapped around her and legs drawn up with her feet pulled inside. Holding a rag of hat in his hand, he kneels beside her. She feels his hip pressing against her, trembling. Without speaking, he stares into the emergent night, his hand moving towards her. Blunt and grey, it looks to Rose like the head of a venomous snake. She does not move as it searches her lap, finds and swallows her own small hand. Still without looking at her, he speaks in low tones about his dream of starting his own empire, and needing a wife, a companion and confidant, to care for him and support him as he seeks their future and glory. In exchange, he promises her fealty and love, and undying devotion.

She looks out over the lead-gray surface of the great lake, the red eye of rising Aldebaran glaring off its surface. For a fleeting moment, she feels an urge to cast herself into its frigid bosom. It feels like the one act of freedom left to her: the slave always having the final choice of the gallows or the shackles. In the distance a grouse booms, the sound so deep she feels as much as hears it. Another male making a supercilious claim to love. Declan mistakes her tear as that of joy, her slight nod as evidence of barely contained emotion. Which, of course, the latter is. Later that night, he and his friends force trade liquor from Turr's stores, and become very drunk in celebration.

~

They find a brown and dead landscape at Fort Douglas. Successive cold nights have flattened the pasture grasses and delicate frost tendrils grow like seedlings on black fallow soil. The thin, blue sky has emptied of fowl and the land holds its breath for the coming, inevitable snow. Night after night, wolves and coyotes praise the return of winter, the season of death.

Fort Douglas is small and shaggy, an outpost intended for the simple gathering of furs, not a beachhead for an empire. It stands alone as a shoal; a dark reef of presumed conquest marked on London-made maps and troubled Indians' dreams. Naked on a featureless plain, obvious, imperious, gnawed by wind and weather, and by a landscape that lends itself to madness. Visible from more than twenty miles, obscured only by the curve of the earth itself.

As most things that survive this land, winter in the fort is usually a time for sleep and rest and patience — waiting for spring and the breaking of the land. Seed waits like hope in the granary, dormant with promise, the colonist's entire enterprise trapped with a few bushels of golden kernels. But the level of seed falls daily in a race to see which will prove the greater: the dilatory yet implacable change of the seasons or the hunger of foraging mice.

The fort is busier now than any previous winter. Due to Nor'wester hostilities and the rumour of war, many who farmed in the area had retreated to the fort once their crops were off the ground, and the place is not happy to receive Rose's brigade — yet another cohort of mouths at the beginning of the hungry season.

Poplar poles are cut and dragged from the river valley, and the crowded, walled-in space echoes with the sound of axe and adze as several new shacks are built to house the newcomers. It all feels a race, a deep breath before the plunge of winter.

Rose marries Declan not long after arriving at the settlement. There being no priest, Governor Semple performs the rites, assuring them that his moral and spiritual authority equaled or exceeded that of a deacon. Several amazed colonists witness them, and the event becomes impetus for a massive, several-day drunk for many of the fort's inhabitants.

Rose has no idea if her choice is wise or foolish, just that events have taken on a life of their own, and it is her fate to follow them to their conclusion. She prays that the child she carries benefits from her choice.

～

"Here, let me help you with that, Mary," Rose says, taking the dish of turnips from her. They are in the fort's kitchen preparing the midday meal with several other women. The hearth fire is roaring and women flit about, chatting like so many sparrows on a pile of spilled seed corn.

Mary wipes a lock of her thin, prematurely grey hair from her eyes and smiles at Rose. Rose takes the turnips and carries them to a table; she sits on a stool and begins cutting the knobby vegetables. The chunks fall into the bowl with a wooden clatter. A raw, earthy smell rises from them. But the knife slips and cuts deep into her palm. Blood appears like a surprise, and Rose's stomach lurches. She runs through the doorway and vomits on the threshold.

Mary rushes to her, and, kneeling, places a tiny red hand on her back. Rose can feel the heat of it through her dress. Frost rises from the ground into her bleeding palm.

"I-I'm sorry," Rose chokes.

"Hush, girl, don't you say anything. Margaret, be a dear and grab a wet cloth?" She smoothes Rose's hair back. "Oh, you have cut yourself … and you are quickening fast," she adds softly, feeling the swell in Rose's belly. Rose hesitates, startled. She looks at Mary.

"How did you know?"

Mary smiles faintly at her. "I am a woman. The signs are not hard to see." She pauses, lowering her voice. "Does Declan know?"

At that, her eyes fill with anguish. A couple of fur traders pass by, giving them both quizzical looks. "Not here," Rose whispers. Margaret arrives with the cloth, and Mary wraps it around Rose's bleeding hand.

"Come with me," she says, taking her hand and helping her to her feet. As always, Rose is surprised at the small woman's strength, her frame as hard and knotted as a birch burl. She leads Rose to a food storage shack; when she opens the door, mice burst from the room, running over their shoes and scurrying along courtyard walls. The cold-soil smell of stored vegetables is strong in the dark space.

They leave the door ajar just enough to allow a slender *V* of light into the room. Mary sits Rose on a sack of pemmican and takes the girl's hands in her own.

"Tell me," she says, kneeling before Rose and looking into her eyes. A vertical band of soft light illuminates the seated figure, and, for a moment, she appears to Mary like a grieving angel.

Rose looks down at the slender, calloused fingers in her own, and her tears fall with tiny pops into the dust. She opens her heart, telling Mary of her trysts and loves and her dangerous games in

Stromness. She tells her about the yearning that drove her, the seeking, and the emptiness that she felt inside that she hoped to assuage in the arms of another. She tells of her many conquests and her few failures and of disasters narrowly averted. She had never worried much about conceiving and never kindled, although she rarely took precautions. Therefore, it was a great shock to her when she missed her time, and the morning illness arrived.

Mary listens to her in shocked silence, wondering how such a life could be; what it meant to her and her family. Sin aplenty she herself was guilty of, but never with such wanton desire, with such conscious will. A fear and jealousy rises for her man and she now has an image of Rose as a succubus. She fights an urge to pull away. But then the door groans open, pushed by a gust of wind burdened by snow. The illusion fades and all she sees is a lonely, lost woman, weeping and afraid.

"Why did you choose such a life?" Mary asks.

"There have been many nights I've pondered that question. It was more than a spoiled brat's distraction, although I was less than honest with myself. Yet I've since found far more meaning in a child's hungry tears than any man's lust. I've become an orphan, and yet it seems to me that I have found myself, waking as if from a dark dream. Your kindness and the kindness of our people have shown me love, if I may call it that."

"Does Declan know?" Mary asks, after a long pause.

"No, no, you are the only one I have told."

"I see. Well, he will have to know about the baby, at least."

Rose looks up at her. "I do not think the baby is his." She sees the unspoken question in Mary's eyes. "Alexander. It's likely Alexander McClure's"

"Alexander McClure? The Half-caste?" Mary says, shocked again.

Rose nods. They sit in silence for a while. "I don't know what to do," Rose says at last, her voice entreating.

"Do? You are not really showing yet, so there is time. And clothing can hide many sins."

"But I will have to tell Declan what I suspect."

"You will do nothing of the kind, girl. As you said, you are not sure. You are to be wed soon and Declan will be the father of your child. Come; let us speak no more of it. We must return to the kitchen. I shall catch my death of cold in here."

~

The sun is low in the sky, its reach withered with the aging season. Blue shadows reach across the square, the palisade logs silver against the white ground. Rose and Mary sit outside in the courtyard, wrapped in white trade blankets and watching the fort's children play. One group represented the marauding Half-breeds, the other the beleaguered colonists. Rose cannot tell which group represented whom, as they took no particular care to dress their parts, but she suspects that the much larger group must have been the Half-breeds. If she had a choice, she knew which was likely to be the winners and would throw in with them. Shouts and mock gunfire and blood-curdling screeching echo in the square.

Rose tells Mary that she yearns for the courage of Isobel Gunn, an Orkneywoman who had impersonated a man and under such guise travelled to Rupert's Land to follow her lover. But someone discovered her true sex, raped her, and she was found out when she whelped a bastard in the great hall of Fort Douglas itself. Gunn was returned to Orkney in shame with her son. As Rose saw it, the woman had the greatest backbone when she defied the core of social convention simply to follow her own heart.

Mary opines that Gunn was a fool, albeit a tragic one. A woman may earnestly love a man, but none are worth such a price. The fact that she had been raped gave further credence to the value of men in general.

Rose considers this, and wonders about her own choices. She had searched for something permanent in Orkney; sought it in the company of old men and young girls, in bankers and fishmongers, soldiers and cripples missing limbs from the wars with Bonaparte and the Americans. All to no avail.

"Perhaps her greatest terror was that she would never find another love, and emptiness would forever haunt her days," Rose says.

"You speak as if love is something to find and keep. That has not been my experience. When I choose to love, I find it waiting; when I do not, love distains me."

After a moment's reflection, Rose realizes that even the sweetest, most tender boy rarely elicited more than a moment's stirring in her heart, and this in a woman who once believed that love was her birthright. She wanted to love, craved it, in fact, but could not get her stubborn heart to respond. Something always seemed to draw down between her and the other that she had thought so promising. Now with a new husband sharing her bed, she wonders about the strange evolution of love in her life; how she had arrived at this place. The cause, if there is one, is not obvious.

"Perhaps not all are fated for love."

"That's not what Jesus tells us."

Rose shakes her head. What did Jesus have to teach about love, other than as something to be tortured and die for? When she was still quite young she had invited Jesus to her heart's bedchamber, but of all her lovers, He was the most demanding and the least satisfying. She clutched at Him with all the ardour at her command, but he stood away, mute and unapproachable. No matter how the priest exorcised her lack of true faith, no matter how hard she tried to surrender her will to Him, His essence lay as cold and unmoved as the type in her Bible. In the end, her love for Him devolved to one of distant warmth: they way one cares for a sweet uncle who only visits occasionally.

"I believe that when one is human, flesh still matters; a theology cannot warm like a pair of strong arms or a lover's breath on your neck."

"Perhaps. But what fruit did that bear you?" Mary asks in a quiet voice, but at the same time opens her blanket. Rose moves into the warm space and breathes deep, as the older woman's arms wrap around her. Rose immediately knows the answer. She had gone into the world with her ache an unseen golem buried under fine powder and a charming smile. And each touch only confirmed her pain.

Her thoughts turn to scones and strawberries and warm milky tea, the fire laid out before her and the comforting sounds of the servants talking quietly in the corridor. It might be dull, but it surely is safe; if she had known the evils the journey to Rupert's Land held for her, she certainly would have refused it. How that simple Orkney girl had managed it, alone and ever fearful of discovery, Rose has utterly no idea. Perhaps *she* simply is no Isobel Gunn. Mary is of the opinion that she is better for it.

Chapter Fourteen

The red glow of a May early morning silhouettes the two horsemen, a warm breeze whispering through the brown foxtail as they make their way across the rim of the coulee. The upper limb of the sun touches the horizon and morning bursts across the prairie, and, as if on cue, a melody of birdsong lifts from the surrounding mats of wet fescue emerging through the snow. From one of the riders a hearty accompaniment — sung with more lust than tune — of "En roulant ma boule" drifts with the wind.

"You are uncommonly cheerful this morning, my friend," Alexander observes.

"It is not I who is gay, but you who is morose. You have a weight upon you, my brother."

"The only weight upon my soul is your song, Jacque. I believe it is melting the snow for ten paces about my horse, for which no doubt he thanks you. Indeed, his stride has increased now that the way is easier. Pray do not cease, I have plenty of gun cotton for my own poor ears."

"The Half-caste has no love of art."

"And the *bois-brûle* have a love of hideous noise. Indeed, only yesterday, I saw one of your clan driving a cart with an ox, and the infernal device made a racket like a hundred rutting toms all shrieking with one voice. I daresay it cleared the country of game for a hundred miles."

"A hundred rutting toms? All pricks and fight? Mother of God, I cannot think of a better description of myself!"

"The noise part anyway," Alexander replies. "But come, my friend, where is this water you promised? I see nothing but withered grass and snow, and my horse is thirsty."

"Why, it is just below us. Where are your eyes? See down there, in the willows?" Without answering, Alexander turns his horse and walks into the coulee. The willows at the bottom are thick and tangled, and, as he enters, the silver branches clutch at him and catch in his gear. The night's dew has collected on every branch tip and soon his clothes and his mount are dark with wet. He sees a spider's web strung with the tiniest of diamonds, refracting the morning sun into glorious colour. The web moves to and fro as the prairie breathes, and the colours shift and flow up and down the threads. He reaches out a finger; it folds, and the light vanishes. He feels suddenly ashamed.

A drift of white petals covers the soft ground and once through the willows, they cling to his wet horse as white spots bright against the darker wetness of its fur. He is almost at the bottom of the draw when his horse stops and lifts his head. Alexander reaches down and strokes the animal on the neck.

"What is the matter, lad?" he murmurs in its ear. The horse tosses its head and its nostrils flare as it takes an elusive scent.

"What is going on up there?" Jacque calls from behind. "Are you shitting yourself, by God?"

"There is something in this wood."

"Indeed, it is called water. If you must fornicate yourself, at least move aside and let a man through." Without waiting for a response,

Jacque knees his horse and passes alongside. Uncertain and wary, Alexander follows.

When he arrives at the edge of the tiny creek, Jacque already has a pipe lit and his horse is drinking deeply, the contractions running up her smooth neck. Alexander moves beside his friend, and his own horse lowers its head to drink. He reaches into the octopus bag tied to his sash and pulls out his own pipe and tobacco tin. Placing a piece of char cloth on the pan of his carbine, he dry-fires and the flare of sparks catch on the cloth. Cupping it with some tinder, he swings his hand back and forth as if preparing a throw of dice and smoke soon dribbles from between his fingers. He takes the tinder and holds it against the tobacco. Smoke trails from the pipe and he lifts it to his lips. Jacque watches without comment.

When the horses have drunk their fill, the men check their flints and proceed along the swamp at the edge of the creek, keeping an eye out for tracks. Mosquitoes swirl about them, heedless of the building warmth of day. The breeze along the creek follows them, announcing their presence to whatever hides in the brush ahead, and Alexander has little hope of catching game at unawares. He relaxes on his blanket, resting his gloved hands on his horse's neck.

Jacque rides ahead on his Indian horse, an almost-white pinto mare with a solitary black mark covering her hindquarters, as if she had sat in a barrel of printer's ink. He too rides without a saddle, although unlike Alexander, who rides without tack of any kind, Jacque's bridle is a colourful affair, with bright ribbons and feather plumes and beadwork that his wife has sewn onto it. Alexander thinks the horse a lovely animal, and so does his own, a fine sixteen-hand stallion. Whenever they ride with Jacque, Alexander constantly has to remind his horse of his proper business. Although normally a wise and phlegmatic animal, when the mare came into heat the stallion became an ill-tempered imbecilic fool, a state Alexander could sympathize with.

He is contemplating on the sorry state that the male can be reduced to in the pursuit of love, when he sees it out of the corner of his eye: a long, tawny shape whisking across their shadows, right under the nose of Jacque's horse. The pinto rears and neighs, almost throwing Jacque into the muskeg. Alexander's own horse capers about, rolling its eyes and tossing its head. The reek of cat fills the clearing.

Alexander reins in his horse and pulls up next to Jacque; their eyes meet and with simultaneous whoops, they whack their horse's flanks and charge through the willows. They burst out of the brush just in time to see the mountain lion disappear over the top of the coulee.

Alexander reaches into his shot bag and tosses a handful of balls into his mouth. As he pounds up the steep slope of the coulee, he pulls his carbine from its scabbard and pours in a measure of powder from his horn. He spits in a ball and whacks the stock against his leg to settle the charge. Both men goad their horses on and Alexander pulls away, tossing great divots into Jacque's face while a string of shouted obscenities lights up his horse's backside.

As he nears their quarry — running flat out, stretching as tight as a fiddle string in its bounds — Alexander takes a bead on the cat's shoulder and fires.

A flash and smoke and a great clod bursts out of the prairie just beside the cat. Alexander curses around the balls in his mouth, spits in another and urges his mount to greater speed. Jacque has veered off to intercept the dodging cat; he too fires and misses.

The cat whisks into another draw and Alexander exhorts the stallion to even greater speed; it leaps from the edge of the coulee, dropping down, down. The wind whistles in Alexander's ears and foam from his horse blows into his face.

They land with a great thud, dirt and turf flying in all directions, and Alexander is almost flung over his horse's neck. He squeezes his knees with all his strength and holds tightly on to the mane, his heart soaring with the pounding of his horse's hooves. He feels drunk on prairie, sky, and the smell of his horse, his senses focused by the ecstasy of the hunt.

Without breaking stride, the stallion surges forward, and Alexander can feel the massive shoulder muscles pumping between his legs, the animal's sweat soaking into his breeches. This coulee is much larger, and a tangle of willow and buck brush fills the valley bottom. Once the cat find its way in there, it will be gone for good; it will be impossible and even dangerous to follow.

It is almost there, dodging and weaving its way over and around the folds of the coulee and Alexander leads it with his gun, guessing its next move. When the smoke has blown clear, he can see the cat on the ground, twisting and leaping and clawing at something unseen. He yanks his horse to a halt; in one smooth motion slides off, spits in a ball, kneels, and fires.

It lies at the bottom of the coulee, ten yards from the brush. Alexander walks forward, loosening his knife in its sheath. As he nears, he can see that the cat is still breathing, with long pauses between breaths. It has been hit in the shoulder and neck, and blood darkens the ochre soil beneath it. A convulsion and it slowly stretches out, limbs quivering. At last it lies still.

With a feeling of triumph, Alexander kneels besides the animal. Except for the tip of its tail, ears, and muzzle, which are charcoal, its pelt is the colour of fall grass, and is in prime condition after a winter of feeding on weak and starving deer. With one deft movement, he cuts its throat. Waiting for it to bleed, he stands up and looks for the arrival of his friend, a few choice words on his lips.

This is home, he thinks, staring up at the spring-blue sky overhead, warm and flawless. The pounding of his heart is now a memory, but he feels as if his moccasins are incapable of bending a blade of grass. *The kill is a fine one, and the cat's hide will bring a good price.* The miserable weeks of portaging and lining boats, of dealing with ill-equipped and sullen colonists — the betrayal and loss have become a distant memory, with a long and challenging winter of trapping and hunting between himself and the river.

He had been melancholy for weeks after leaving the brigade, with many a night passed in rum's dulling embrace. But with the challenges of simple survival always at hand, he had found himself thinking less and less of her, and over time his old spirit returned. He exulted in his reclaimed life — one of wind and freedom and prairie. He swore he would never again place his heart in another's keeping.

By the time he has smoked a pipe and thrown the lion over his horse's back, Jacque still has not appeared. Alexander follows back along his trail, giving his horse its head, surprised to see just how far they had run. No wonder the stallion had felt so hot beneath him. He sees Jacque long before he catches up to him, a dark image on the horizon, and he is on foot.

When he walks up, his friend is headed the other way, his tack carried under his arm. Looking out over the prairie with his hand shielding his eyes, Alexander sees a couple of crows perched on something in the distance.

They walk together for a while. "What happened?" he asks at last.

"Prairie dog hole," Jacque replies. Alexander nods. He had not heard the shot, but had been down in the coulee and caught up in the chase. God could have farted, and he probably would have missed it.

"Give you a ride, my friend?" Alexander lowers a hand. Jacque turns toward him, his face covered in dust and two telltale tracks line his cheeks. He takes the hand and swings up onto the stallion behind Alexander. The horse gives a mournful sigh and heads off.

～

The sun is low and cold begins to creep out of the ground. The line of dark clouds that had spent the afternoon hugging the southern horizon now roll toward the zenith, all saffron and lavender, their edges burning with a final caress from the setting sun. The air is still and silent, and the sound of the horse pulling at the new grass carries a long way. Coyotes yap in the distance.

Jacque examines the sky a moment, sniffs, and frowns. "You better hobble that horse. By the smell of the air and the look of the sky, I will wager my left testicle that it will be an ugly night."

Using his knife, Alexander quarters a skinned and gutted jackrabbit and impales the meat on willow sticks, jamming an end into the sod so that the meat leans over the buffalo-flap fire. The rabbit is fat with spring grass, and the pieces drip hissing into the flames. The smell is glorious.

He glances up at the sky. "It is strange, is not — this time of year for a storm? I would swear by your mother's tit that it is nowhere hot enough."

"You are right, Alex, and I think those bastards hold more than rain to piss upon us. This early in the year — Mother of God, if there is not a blizzard hiding behind those pretty colours, I will tongue a priest's anus. We are fools to be caught out in the open like this."

"It is not far to your house."

Jacque shakes his head. "We have walked many miles on top of that spavined turd you call a horse, and he is well spent. I remember that there is no shelter, no coulee for many miles around. We can do nothing but see what the night brings. I am worried for your horse."

"He will carry us to the ends of the earth if that is your need. However, have a smoke and a bite of rabbit. There is rum in that pannier; fetch it will you?"

~

The lightning cuts a jagged swath across the night sky, for the briefest of moments illuminating the silhouette of two riders on a solitary horse. The thunder is an almost constant cannonade, filling the gaps between the blinding flashes. A cold wind roars across the prairie, flattening the grass and forcing the riders to hold dearly to their horse — hats long since lost. Another flash, much closer, and Jacque breaks out laughing.

"What is it, you ass?" Alexander says, in no mood for humour.

"Your hair … it stands as if you have seen a ghost." He is laughing deep and full, slapping his breeches.

Alexander frowns and turns toward his friend. Another flash and he sees Jacque's long hair also standing on end, reaching for the heavens. With a cry he knees his horse, and it leaps forward with a lurch, almost dropping Jacque onto the prairie. They thunder along, the sound of their footfalls utterly lost in that immensity of sound and noise. The air about them sparks and crackles, crawling with fairy-light.

"*Merde!*" cries Jacque, clinging to Alexander's jacket and wondering what the hell is happening. The horse pounds along zigzagging this way and that, throwing great divots from its hooves. Alexander is terrified that they will step into a gopher hole in the darkness.

But the lightning illuminates the valley of the Assiniboine River and the belt of trees growing along its bank. With a great, stomach-churning crash that rolls and tumbles and flattens the very grass, and compels the now thoroughly frightened Jacque into crossing himself, they charge into the valley and the safety of the trees, lightning flicking their mount's streaming tail.

They give the weary horse its head as it picks its way through the cottonwoods. It knows the area well, and soon they find their way to a small cabin and corral, not a stone's throw from the river. Pulling up to the gate, Alexander strokes his horse on the neck and dismounts, Jacque following.

"What was that all about?" the big man grumbles, rubbing his buttocks.

Alexander turns to him in the dark. "Lightning. If we had stood there another moment we would have been blasted to hell."

"I thought you had more balls than that, my pale friend. And your horse — I was certain he would step in a hole, and we would have our necks broken. Ah, my poor little *Marie*." He shakes his head.

"I have seen it before," Alexander says. "On a buffalo hunt. The man, Pardie, was sitting alone at a fire while the storm banged around us. I was checking my horse's hooves, and when I looked up Pardie's hair was all on end. We were all laughing at him when a great crash flung us about like dolls. Pardie's hair was all scorched, and he was gibbering like an idiot. All his clothes were burnt off. He lived, but was never right in the head after that. Whenever we visited an Indian camp, he would tear off his clothes and chase the women. The Indians thought he was possessed by a demon, so they didn't kill him, but our trade suffered."

Jacque whistles, and spits. "Piss!" he says, shaking his head again, and then after a moment's thought, crosses himself. The door to the cabin opens and a small figure stands in the doorway, lit from behind by warm firelight.

"Who is there?" a woman calls.

They let the horse into the corral and walk to the cabin. They see that she carries a fowling piece and lifts it toward them as they approach.

"Oh, my little pig!" Jacque cries, spreading his arms. "It is your husband, home at last."

"Jacque! I was wondering what had happened to you, great fool." She steps from the doorway and wraps her arms around her husband, who bends over her and kisses her long and deeply while Alexander takes great interest in a rusty plough leaning against the house.

When the couple at last pause for a breath, she scolds Jacque for being away so long, then sees Alexander standing in the shadows, his eyes watching her with great affection. He reaches for the brim of his cap, and then remembers it is somewhere out on the prairie.

"Hello, Elise," he says.

"Dear Alexander, I did not know you were to come. Jacque say nothing to me. Welcome, dearest friend," she says, taking his hand and Alexander bends over, giving her a light kiss.

"No, no, wretched woman, keep thy tongue in thy mouth," Jacque says. "And for the disgusting fire in your loins, Alex, we have a goat in the back, a good prime goat I save for you and any other English or damned Half-caste."

"A godly man never sets his eye upon a friend's true love," Alexander replies.

—

The men stomp into the house, throwing down their gear and tracking in grass and mud onto the sawn-wood floor. There is a birch fire burning on the stone hearth, and it is warm in the tiny room. Alexander sits at the table while Jacque retrieves a jug and two tin cups. He fills them both brimming.

"And what about me?" Elise asks, her hands on her hips.

"Food, little pig. Food first, then you will drink. We have ridden hard and long under the very bolts of Thor himself, and only escaped with our necks by a cunt-hair, praise God. Fleeing is difficult work, and at this moment, I believe I could eat a skunk's asshole."

"I think I do much better than a skunk's asshole," says Elise smiling and lifting a heavy frying pan from a hook on the wall.

As he drinks his rum, Alexander watches Elise prepare a meal of buffalo tongue and bannock. She is a slight Cree woman from a tribe near Cumberland House. She had married Jacque earlier in the year, *à la façon du pays*, and once as slight as a slip of thread-paper, she already shows a swelling belly. Her Cree name had been Pinackopicim, roughly translated as "autumn moon," a name given to her for her fair skin and reddish-dark hair, the result of some forgotten liaison with a fur trader somewhere in her ancestry. Alex thinks her Indian name is beautiful, but she insists that only her French name be used. Watching her movements, he feels a stirring in his breeches and is immediately reminded of Rose.

"Drink, drink, my friend," shouts Jacque in his ear. "You look a man sentenced to hang, not one who has escaped the gallows. Drink!"

They drink, all three, until late into the evening. They are accustomed to the vicious solvent that Jacque nursed in his barn, though an outsider would be startled by the sheer quantity of liquor a native of the country will consume and still be able to carry on an intelligible if not respectable conversation.

Somewhere along the way, however, the mood changed; about the time Elise mentioned in passing that Cuthbert Grant had stopped by, seeking Jacque.

"Cuthbert Grant! What the hell does that pig turd want?"

"He would not say. Something to do with colony, the new people at the Forks."

"Damn him, damn him to hell. He is always poking and prying and raising mischief. You see, there will be trouble again, more than before. When it smells bad, you look for shit, and it has smelled bad around here for too damned long. Piss on him, I say."

"Now Jacque, must not speak like this."

"Who is Cuthbert Grant?" Alexander asks.

"The fornicating son of a cross-bred goat, whelped by a bitch-dog and nursed by a half-penny whore."

"He our chief," Elise says with a smile. "One of them. Jacque mad because he not pay debt for pemmican. Grant owes Jacque new musket."

"Damn right he does, that foreign son of a poxed whore's left tit. But it is more than that, little pig. When he and his doxy Duncan Cameron are not busying tonguing each other's holes, they raise so much shit that the redcoats must surely come. He could have let those Scottish half-wit peasants freeze or starve, but he has to burn them out, and now the mad King George will be pissing himself and sending in his troops."

"What do you mean, 'foreign'?" asks Alexander, trying to make his eyes focus on Jacque.

"He's a foreigner, by God. He might have been born an honest Half-breed, but he was sent by his papa to Scotland, grew up on the fucking moors or heaths or whatever the hell it is called. Came back to Rupert's Land dressed like a doxy with his pantaloons and boots and hats. Shits gold dust and diamonds. Yet, just last month I saw him dressed like one of our warriors, with paint and feathers. I would have shot the fool right off his mount, but I was afraid of hitting the horse."

"Didn't you grow up in Montreal, Jacque? Your people so rich you were nursed by saints and had angels wiping your arse?"

"Yes, I did, by Christ," says Jacque with enormous solemnity. "I went to school for four whole years, before I kicked the good Father in the balls, and they threw me out, the whores. My dear Papa put me on the next brigade westward, and here I have been: a true Voyageur and trader and hunter while Cuthbert Grant was still in Scotland, stuffing his scaly prick up every cassock he could find."

"What is happening at the Forks now?"

"*Merde* is happening, my friend. I hear that the fucking colonists have since come back, and they recaptured Fort Douglas, stormed Fort Gibraltar across the river, and even arrested Cameron. Grant is running all over the country rousing our people to war. Piss on it all, I say! Here, little pig, pass the drink, won't you?"

~

Alexander is awakened by a grunting in a corner of the room, the place where their willow bed is pushed against a wall. Confused, he turns over just in time to see Elise take Jacque's penis in her mouth. Jacque looks up, sees Alexander watching, and winks at him. Alexander stares for a moment, in his confusion not understanding what he is seeing, but, as awareness dawns, he flushes and quickly turns away.

After a while the sounds die away; he tries to sleep but cannot, and lies in the darkness listening to the shrieks of owls and the occasional snap from the fire, long since burned down. The air in

Chapter Fifteen

Alexander is roused by Jacque groaning, "Mother of God," and the sound of vomit splattering the floor. His own head is pounding after the past night's heavy drinking, and he scrabbles up, heading for the door. His head is swimming and he hits the door hard, sending it crashing back against the outer wall.

"Be careful of the portcullis, you clumsy English bastard," Jacque shouts at him, followed by a pained screech from Elise. Alexander staggers into sunshine reflecting off a glorious patina of frost covering everything about him. He gulps the cold air to clear his head as he walks toward the corral. His horse is standing there steaming, one forefoot tipped onto the edge of its hoof. He had been frisking about the enclosure in the cold morning, judging by the sweat and proud toss of his neck as Alexander approaches.

"Good morning to you, my old friend," Alexander murmurs to it as the horse lowers its head and nibbles on his ear. The bubbling song of a meadowlark calls from the top of a nearby cottonwood, and a pair of crows sweep overhead, cawing as they pass by.

He throws some hay into the corral along with a shovel of grain. He is examining Jacque's colourful bridle hanging off a corral post when he hears the thunder of several hooves approaching at a run. Soon there is a flash of many colours and a group of horseman pound into the yard. Alexander approaches the nearest rider, taking the restive animal's bridle as it tosses its head.

Some of the Métis are dressed in the capotes and paint and feathers of their mother's tribes, but most are in beaded leather buckskin and leggings and wear a broad red sash around their waists. Some have jaunty feathers in their caps. All are armed with knives and muskets.

"Hallo, Alexander. Good day to you."

"Hallo, François, and a good day to you." He turns to the rest of the band, all lined up and watching him, their horses chewing at bits and capering. "And what is this? Off to find you a wife at last? I think you will need more men to assist you."

"The hunt, the hunt!" François replies. "There was a council and it was decided that it is time."

"François!" Jacque shouts from the doorway, dressed only in his long red woollen underwear, the rear flap hanging down. "Come in, come in, we must have a drink. Get up little pig, get up my love, we have guests. Food, we must have food."

"The last time I was a guest at your house, I had the running shits for a week," one of the horsemen call.

"That is because you are not used to solids, Théophile. It really is time your mother weaned you. But there is no worry, I will do you a great favour and shoot the ill-bred nag you ride, and there shall be fresh meat for all. Come in, come in, everyone."

By the time the good-natured party has jammed their way into the cabin there is hardly room to move. The riders have their own kegs with them, and it soon becomes apparent that the buffalo will remain unmolested for at least another day. Elise insists on a roaring fire — likely an ill-fated ruse to ensure that the guests do not overstay — and the space not filled with sweating bodies is occupied by several voices, all speaking at once and loudly discussing everything from the imminent hunt to the spring weather, but mostly the certainty that all-out war will be declared on Selkirk's settlement.

Somehow word gets out to the surrounding community, and even more riders show up, many accompanied by their womenfolk. The corral fills with horses and the gathering thankfully moves into the barn. Someone has brought a fiddle and the little farm on the banks of the Assiniboine River echoes with lively jigs and rumble of buffalo-hide boots on wood.

The gathering lasts all day and into the night, and after a time Alexander wearies of it, retreating to the house. It is cold and dark inside and he pokes up the fire before taking a burning brand and lighting his pipe. He sits back in the darkness, resting his moccasined feet on the table, the music and drone of the crowd faint through the log walls. He is barely into his second pipe when the door opens, and Elise steps inside. She looks around and seems surprised to find Alexander sitting there in the dark, the fire warm. Her face is rosy and flushed, her dark hair long and hanging down her back. Drops of sweat shine on her forehead, reflecting the fire like tiny suns.

"Excuse me," Alexander says, preparing to get up.

"Just sit there," Elise replies, looking around and lifting her damp hair from her face. She takes a tin cup and fills it with rum, collapsing in a chair beside the table.

"Jacque will leave tomorrow," she says, and sighs.

"Will you not come, too?" Alexander asks after a pause. The question feels heavy; she can feel him searching her.

"Jacque does not want me. Want me here for the baby." She drops her hand on her belly and squeezes.

"I am surprised to hear it," he replies. Neither Indians nor Half-breeds gave any special exemptions to pregnant women; they pulled their weight along with everyone else.

"He is afraid … afraid for baby. I lose before, once. Baby did not live, you understand?"

"I did not know. I am sorry."

"I am lonely, Alexander. Jacque, he hunts all days. He is never with me. I am alone in this place. It feels so dark to me now. Once I was happy, so very happy, but not now. I miss my family."

Alexander clears his throat and begins a few inadequate sentences, then falls mute. His hand reaches across the table and gives hers a few cautious pats. It is wet with her tears. She is suddenly furious with him and turns, staring at him. She cannot see his face in the dark.

"You are just like him!"

"Eh?"

"Another asshole hunter that would rather sleep with buffalo than woman. Or with men. Do you fuck men, Alexander?"

"What the Christ are you saying?"

"You all alike, fuck each other. Probably fuck buffalo too, right? Maybe even bitch coyote. Do you roll on the grass with my Jacque, that why he no come home?" She is shouting now.

He stands up, kicking away the table. Elise leaps to her feet, her eyes glaring in the firelight. He steps towards her with his fists clenched. He expects and hopes that she will pull a knife. Half-breed women could be incredible vicious in a fight, much more so than their men.

He is surprised when she lowers her fierce eyes, and shocked when she pulls a shoulder free of her dress, and then another. With a sigh, it whispers down her body and piles up around her feet. She stands in the firelight, gazing at the floor. Her body shines in that unearthly glow, more shadow than substance, the light flicking across her breasts, small, round dome of her stomach. She pulls her shoulders up and raises her head. Tears are on her cheeks, and she looks so forlorn that Alexander just checks himself from wrapping his arms around her. He takes both of her hands and squeezes them.

His head is spinning, but he knows that much is at risk now, and he must be careful. For all their sakes.

To reject her would be dangerous. You don't fuck with Half-breed women. But Jacque … with her standing so lovely there, so incredibly desirable, he pulls her toward him and the memory of Rose crashes into the room. He freezes, caught in a triptych of fear and grief and desire. Elise looks at him closely and knows that they are no longer alone.

"I … I will speak to Jacque," Alexander says in a choking voice, his hand of its own accord running along her side, until he feels the weight of her breast on the back of it. He makes a motion as if to leave, but finds that his other hand is around her, moving down. Her lips are on his own in a heartbeat, the pain that fills them both moving across the moist touch like lightning, and they are sure of one another.

~⁓

"You must let her come on the hunt."

"Oh, ho, listen to the English telling me, Jacque, what I must do with my wife. Your testicles are big enough for the both of us now, are they? And what do you know of it? You are still a damned virgin, by Christ. What do you know about keeping a wife?"

They are in the muddy corral trying with little success to corner Alexander's stallion, which is unusually stupid this chilly morning and will not allow anyone to approach him. Several Half-breeds sit on the corral rails watching with vocal amusement.

"Look, my friend, Elise spoke with me last night. She is very unhappy living here alone, and it will be worse now that you and everyone else is to leave for the hunt."

"Bah, in my home is her place. I will take my belt to her back and then she will know the meaning of misery. I've got you now, you great oaf." He lunges for the stallion with the bridle, but the horse easily dodges and thunders off with a flick of his tail and mud flying from his hooves. The watching assembly cheers.

"Shit on a priest," moans Jacque, holding his temples. "It feels like there is a brat with a drum inside my head this morning."

"You know Half-breed women will not endure such treatment, Jacque. If she doesn't leave you and return to her family, she will cut your throat one night while you lie beside her."

Jacque pauses for a moment considering. "You really think so? *Mon dieu*, I must consider this. Elise can be a bitch when the mood is upon her. No, no, I have no horse for her. That bastard Lefebvre tells me he will sell me a horse, but he wants thrice what it's worth, the Jew. I offered him a musket ball, but he showed little interest. Told me to fuck myself in the ass. I told him it was impossible, as his mother's tongue was in the way. But I cannot afford one for Elise as well."

Alexander stops and looks down at the mud. "She can ride with me. My horse is big enough for the both of us, as you well know."

Jacque frowns and spits on a fencepost. "Ride with you? Fuck all priests and bishops. I do not know …"

"I did not want to tell you this, my friend, but she said that she is so angry that she desires not to slit your throat, but to cut your prick off."

Jacque blanches and crosses himself. "Why do did you say that? God in heaven! You are an evil man, worse than the English, Half-caste. Why would thee say such things to me, your friend? That damned bitch …"

"Hand me the bridle; you are making the horse nervous with your frightened gibbering. I will catch him myself."

"Truth, did she really say such a terrible thing, Alexander?"

"Indeed she did, promising to nail the thing to the door, for the crows to peck at."

Jacque's hands went instinctively to his crotch. "God save me. But you will do this for me, will you not? You will carry my Elise with you, so that I may not be gelded?"

"I said I would, now stand still! I almost have him." Alexander manages to corner the horse and is approaching slowly, the bridle held forward. Normally he rides without one, but with all the horses they will be riding with, including many mares, he wants to take no chances. The stallion's nostrils fill with their scent, and they flare as his eyes roll red; he stamps the ground and snorts. Alexander watches him, thinking himself a fool for ever imagining this is a broken horse. It is as likely to kill him as to let him mount.

The catcalls and hooting at the fence stop as everyone waits to see what will happen when the hide is looped over the horse's face. All of them, including Alexander, expect an explosion. The watchers are very disappointed when the horse lowers its head and nuzzles Alexander as he slowly pulls the bridle on. He leads the now docile animal back to Jacque. The Half-breed pats the horse's flank.

"My God, he is a beautiful animal."

"Not on your life, Jacque. Take that worm-eaten screw of yours and load up. Make haste, as we are late. See, the sun is halfway to noon. Make haste."

~

When he awakens, sunlight is already streaming through the saffron canvas of his tent. As he lies on his back, his eyes follow a blue bottle fly as it wanders back and forth along the ridge. Outside he can hear the camp awakening: the bark of dogs, clatter of kettles being filled with water. The smell of buffalo dung fires. Muted voices carried, half-heard, sounding like the muttering of a distant shore.

He sighs and throws off his blanket. Pulling on his moccasins, he sees that the sole is almost through on one of them, and he will have to mend it soon. Hopefully after today, there will be no shortage of the thick hide required. He sighs again.

When he pushes his way outside the tent, he sees that the sun has barely been up an hour, and the dew on the grass shines with all the colours of imagination. The smell of wet grass lightens his heart. Straightening his back, he looks along the trail that they had passed the previous day: a dark broad river of crushed grass and prairie rutted by the passing of hundreds of wooden carts, horses, and dogs.

All the carts have been circled as a defensive perimeter against the Sioux, and inside this barricade the camp is astir now, with breakfast well on its way. There are dozens of fires burning and Alexander moves to the nearest; with a nod to the woman tending it, he pulls out a burning piece of dung and lights his pipe. She offers him a slab of fresh bannock fried in buffalo fat and Alexander accepts it with a smile, placing it in a pocket for later in the day. Standing up, he sees the captains gathering, and, with a touch of his hat to the woman, he hurries away, finding a spot in the circle of men.

They all sit cross-legged, with their guns on their laps and their pipes burning. Conversation flows back and forth, and although there is concern about the coming war, most of the talk is of a more personal kind, problems with a mate or a neighbour, hopes for the future, memories of the past. Their costumes are as brilliant and varied as the individuals wearing them, and there is much laughter among the elected captains, a light-heartedness that belies the hardiness of the men and the difficult lives they lead.

Soon the conversation flows on its own account to the buffalo, and plans for that day's hunt. No call to order is given; no chief stands up and addresses them. But gradually, like the collecting of birds in an autumn sky, individual conversations gather toward a common topic, and evolve into a general discussion of plans for their day, and about how the hunt will proceed.

Jacque sits opposite Alexander, the great Half-breed a head taller than his neighbours. Alexander smiles faintly at him, but he does not respond, just continues staring with the same intense look he had given his friend for many days.

Conversation between them had withered until it ceased entirely, his friend forsaking his companionship for the company of others.

When Alexander had the rare opportunity to ride alone with him, the man said little, just turning every now and then and looking at him as if considering, as if pondering what he should do. After a few days, Alexander had given up trying to break through his friend's sudden taciturn mood, and with a sense of both relief and foreboding, had turned to the company of others.

As they had slowly walked along the dusty trail in search of the buffalo herds, he had many hours to wonder if Elise had spoken to Jacque of what had passed between them that night in their cabin. She had long since abandoned the place on his horse behind Alexander, riding instead in one of the many carts with the women. She was never alone, and so he had not the opportunity to question her. But this sudden change in mood from his friend made little sense otherwise, although if he had known, Alexander is surprised that Jacque has not called him out.

Perhaps it is out of respect for the hunt; it is too important to risk division or fracture, and discord will not be tolerated. Any serious conflict is expected to be dealt with in private or when they return to the Forks. Perhaps something has been whispered about him; Alexander was a Half-caste, not a true Half-breed, and while most were willing to forgive him this failing, there were those who thought his presence an intrusion, not least because of his previous alliance with the Hudson's Bay Company. Some think him a spy, and under Cuthbert Grant's orders, they keep a suspicious eye on him. Although Jacque is a man who avoids politics of any kind, like all of his people he loathes duplicity, and betrayal of their community is the most capital of crimes.

Returning to the discussion at hand, Alexander hears that scouts have located a large herd at a distant wallow, and the men begin discussing how best the hunters should approach, and the rules they all agreed to abide by. One ambitious fool could scatter the herd before the rest had a chance to take position, so great care and planning is required to ensure a successful hunt. They nominate a chief of the camp to take charge and organize the hunters: Jean-Baptiste Dumont, recent of the Saskatchewan country. It would be he who must hold back the impatient hunters until the proper moment and the cry given. Dumont stands up and bows before them, to many a crinkling eye and puffing of smoke and soft laughter.

With much back-clapping, the captains stand and head off to prepare their people. One man goes to a nearby cart and unfurls their new flag, a white lemniscate horizontal against a navy background, which is the signal to all to prepare for departure.

Although it appears from a distance that the camp has descended into chaos, there is in fact great order in the organizing of the carts and hunters. There are more than 450 Half-breeds attending this hunt, this annual pilgrimage to seek the buffalo, and, as a communal event, women, children, and the elderly are included. Even the feeble and sick attend when possible, jostled in the back of a cart piled deep in buffalo hides. All have a role to play, and within half an hour the carts are bound to oxen, gear is packed up and stowed away, then they are ready to begin.

Dumont moves to the front of his people and, without looking back, begins the march. Under the shouted directions of the captains, one by one the carts pull away, like the unspooling of a thread, each one surrounded by many horses and dogs. Dust and the unholy head-splitting creak of wooden hub on ungreased wooden axle rises into the hot prairie morning.

Before long, all are caked in dust, each man, woman, and child breathing as best they can through handkerchiefs. The sun swings higher and higher, and dribbles of sweat clear paths down saffron-caked faces, making even the children look unearthly and ferocious.

The land is empty and barren, the year's grass already withering in the rainless heat. But among the thin tussocks and weeds lies a garden of bleached buffalo bones, running from horizon to horizon. Like grotesque topiary, cluster here and there, gathered sometimes in piles; skulls and pelvises and ribs, femurs and vertebrae. They clatter as the horse's hooves push them aside.

Far more interesting to the hunters than the bones is the churned-up soil, the fresh buffalo flaps not yet burrowed by flies. Alexander is examining the trail when he sees a crow descend behind a knoll. He stares after it awhile, and then reins in his horse. The next captain following, a young man in a blue capote and bright red sash, soon catches up to him.

"What is it?" he asks. "Forget which way to go?"

"There may be something over that rise, Andre. Let us go see."

Andre looks to the front of the column. "What is it? Should we not speak with Jean-Baptiste?"

"And tell him what? I may be mistaken. We will ride together, you and I, to see what there is to see, if anything."

The men veer from the column, walking their horses up the rise. Many eyes follow, but no one moves from their position. The air away from the brigade is clean and sweet, and both men pull down their scarves and breath deeply of it. After the hideous racket of the carts, the soft rhythm of their horse's hooves sounds as peaceful and relaxing music.

Upon reaching the crest, both men grab their guns. Lying down in a small draw on the opposite side are the carcasses of two buffalo. As they descend, several crows fly away cawing, lighting in the wiry branches of a long dead cottonwood and furiously complaining at the intrusion.

Alexander and the youth slide off their horses and lead them beside the carcasses. Flies buzz, circling and swirling around the red bones, the kill so new not even the coyotes have found it yet. Nothing edible is left, just scraped bones. Even the skulls have been broken open for their contents. Alexander crouches beside the nearest, poking it with the barrel of his carbine. He looks up at the distant tree and the noisy garrison perched in its branches.

"Sioux?" Andre asks.

"Maybe. Could be Cree, even Stony. They have been raiding into the southwest."

"I better let Dumont know."

Alexander nods. Andre leaps onto his horse and, reining it in, turns and races up the slope, quickly disappearing behind it.

Alexander examines the ground around the kill. The buffalo seem to have been butchered where they were dropped. He spots a narrow trail leading eastward, a faint disturbance in the grass. As it is the habit of the plains Indians to ride single file to disguise their numbers, he has no idea how many where there, whoever they are. Most tribes are peaceable enough, but the few exceptions are noteworthy in their violent opposition to others in their hunting grounds.

The freshness of the kill means that these hunters are in all likelihood aware of the brigade; it is hard to move around the country unobtrusively: sheer numbers aside, the dust cloud and noise announces their presence for miles about. At least on this side of the rise, the sound of their passing is faint. He stands up and looks again at the crows. Climbing back onto his horse, he makes his way back to the column.

"What do you think?" asks Andre as Alexander catches up with him.

"Whoever they were, they're gone now," he replies. But as he is reassuring the youth his mind goes back to the noisy squabbling of the crows, certain in his gut that other eyes had observed them with keen interest.

Chapter Sixteen

The Métis column plods on. Men elected as soldiers and guides keep close order, and even those on horseback are required to keep alongside, eating dust with the rest of them. While the air is clear a little way to the side, if not checked the line will spread farther and farther as each man seeks to escape the pall from his fellow in front until all is in disarray, and outliers are at risk of spooking the buffalo or being picked off by stalking Sioux. With shouts and curses they are herded like the beasts they pursue, driven to the next camp.

The distance to the wallow is not great, and the day's march is blissfully short. The wind has died completely, the heat and dust intolerable. The scouts surround Dumont; while the people wait, an anxious conversation ensues, with much head-shaking and pointing of fingers to the horizon.

Visibility is very poor, with a yellow haze obscuring everything beyond a mile. Alexander moves forward with the rest of the captains — fifty in all — and listens as the scouts indicate the location of the wallow, and Dumont assigns position. One scout slides off his horse, picking up a handful of grass and lettting it fall through his fingers. They all watch as it scatters down, flicking to the east in a sudden gust.

As one, all heads swivel to a dark line of clouds building to the west. Thunderstorms have arrived with the afternoon for the last several days, pounding the prairie with torrential rain and noise. It appears that today is to be no different. Distant grumbling carries along with the breeze

The riders turn southwards, in a broad line; Alexander finds himself beside the mute Jacque.

"A good day for a hunt, brother," he says.

Jacque looks around as if he has just woken from a dream. He nods his head. "I have yearned to shoot something in a great long while," he says, lifting his musket to examine the flint.

Alexander is about to reply when a shout carries down the line. The riders move closer together. The herd appears as a shadow covering the prairie, a darkness that drapes over the rolling landscape without break, moving and flowing here and there, but maintaining a contiguous mass of life from horizon to horizon. It is only by shielding their eyes from the sun and squinting that the hunters can tell that the shadow is in fact an unimaginable number of tiny, discreet objects. The strong tang of dung and buffalo drifts toward them.

Coyotes flit along low to the ground with that lope, stop, stare manner of the wary predators. Shadows of the shadow, hoping to scavenge a carcass left by grizzly, mountain lion, wolf, or Indian. The noisy passing of crows saws the air.

Word comes down the line that the hunters are to bear east and follow a narrow hollow, a remnant of ice, wind, and cataclysmic water that fissures the otherwise smooth breast of the prairie. One by one, the riders dip into this hidden place, each man checking his load and prime. Mouths fill with balls and whispered hopes and comments become mute.

Dumont sends a scout ahead on foot. The waiting for his report is interminable, and when at last the man returns, he informs them that further progress is impossible without revealing themselves. Dumont orders the men into a broad swath, and the horses, sensing their riders' excitement, stamp and chew on bits, capering sideways and flicking their tails. Dumont rides up the side of the hollow to see the herd for himself and check the lay of the land. It is rolling country, with many dips and rises between them and the herd. But it will be impossible for the hunters to move any closer without detection.

He draws out his spyglass and scans along the herd, feeling for their feelings, judging their alertness. It is late afternoon and the image dances with the rising heat. Flies buzz about his ears. A great many of the animals are lying down or rolling in the dust. The wind gusts stronger now, blowing across the top of the rise and shaking his glass, his long, dark hair streaming beside him.

Dumont knows that no matter how sleepy and peaceful the herd appears to be, there are always old bulls around that keep a wary eye on the horizon. The wallow is in low ground and with the approaching storm, the animals will be more nervous than usual. As this thought forms, a deep boom descends from the darkening sky, crawling over the prairie and startling many buffalo to their feet. A few drops flick nearby grass.

As usual, the youngest and most desirable animals are concentrated in the centre of the herd. His glass picks up one ancient, black bull raising its head and taking scent. It paws the ground and snorts, its neighbours turning to watch him.

Everything depends on his choice: he can wait for another day when the buffalo are more settled, or they can attempt the long run to the herd. The snorts of the hunter's horses behind him are filled with impatience, and he can feel the energy of his people to begin.

Worming his way down from the edge of the coulee, he returns to the waiting hunters.

"They sense something — the coming storm or maybe they have caught a stray scent. We must begin before they panic. Métis, *start!*"

At that word, all the riders explode from hiding, galloping as fast as ever they are able, determined that their fellows will not leave them behind. But as in his race with Jacque pursuing the mountain lion, Alexander pulls ahead on his stallion.

Almost immediately several old bulls spot the riders: huffing and pawing, they toss their vicious-looking horns. Tails lift, and some of the animals begin trotting away from the approaching hooves. A few of the largest bulls move toward the hunters, bellowing.

The wind whistles in the hunter's ears, and if their mouths were not filled with shot they would let cry, knowing that their quarry is close enough that escape by stampede impossible. Their hearts sing within their breasts, glorying in the killing and slaughter that is to come. More and more buffalo leap to their feet; calves bawl and cows bray, and with the inertia of a great organism, the shadow on the prairie begins moving.

At last, even the guardian bulls turn to flight, and the prairie fills with a new thunder, and the sky above the herd boils yellow as an enormous cloud of dust overcomes the lowering storm. The hunters pass into the animals, and, from the corner of his eye, Alexander sees a rider go down, gored by the swinging head of a bull. He digs his heels into his mount, and he presses him onward into the sea of roiling backs, dust swirling like wind-blown spray, the travelling rumble of countless hooves through the grit and grass echoing in his ears. Dust fills his eyes and he blinks it away, tears pouring down his cheeks.

The dust thickens, and he can no longer see where he is, his world reduced to a small circle of ragged humps and black horns shining in the tallow light. He hears a shot in the distance and decides to follow this man's lead. He pulls his horse up, and for a moment stands like a frail, tiny island of sand in danger of being swept away by a flowing tide. His legs are banged and bruised by the passing of animals, and, with a kick to the flank, his horse turns and charges, Métis fashion, against the living current. The buffalo veer aside at the very last instant, their horns lowered and snicking along his legs.

At last, he raises his carbine, and, correcting for the roll of his galloping mount, sights a young cow emerging from the screen of dust.

Alexander fires and the animal goes down, tumbling in its inertia, several others tripping and falling over it. His horse leaps and sails over the roiling mass. He swings his gun down, charges it, spits in a ball, whacks it against his leg, primes, and cocks. All about him bursts of gunfire ring over the cannonade of hooves. He shoots at a passing bull, and it sheers away, taking several of its fellows. Dust roils and billows, breathing almost impossible.

Several kills later, Alexander emerges from the herd and sits a moment, gasping for air, staring with amazement at the pounding black mass hurtling its way across the prairie. At the horizon, the buffalo appear to meld with the ferocious sky, as if ascending to heaven.

With a shouted "hee-ya," he spins his horse around, and, reaching into his shot bag, refills his mouth and charges back into the river of fleeing animals. A tremendous clap of thunder sounds overhead, and the terrified buffalo swerve away from him, like the sea parting around a reef. He knees his mount to greater speed and looks around for a fat animal. Spying a tawny yearling, he brings his carbine to bear.

At that moment, a passing cow swings its head and catches its horns beneath Alexander's horse. With hideous strength, the animal lifts the stallion's chest, and tosses horse and rider aside, tearing a great gash from barrel to withers. Alexander collides against the flank of another buffalo and bounces away, falling to the ground; his eyes and ears fill with dust. The ground trembles beneath him. Another peal from the sky and the clouds release their burden, deluging the churned soil.

Alexander lifts his head and through the downpour sees the blur of the passing animals, his carbine gone, and his horse on the ground in front of him, legs pawing the air and screaming in agony. Blood spurts from its side, running in a red torrent into the sucking mud. Blue loops of guts hang obscenely against its darkening coat.

The dust settles quickly in the rain and Alexander can see their tiny island is about to be swamped as the running buffalo edge closer and closer, their black eyes and wet horns reflecting the flash of lightning.

With a gasp of pain, Alexander struggles to his feet, and, dragging his injured leg, hobbles through the mud to his horse. His hat is gone and his clothes run dark with mud. His hair lies in streaks down his face. Standing helplessly beside his wounded horse, the racing buffalo are so close he can reach out and touch them. Mud from their hooves splatters him.

"McClure!" a voice calls from behind, scarce heard over the overwhelming din of rain and thunder and hooves.

He turns and through the storm sees Jacque sitting astride his horse, buffalo stampeding past him. Water runs down his red face, and his eyes are filled with hate. His horse is black with the wet. Jacque lifts his musket and stares down at him, Alexander closes his eyes as the report sounds. The awful sound of his mount's agony goes silent. When he opens them again, Jacque is kneeing his horse; he pulls up and lowers a gloved hand. The whites of his horse's eyes are visible, the animal near panic at the smell of the stallion's blood.

"Get up!" he shouts.

"I thought you were going to kill me," Alexander yells back, wiping the rain from his eyes.

Jacque spits on the ground. "I wanted to, with all my heart, my friend. But not here, not now. I will spill your blood another day."

A buffalo sideswipes Alexander, knocking him into Jacque's horse; she neighs and rears, her rider cursing and pulling hard on her reins. Alexander begins to slide into the mud. Jumping off his horse, Jacque grabs him and with his great strength pushes him up onto the horse's back, where he sits swaying.

Jacque swings himself up, then immediately pulls the horse about, and they ride with the flowing buffalo, slowly working their way diagonally out of the mass of terrified animals.

Soon they come to the edge of the herd and turn back, the sound of the last of the buffalo diminishing in the distance. Through the rain, the two men see hundreds of slain animals littering the bloody prairie, dark carcasses that will feed the people for many months. Shots fire in the air, and the whoops and hunting cries of the Métis drift down the wet wind. But as the hunters gather, the blanket-covered body of the man gored to death subdues their jubilation. Several have wounds, some serious. Alexander's hip has been torn by a buffalo as it passed by Jacque's horse, and he is pale with loss of blood.

A rider gallops ahead to let the camp know the hunt is finished; the long and arduous job of preserving the tons of meat — the skinning, butchering and cutting into strips for drying and eventual grinding into pemmican — now passes to the women and children and elderly.

. The wounded also need tending. Jacque walks into camp with Alexander clinging, barely conscious, in front him. He stops in front of a tent, and Alexander slides off the horse and falls into the mud where he lies unmoving. Overhead, the clouds break apart and rays of welcome sunshine light the camp. Thunder mutters in the distance, answered by the warble of a meadowlark. Jacque turns his face toward the sun, closing his eyes for a moment. He takes a deep breath.

A woman emerges from the tent. "Take care of this son of a bitch, will you Isidore?" Jacque asks. "It would be a poor thing if he was to die today."

⌁

At the sound of drumming, the old carpenter drops his adze and stands up. He places his hands on the small of his back, and stretches, the vertebrae popping and snapping like a squirrel breaking nuts. Taking his pipe out of his mouth, he spits, brown saliva running down his beard. He wears no shirt in the scorching heat and, scratching his belly, he walks languidly over to the gates.

HBC fort Brandon House is almost empty in late spring, the courtyard silent but for the soft bark of the carpenter's adze squaring timbers. Looking across the Assiniboine River to the hated Nor'wester post, the carpenter can see that all there is quiet. The drumming is coming from an unseen source to the left.

"Cor, what the bleeding 'ell is that?" asks the butcher, walking up and wiping his hands on a bloody apron. He had been carving buffalo meat all morning, and his hands are covered in blood.

The carpenter does not reply, just takes his pipe from his mouth and points with the stem as a contingent of fifty or more Métis, Indians, and Nor'westers ride into view. They are on horseback and ride in formation, a drummer in their midst pounding a beat to a song that carries across the plain. A strange red-and-black flag snaps from a standard carried at their head.

They follow along the shore of the river, the two men watching from the fort gates. When the formation reaches a point directly opposite, they suddenly turn their horses and pound their way towards them. The butcher flees, but the carpenter remains standing at the gate, his eyes widening as the contingent approaches. He removes his pipe and spits.

At the last moment, he stands aside as the attackers pound into the fort, followed by a cloud of dust. Shots are fired into the air, and yells echo from the palisade. Men leap from their horses and charge the buildings. Doors are kicked in. Women shriek and pray as the few trader families in the fort scramble for the gates. In a few moments, all inside the fort at the time of the attack — HBC servant, fur trader, or their women and children — are running pell-mell across the prairie.

Within an hour, Brandon House is sacked. Ammunition and trade supplies and a great quantity of liquor are looted; the victors start a fire and celebration in the courtyard. Those from the fort across the river join them; a fire is lit and they drink, sing and dance at this great victory of all the Freemen of the west against the hated usurper from England.

Chapter Seventeen

"I have found one," Declan says, lifting a rat-gnawed leather bridle from a heap of tack. "It is nae very good, but will do in a pinch. Much better than nothing."

Rose nods to her husband. She is competent on a horse, but with full saddle and tack only, and is unfamiliar with the Indian style of riding. At least the bridle will help keep the beast in check. The animal she is thinking of for their ride is the shaggy Indian pony standing beside her. The smell of fresh, March snow is in its nostrils, and it is restive and fiery, capering about and snorting clouds of breath over her shoulder.

"Are you sure you want to do this?" asks Declan over the back of his own horse, a piebald mare he had bought from an intoxicated Half-breed for a small keg of diluted liquor. When Declan had informed Rose of his intent to hunt partridge the following day, she had surprised him by asking if she could attend.

"It is beastly dull here," she had told him. "Boredom and stupe-fying conversation all around. I must get away, if only for a day."

As they prepare to depart, the thought occurs to him. "Will I teach you to shoot?" he asks, his eyes crinkling as he checks the load in his fowling piece.

"If you would do so," Rose replies, "I would much appreciate the skill, but do not wish to be a bore. Only if it will give you pleasure."

"It is in the natural way of things that the student shall one day become the teacher," he says, and they both become awkward at the reference to Alexander. His horse lifts her tail and drops a load of steaming clods.

Rose wishes she could mount and ride off alone into the morning sun, but without stirrups and burdened by her long skirts, all she can do is grip the horse's mane and stand waiting, her nose buried in its aromatic coat.

Declan hesitates and then walks over, offering her his cupped hands. She steps into them and he heaves her onto the horse's back. Without waiting, she pulls the reins across the animal's neck, and they bolt from the stable, chickens scattering.

"Ho!" Declan shouts, but she is gone.

He catches up with her, waiting about a mile from the fort gates. Her face is frost-cold and red when she turns towards him, but lit by a broad smile.

"It is delightful," she says as he walks his horse alongside. "It is far brighter outside the fort, the air so clear and cold that sound carries many miles; listen, is that the river?" Indeed, the voice of the Assiniboine groaning under the weight of ice and new snow, carries like distant thunder.

Declan nods. "I dinna like the manner of your leaving. What a fool I look to be chasing after my wife. You will please wait for me next time. However, yes, it is indeed peaceful and empty. Hardly a track to be seen." He stares after the coal-black motes of crows as they lift from the naked branches of a distant cottonwood.

Rose looks down at the furrowed snow by her horse's hooves. "It seems a shame to disturb the peace with our hunt," she says.

He approaches her and pulling off his glove, awkwardly reaches out to caress her cheek. "Thou are in the bloom of health. So lovely you seem to me, and such a tender spirit to not wish to disturb newly fallen snow."

"Thank you, sir," Rose replies, looking intently at Declan, her grey-blue eyes startling him, as they always did. He suppresses a shiver and audibly sighs.

"Well, the hunt can wait if it must, but I would prefer to return with meat if I can. I promised Jack something for the pot."

"Thou art a true Nimrod, sir. Very well, show me your sport."

For sport it was. Declan had never before hunted the wily birds, and they proved elusive and flighty, made nervous by the previous night's storm. All living things felt it, from Indian to coyote to colonist shivering under their blankets; the night's wind had a voice that suppressed all warm-blooded speech, and all things had hunkered down as best they may, waiting for nothing but its passing.

But as in all games of chance and skill, eventually chance prevails: Declan takes down a grouse in a puff of white feathers. They had ridden many miles along the shrouded valley of the Assiniboine, and, after collecting the bird, they unpack the lunch that Rose had prepared the night before.

"It is only a bit of buffalo sausage and bread," she says, almost apologetically.

"It is enough," Declan grunts. "Shall I make us a fire to warm ourselves?"

"As you wish."

He wanders through the woods, breaking off branches, often releasing billows of snow that sigh down upon his head. When he returns with his bundle fairly covered in snow, Rose suppresses the laughter that spills from her lips.

Declan glares at her. "Titter, titter, what is this? I am glad I so amuse you. Sure, there has been little enough mirth from you of late."

That clapped down her humour as if he had struck her. There had been doubts about her and Alexander, suspicions without accusations, he refusing to bring the issue to a defining head that would force him into irrevocable action. So he spent many a dark hour wondering and musing, the heat within him building until it became a wall that separated them more effectively than many miles of empty prairie. He sought and found fault in her — her dress, her meals, her elevated manner of speech among the people: who was she to hold herself so high? He told her many times that it is not who you are, but what you do that matters in Rupert's Land.

As he struggles with the fire, his own speeches on competency return to goad him, and he feels a rising wrath toward his wife. He is certain she is watching him with cold, amused judgment, but no matter how he tries, he cannot get the flint to light the frosty tinder. Despite his belief to the contrary, fire is not his nature.

"It is time to leave," he finally says to her, taking control of the situation as best he may. He drags a cold hand down his frosted beard. "We have farther to go this day, and I would rather show my face at the fort empty-handed than with one shitty bird."

They wander up and down ridges, and in and out of snowy folds without sighting any other game. At times, the drifts are so deep it is as if the horses are swimming in clotted cream. The sun becomes haloed, as if ringed in tears, and is dimmed by the lateness of the day.

"Do you not think we should return now, Declan?" Rose asks in a quiet voice.

He looks up at the sky, frowning. "You are tired, I suppose? I knew I should have gone alone. Damn my eyes, I hoped for more than this. Still, we may come upon more on our way back. We will return through the valley, among the willows where there may be more game."

At that, they descend into the valley of the Assiniboine until arriving at the banks of the river itself. Turning left, they wander among the willows and cattails, Declan's hand impatiently twitching around the gun in his hand.

But the snow is even deeper here; the going difficult for Rose's slight horse. At times, it reaches to the animal's breast and it churns along in the bigger horses wake, breathing hard.

"This is too much for the horse," Rose says at last, feeling irritated that she has to be the one to state the obvious.

Declan shoots an angry look at her. "I suppose you are right, my love." He says at last. "We are still far from the fort. We must climb out of here … what is that?"

They have come upon a trail, as the way suddenly becomes much easier. The snow is packed by hooves, many horses' hooves that had passed sometime since the night. They move forward on the trail until they come to a place where the river ice has been chopped open; they walk up to let their grateful animals have a long drink.

"Who made this trail?" Rose asks, looking around her.

Declan shrugs. "Savages, most likely."

The sun has turned into a brilliant fireball watching them over the far bank of the river. The willow and birch surrounding them, grey in the full light of day, now glow scarlet, as if the woods are lit with fire. Long, blue shadows lean from every bole, undulating over the thick folds of snow.

But an approaching cloud bank, unseen from the bottom of the valley, now swallows the sun, and grey shadows drop among them. From across the river, a fox yips twice and falls silent.

"We must go," Declan says and pulls his horse around. They climb quickly out to the open prairie where they can clearly see the massing clouds piling up behind them. Wind stirs their coats. Declan reserves his thought that it will be a near thing to arrive at the fort before the weather strikes; he does not at all like the notion of spending the night outside.

At least the way is clear to them. The river valley is a trail they cannot miss. If they go too far they will arrive at the junction of the Red River, and have but to turn north a few miles to arrive at Fort Douglas. He feels grateful for this accident of geography, for he would not want to trust his skill as a woodsman to find their way home. Indeed, he has not even a compass with him, in his foolishness thinking of the many hunts in which he participated on his beloved Highlands. If he becomes disoriented, there will be no peasant to remind him of his way.

A few flakes begin to appear, drifting lazily about them, but before long the air fills with falling and wind-blown snow. The wind increases at their back. As the final light begins failing them, Rose glimpses something on the trail ahead.

"Did you see that?" Rose asks, pulling up her mount.

"See what?"

"Ahead — there is something there! I saw it through the snow."

"What was it, an animal, a buffalo perhaps?" His heart pounds at the thought of the glory such a prize would be.

"I do not know; I only saw it a moment. It is that way I believe, if any clear way can be defined in such weather. I cannot see past the nose of my horse."

Declan checks his fowling piece again, wondering if such a light weapon could indeed overcome one of the mighty beasts. He hopes so. Perhaps, it was only a deer. Without a word, he nudges his horse and pushes past Rose, looking from side to side, searching for tracks. The snow swirls as a shape appears in front of them, shaggy and black. Declan's heart jumps. He lifts the gun and fires. Snow falls from the beast as it slides to the ground.

With a cry, Declan urges his horse forward, hastily reloading the gun; he cannot believe his luck. Rose follows behind, her mind dark with doubt; she had not seen any buffalo for many months and it seems to her unlikely to find a solitary animal out here in the storm.

Jumping off of his horse, Declan approaches the beast; the shaggy black fur blows in the wind as Declan prods it with the barrel.

"Something is wrong." Rose says, sitting beside him on her horse. Her hair loosens from her cap and twists about her. Declan looks up at her; surrounded by blowing snow; in the gloom she looks like a wraith, grey and shrouded, her face masked by winding hair. The wind whistles in his ears.

Something wrong. He prods the shape again, and there is a moan. A human moan. He bends down and pulls away the buffalo hide to find a woman, a Savage woman, badly wounded by his shot. Her shoulder is ragged and running with blood, her neck and the side of her face peppered red.

"Oh, dear Jesus," Declan says, dropping the cloak.

"What is it?" Rose asks.

Declan considers lying to her; it would be so easy to jump on his horse and both of them ride off.

"It-it's a woman. A Savage. Wrapped in a buffalo hide," he adds defensively. Rose drops off her horse and hurries beside him. "A woman? And you just drop her into the snow?"

"Rose, I don't know …"

She pushes the robe aside and sees the woman's wounds. She is young, about twenty, unconscious. The robe is filling with blood. Rose pulls at the hem of her skirts and tears away pieces of it.

"Come here, help me bind these wounds. Do you have a knife?" Declan hands it her and she cuts the strips into lengths.

"Do you know what you're doing?" He asks her, surprised.

"Of course I don't, but we have to try something — there's so much, so much blood. Here, hold this while I try and wrap this around her shoulder." He kneels and presses a pad against the wound, feeling the hot blood well through it. Rose wraps the strips around the woman's arm and shoulder as best she can.

"That's all we can do until we get her to the fort."

"Get her to the fort?"

"Of course, we cannot leave her out here." She is surprised to hear how much her last words sound like a question. She looks down at the blood on her hands and wipes them into the snow.

Declan looks out at the surrounding storm. "What the hell is she doing out here anyway? She would have died there like that. She has no gear, nothing."

Rose looks up at him, brushing the hair out of her eyes. "We must take her," she repeats.

"Get on your horse, Rose." Declan is certain that he has seen the girl before, in the company of local Cree with whom he has worked hard at developing a trading relationship. The Company and the Nor'westers might be at each other's throats, but their distraction had provided robust opportunities for an independent trader to exploit. He had only just begun entertaining visions of a trading empire of his own, and now this. It wasn't fair. It wasn't his fault. The damned girl.

Rose stands up, facing him. "Declan ..."

"Now, Rose!"

"And if I refuse?"

He looms over her. "Listen to me. You are my wife and will do as I say. You will tell no one about this. She's just a fucking Savage."

"I will tell everyone."

Declan's face is split with scorn. "Will you, now? And I wonder what they will think about your bedding the Half-caste? Do not deny it! Tainted and foul you are, and they will run you out to live with the Savages that you carry such a passion for."

Rose knows that he speaks the truth; all it would take would be an accusation, proof would not be needed. She fights back her tears. "Why are you doing this?" she asks. "I am your wife. This poor girl."

"My wife? Yes, you are indeed my wife: I bear the shame and grief of that truth every day. I will hear no more of it. Get on your horse, or I will leave you here as well, I swear."

Rose at last sees the jealous hate that has consumed him these many months and knows that he will do as he says; she doubts she can find her own way back to the fort. It all comes clear to her now: the dark moods, the strange, probing glances. She had tried to be a loyal, dutiful wife to him, but knew in her heart that she did not share his love. It was this unhappy truth that she had blamed for his cold reserve, never suspecting he might know anything of her time with Alexander.

She has looked for love in many strange places to no avail, and it seems to her the bitterest grief that her marriage too should be so barren. Against all her being, all herself that demanded autonomy, she has tried to make her heart succumb to him. But despite all the coaxing, it remains as cold and dead as the partridge now stuffed in his pannier. It feels to her the final insult of her dead father: to condemn her to such a life.

After helping Rose on her mount, Declan leaps onto his own. He turns and with a last, angry look at the dying woman, nudges his horse into the flying snow.

Chapter Eighteen

The riders approach the Métis camp with a great deal of firing and screeching, and for one terrified moment, several Half-breeds believe it to be a Sioux attack. But many of the riders' costumes are too bright for the wearer to be mistaken for full-blooded Indians, the scarlet sashes visible from a long way off.

Arriving at the camp at full gallop, they run about the circled carts raising a swirl of dust, the people staring and wondering what is afoot. Eventually, one of them reins in his horse and drops to the ground, his men following.

"Pierre, my friend," he cries. "Rouse your captains. I have great news! We have taken Brandon House!"

The men gather around a fire. Pipes emerge; they smoke and swat mosquitoes, and wait for the stranger to begin speaking, for word has passed that the great general Cuthbert Grant himself sent the messenger. A keg of rum is broached and passed around, poured into proffered tin cups.

The stranger is standing in front of them, a cup of brandy in his hands, eyes twinkling with excitement.

"My name is Boucher, and I bring news from our general." He pauses for a moment, before blurting out, "The Métis have overwhelmed the garrison at the fort, and the English no longer foul the Assiniboine with their presence."

"Tell us the story," a captain shouts.

"I wish you could have seen it, my friends. The flags of the Métis Nation flying high and proud, the war songs, the sound of our drums. We made as if to pass the fort when General Grant turned and lead the charge straight through the main gates. The affray was hot; I assure you, but we had the favour of God, and soon victory was ours. After their meek surrender, we took what we wished from the invaders and many cartloads of pemmican, furs, and ammunition there were, and many Canadian slaves, whom we freed. We then put the house to the torch."

There is much grinning and backslapping among the captains, but the stranger interrupts them, beaming. "There is more, much more, my brothers. We intercepted the English's brigade at Qu'Appelle and have secured countless furs and tons of pemmican without which the usurpers at Red River must starve. We have them on the run!"

Cheers rise from most, but not all seated there; a few hats fly skyward. Brandy is poured; a gun is let off.

"So what now? What does General Grant intend?" Dumont asks.

"Now we will carry the furs and pemmican to the North West brigades on *Missinipi*. After that, only the general knows. But those trespassers of a stubborn and stupid nature will find the days warm indeed, as the general has sworn that come this autumn, there will be no English between the Bay and Pembina."

~

Alexander's shadow stretches far ahead of him as he shoulders his pack; the prairie is lit with the rosy light of dawn. A few fading stars twinkle in the west, hugged by scarlet-fringed clouds the colour of royal velvet. Birdsong rises from the surrounding grass and, as he walks, small yellow finches burst from his path to undulate over the ground a ways before disappearing back into turf made ragged by the stampede. The sound of his footfall silences nearby crickets.

After weeks of hard labour, the camp is breaking up, the tons of buffalo meat dried and loaded. The plain around him is scattered with reeking carcasses, the rising sun shining through arched ribs and illuminating the dark orbits of skulls. Some have been stripped of little more than hide, hump, and tongue, and glow a dullish red. Crows lift at his approach, and wolves flit from shadow to shadow. Coyotes yap nearby. Even a badger partakes of the feast, scurrying away as Alexander's shadow moves over it.

The field of slaughter is dappled with brown-eyed Susans that have emerged since the rains, and, nodding in the morning breeze, they seem to Alexander a memorial to the bones, red and white, that scatter like thistle seeds across the breadth of the prairie.

Distant shouting, then the din of carts begins as the Half-breeds make their ponderous way back to the valley of the Assiniboine. His horse dead, Alexander is on foot, taking only water, pemmican, his carbine, and a bedroll. His path is more northerly than that of the hunters, to the shores of lake *Missinipi*, where he hopes to intercept a passing Nor'wester brigade from Montreal or Athabasca.

As Alexander moves away from the path taken by the stampeding buffalo, he encounters an ocean of fescue, waving and billowing in the ever-present prairie wind. At times he is forced to focus on the horizon, the swaying of the grass filling him with a kind of vertigo, and, with his weakened leg, he is in danger of tipping over sideways.

In the days since the hunt his leg has mended well, but he is careful not to exert himself and rests often, sitting so that only his head and shoulders are visible above the grass. Sometimes, he lies down, undetectable to a man walking but five paces away. He had been gored in almost the exact same spot as years ago, and the loose chunk of bone that sat inside there all that time had been popped right out. The experience brings back memories that he would rather forget: memories of community and belonging. What was the point in dwelling on what has been?

At such times, he likes to cross his hands over his breast, like one laid out for a funeral, his head often crowned by the profusion of wild prairie flowers mingling with the grass. He stares up at the sky above, his perfect view crossed now and then by a booming bumblebee or the distant shape of a wheeling Red-tailed hawk.

Day follows day each much as the same before, the sun arcing just a little higher, burning down on him with increasing heat. The grass parts and closes behind him, the wild, green dew-wetted scent rising. Like a schooner in the mid-Atlantic, little trace is left of his passing.

Every emerald pond or slough he walks by is filled with ducks and geese, the surrounding marshes and reeds reverberating with the whistles and pipings and territorial cries of hidden birds. Redwinged blackbirds bob on cattail stems, flashing scarlet epaulets and scolding their neighbors. At the passing of an eagle, shorebirds wheel and slide along white alkali shorelines like schooling minnows pursued by pike.

As day is replaced by the glow of star and moon, birdsong is supplanted by the boom of bullfrogs, ring of peepers, shriek of owl, and the singsong chorus of wolf and coyote. Badgers dig and snuffle in rodent holes and stricken rabbits scream as owl talons lift them from the grass. With the cool and damp coming of night, the delicate and bloodthirsty mosquitoes emerge in numbers that only an apocalyptic horseman can imagine. But he is a man wild of the prairie as well as forest, and is burdened only by his memories.

$\sim$

The shot comes from the north, pulsing with distance, and instinctively Alexander sinks into the grass. His gun is primed and loaded, but he glances at the flint just in case; it is cracked and worn, and therefore dangerous. He wonders how he could have forgotten to check it after the hunt, but with no spare flint, there is little he can do until he meets up with a brigade or arrives at a trading post.

The shot is not far off, perhaps a mile. He can see the shadow of a creek valley, one of the many that flows south to feed the Assiniboine River. Knowing it is better to know who *they* are before they chance to discover him, Alexander makes his way toward the gulley, crouching.

The awkward stance is difficult for his game leg, already sore by heavy use, and by the time he arrives at the gulley's edge, he is limping badly. For the last several yards, he moves forward on his elbows. A curlew bursts from the grass by his very nose, the large, long-billed bird shrieking *kewkewkew* as it flies away.

Alexander flattens in the grass, his heart in his mouth. To his right, he spots the tips of a patch of shimmering wolf willow. As if swimming through the grass, he moves deep into this shrubbery. The wind hisses through the wolf willow, setting its silver leaves dancing and twisting, and Alexander is suddenly aware that the flickering might draw attention. He buries himself deeper into the little copse and waits. He does not wait long. There is movement along the gully's upper edge, and soon a feathered, black-haired head emerges, scanning the horizon. Almost to his immediate left and much closer, another appears, equally alert.

Rising from the ground like spirits, the two men emerge from the gully, rotating this way and that, their muskets levelled. Their movements are lithe and predatory, and although they see nothing untoward, they remain suspicious, crouching in the grass in much the same manner of Alexander.

He recognizes them as young Sioux, and sweat beads on his forehead. They are a people long warring on the plains with *Asinepoet* and Cree and Half-breed alike, but these two have been raiding deep outside their own lands. His senses become attuned to every detail of his surroundings, the chitter of grasshoppers, the rolling burble of a nearby meadowlark, the sun reflecting off the sweaty black paint adorning the nearest Sioux's cheek.

The farther Sioux makes hand signs to the nearer, who responds by crouching in front of the very willows covering Alexander. Behind him, Alexander wishes that he knew an appropriate prayer, forced to silently plead with a crude and generic begging.

The further Indian stiffens and aims his musket for a moment before slowly lowering it. "Shit," he says.

"What is it?" the other says in a low voice.

"Just a coyote."

"Fuck all coyotes."

"I told you, Wah-pah-shaw; you're as nervous as a jackrabbit on a hilltop."

"Do you blame me? We shouldn't be here. This is Cree territory. Those assholes will split and gut you faster than you can shit."

"I told you; I have to find my horse."

"Never mind the horse, we must get out of here."

"There's the jackrabbit again."

"Say that again, and I'll whip you. I've had enough. Bring up the horses, and let's get out of here."

There is something in Wah-pah-shaw's voice that tells his brother that there is no more room for argument.

"You know father will beat us when we return," he says, as if that fact somehow helps his argument.

"I know it, Chan-ta-pe-a. Just get the fucking horses!"

Looking sullen, his brother's musket droops, and he slouches down into the gulley.

Wah-pah-shaw moves farther back into the bushes and squats. A fart carries from beneath his loincloth, and the dried leaves rustle as he drops dung. With a sigh, he stands up and rearranges the cloth. At the smell, Alexander pulls slightly back, and a branch snaps beneath his foot. Wah-pah-shaw freezes.

Alexander erupts from hiding and claps his hand over the youth's mouth, cutting his throat; the heat of the man's life bursts over Alexander's hand and down his arm. He hurls the body aside.

He grabs the Indian's gun, a very worn trade musket, and removes the flint. He tosses the weapon aside and, with shaking hands, picks up his carbine, loosens the hammer screw, extracts the old flint, and inserts the other, just as Chan-ta-pe-a climbs out of the gully on horseback, another following on a lead.

Alexander raises his gun and fires, the Indian disappearing behind a cloud of smoke. The well-trained horse barely flinches as its master falls to the ground. Alexander runs over, prepared to thrust his knife into his throat. With a heaving sigh, he drops down on his haunches. The top of the man's head is missing, the eyes staring at the uncomprehending sky.

He spends that night camped in the gulley, the ringing of crickets punctuated by the sound of coyotes fighting over the two corpses. He passes the night tending the tiny fire and staring into the flames. The murder of the two men does not particularly concern him as much as the significance of their presence and the feeling of impending disaster. He cannot find the answer in his heart or mind, but something tells him that darkness is coming fast. As he watches the flames consume stick after stick, he wonders what it all means.

At first light, he is awakened by the nearby flutter of pipit wings; his legs are stiff and sore. He rouses the ashes of the fire and lights his pipe, counting in his head the miles left to the Great Water. He had contemplated stopping at the Nor'wester post of Fort Gibraltar for provisions — located across the Red River from Fort Douglas, to the great ire of the Hudson's Bay Company — but with those left by the dead Sioux, it will no longer be necessary. He will take a more northerly route, bypassing the Red River settlement, and all the misery it represents.

After a breakfast of dried buffalo tongue and another pipe, he loads his pack onto one of the horses and rides up to greet the morning. A herd of feeding pronghorn antelope gallops off, and at a distance they stop to turn and stare at him, white rumps flaring. Nearby, there is a noisy flapping of wings as several crows protest the interruption of their scavenging. Alexander ignores them, turning his face to the sun.

On horseback his progress is much faster, and soon he finds himself back in the valley of the Assiniboine River. He descends into the cottonwoods and follows a well-worn path along the shore until arriving at a ford. He edges his horse into the river and soon the two animals are swimming, Alexander floating alongside and clinging to his horse's mane, holding his Baker carbine aloft. When the horse finds its footing on the opposite shore, he climbs back on, and all three emerge from the river, cold and dripping. While checking his rifle, he hears a dog bark, and frowns, realizing he is closer to the forks and the Half-breed settlement than he had intended.

Hanging his rifle along the side of his horse, he knees it forward through thick buck brush; he has no intention of following the trail any farther. At first it hesitates, then pushes forward, the branches scraping along its side. Alexander lowers his head, protecting his face with his hat.

Soon they climb out of the bush, horses and rider looking rather dishevelled for the effort. The upper edge of the valley is mounded and rolling, and to his right he sees smoke rising from a nearby fold.

They climb out of the valley. A gust of wind hits them, and Alexander snatches at his hat to keep it from blowing away. While down in the valley the air felt stifling and hot, but now the open prairie feels fresh and cool, especially in his wet clothes.

He pauses long enough for a pipe and a scan of the sky. A thin layer of cloud veils the sun, and the usual effulgent blue sky is pale and uncomfortable, heralding a coming change in the weather. As he stares, he sees a red-tailed hawk soar against the watery sun, its backlit tail feathers seeming on fire.

He knows the Red River settlement is many miles eastward, and so he turns north. But soon the land dips again, and he finds himself in wet, bogging land — not the well defined alkali-lined sloughs, but a region of amorphous earth where water lurks close to the surface; cattails and sedges and coarse grasses stretch from horizon to horizon.

He can go no further; the Indian horse is sinking past its fetlocks, its beautiful tawny hide stained black. To turn west could take him many miles out of his way, while eastward would take him close to the settlement, closer to her. Angrily, he shakes his head and knees his horse forward. Suddenly he pulls it up; faint in the distance, a large body of horsemen also follow the southern edge of the bog. He watches them for a while and sees that they are heading east, away from him.

Nor'westers or Half-breeds. With an inner shrug, he knees his horse forward. But, as he follows, his unease increases; the group of men is proceeding very slowly, encumbered by a large cart pulled by an ox, a cart uncharacteristically silent. They are heavily armed, even for Rupert's Land, with guns bristling in all directions. But even more than their weaponry, it is their attitude; although they have not yet spotted their shadow, they are nervous and on their guard. Men continually rise on their horses and stare east, and they are in close formation as if expecting attack. Sioux territory is far to the south, and the Cree and Stonies of the region are not violently ill-disposed to the Whites and Half-breeds squatting on their lands.

For some reason he is unable to define, Alexander feels a need to hide himself. He moves the horses into the cover of several willows and dismounts. Leaving them behind, he hurries through the edge of the bog as quickly as possible, making his way closer to the slowly moving brigade.

After a long, sneaking march interrupted by more than one misstep into deep, gurgling mud, he is close enough to hear voices; one is louder than the others, giving orders. Although the words cannot be made out, the tone of the voice is concerned and impatient, the ox and its cart apparently slowing them far more than the man feels proper.

Alexander watches him closely. He has dark, arching eyebrows and a stern gaze. Clean shaven unlike his fellows. A young, handsome face, especially for this part of the world where exposure to ice and wind and heat erodes a face like the land itself. Suddenly, he realizes that this must be the famed Cuthbert Grant; no wild Half-breed or itinerant fur trader, the face and voice is that of authority and learning. The dam has burst at last. This must be a war party intent on driving the settlers out of the Forks once and for all.

There had been talk all spring, a rousing and a muster that had disturbed him greatly. Divided in his loyalties, he had wanted to warn the settlement, but such intervention would result in his becoming a traitor to his own people, men and women who valued community and fealty above all else. The fact that it might also bring him face to face with Rose was an additional deterrent that he refused to acknowledge to himself. He wonders why he even gave a damn, but a part of him still feels that the souls he had guided from York Factory are still his responsibility, despite his abandoning them at Jack River House. Guilt plays a large part of this, his conscience unmoved by whatever rationalizations he offers his burdened heart.

Teasing out the threads between the North West Company, the Hudson's Bay Company, and Selkirk's adventures at the Forks is not simple in any case, regardless of what Cuthbert Grant had to say about it.

He pulls back into the rushes and walks thoughtfully back to the horses. He rests his head against one of them, stroking the animal's warm flank while he stares at a redwinged blackbird clutching to a bulrush in the face of a rising wind. The voices of the Half-breeds diminish in the distance.

After a long while he shakes his head and looks up at the horse; its ears rotate forward and it lowers its nose to his scalp, nuzzling him. Alexander smiles at it. "Patience, my new friend. I am muddled in my mind. A fork in the path has emerged and a poor choice lies before us. Darkness no matter the route, no doubt. God be with me."

He settles in the willows while the sun passes the zenith and begins its daily pursuit for the western horizon. It is low in the sky before he again stirs. With a final peek to check that he is indeed alone, he jumps onto his horse's back.

"Run now, run as ever like the wind you can, my friend. I have killed your master, for which I beg your forgiveness, and ask that you show flight like never before seen by Half-breed or Indian. Many will die this day; I feel it in my heart. Run and show me your speed." With that the horses leap away, their hooves in perfect cadence, drumming across the grass as the rolling prairie flashes away beneath them.

He turns far to the south to outflank the war party before turning east again. He gives the horses but one rest and drink when they pass through a narrow creek, and when he at last spies the palisade of Fort Douglas, his mount is footsore and weary, foam caked about its muzzle and darkening its breast. Damp heat rises from it.

The gate is ajar when they walk into the courtyard, abandoned but for a few scrawny fowl. The sound of his hasty approach has frightened the people, and he can feel eyes watching from several buildings of rough-hewn poplar. The clop of his horses' hooves sound loud in the yard. The sun is below the palisade when he slides from his horse and ties the animals to a hitching post. He hurries towards the largest building and crashes through the door.

"Semple," he cries to the startled clerk. "I must speak with him. On your feet, fool! For your lives!"

Chapter Nineteen

Soon the courtyard is crowded with colonists; word has spread fast through the scattered settlement, and people are arriving from the surrounding countryside. Many are terrified that they are to be burned out yet again, or worse. Their voices rise in anger against the governor, who stands in the courtyard with a hand in his vest pocket, waving the other over his head, as if dismissing an irritating gnat.

"Gentlemen, gentlemen," he calls to the crowd. "There is nothing to fear. We do not know what these rascals are about, but we shall learn soon enough."

"We bloody well know what they are abouts," a man shouts at him. "Killing and pillage, by God, and what are thee going to do about it?"

"If you give me but a moment, Mr. MacDonald, I shall explain," says Semple with a frown. "I have decided to intercept these rogues and inquire as to their business. We have men aplenty here, weaponry they do not possess." This said with a nod toward the small field-piece near the gates. "If we are not satisfied as to their purpose, we shall blow them to the hell that they deserve. Now who shall accompany me? Remember your crops of last year, remember your farms burned and razed!"

Shouts erupt from the dusty crowd. Many present had been chased off the land the previous year by the Half-breeds, a shame and humiliation difficult to bear. They are hungry for revenge and gladdened that this governor would see their backs up. This time there will be no running.

As the men prepare to march, their women crowd together, almost clutching each other in anxiety. Alexander spots Rose among them, Declan approaching him.

"Hello, Alexander," the Highlander says rather stiffly. He looks uncomfortable dressed in a new frock coat and Hessian boots. His purple cravat gleams in the waning light. Alexander touches the brim of his hat and nods.

"I see it has come at last; the fight has arrived, and I for one am glad of it," says Declan. "These people have run wild through our days and tormented our dreams, and the matter of land and rights must be settled. I am glad to see you with us," he adds with a cautious glance at Alexander.

"You must not come," Alexander says.

"Eh? What was that? What did you say?"

"The action will be sharp, more than you can know, and you are no soldier."

"Indeed? Well, I decide my own course of action. I will nae stay and cower here with the women."

"You speak like a fool, Declan. Many must stay behind; there is no place for those unskilled in hot work, and I fear that most men here are not the thing at all. And I see that Rose is with family; you must stay with her."

"Fool is it? Perhaps I am. But I am nae coward, and I will take my place beside the governor. And of Rose, I have naught to say. Good luck to you." He turns his back on Alexander and walks away.

Alexander pushes through the knot of anxious women. "Will you not speak to him?" he asks Rose. "He must not accompany the sortie."

"You know him, Alexander. He will do as he sees fit."

He looks down at her, sees what he has feared most; the light has gone from her eyes and lines of care and toil have edged onto her face. He can almost hear the cracking of his heart.

"Rose ..." he begins.

Declan marches up, places an unfriendly hand on Alexander's shoulder and spins him around. "Rose? What is this, Rose? Why do you speak to my wife thus? Rose, go with the women." To Alexander's great surprise, Rose nods and shuffles away, burdened by her great belly.

"We were friends once, and for that I forgive you, but it is enough. Dinna speak with my wife, nor interfere in my actions. Do you understand?"

"Very much is clear to me Declan, and yet I am loath to have Rose a widow. She is positively bursting with child, and what will she do if you are killed?"

"It's none of your business."

"What have you done to her, you pox-ridden bastard?"

Declan's eyes harden still further. "Do you stand by that remark?"

"Go to hell."

"Then I am forced to call you out. Mr. Gordon, will you be my second?"

Seeing something amiss, Governor Semple hurries over and interrupts them. "What is this? There shall be no calling out. Mr. Cormack, I beg you save your spleen for the Savages. Come, we must organize this sortie."

Declan hesitates, struggling with his emotions. "The real question," he says to Alexander, "Is what have *you* done to her?"

$\smile$

Alexander leans against a post and wipes the sweat from his forehead. He was more than ready to take on the Highlander before Semple interrupted, and is now glad the man did, for Declan's blood on his hands would have been too much; he has cut a swath of destruction in his wake for a long time. Although he knows not the cause, he has to put a stop to it. But Rose, why her? Why had he not been able to save her?

He had watched her enter one of the several small cabins scattered within the fort walls. He makes a sudden decision, and walks over, and, after a glance around to make sure he is unobserved, opens the door.

The cabin is almost empty but for a poplar-framed bed covered with a straw mattress and a rough-hewn table burdened with a Bible and a tallow dip. There is a bucket in the corner, and Rose is sitting there in the shadows, washing her feet. She looks up in surprise and shields her eyes from the low sunlight streaming in from the open door. Suspended motes swirl in the disturbed air. Alexander is an unrecognizable silhouette as he enters, but when he closes the door behind him his pale face emerges from the darkness, floating disembodied like a wraith. They stare at one another without speaking; the only sound is of men running and the jingle of metal carrying from outside.

Eventually her gaze drops, and she asks him in a quiet voice for the towel. Alexander looks around and sees a square of old muslin on the bed. He walks over to her, and, kneeling, takes her dripping foot in his hand. Her rubs it with the cloth, but does not release it, cradling it like a nestling, drawing a finger across the top and over her toes. With a sigh, he leans against her. At first, she does not move, but slowly her hand falls from her lap. At the caress across his shoulder, he closes his eyes, his thick arms wrapping around her legs as if he will never let them go.

"You have been gone a long time." The voice holds accusation.

"I could not stay. Not as long as you were with him. I would have gone mad." He lets go of her legs and raises his face towards her, searching her. "Did I really do so wrong? You made your choice, and I was left with nothing. I had to find my own salvation."

A tear forms in the corner of her eye. "The night before my father died, he wrested a promise from me that I would wed Declan if it were offered. My oaths count for something, Alexander."

"Unlike mine, you mean to say?"

"You abandoned me — no, you abandoned us. My husband is no match for this country." She looks at the window as if her gaze might penetrate the skin and palisade logs to the rolling landscape outside the fort. "There are some this land feeds, but most it seems to destroy. Like my father. Like my husband, who will soon be destroyed, as you have foreseen. The land may be promised, but the gift is an ill one. You are a survivor here; you could have led my people to success and a fragment of comfort I have no doubt, but instead we have fear; fear and war."

"How can you cast me aside and then condemn me for leaving? Where is the justice?"

"I am a woman, Alexander, and know little of justice. My choices are hard and few, yours not so much. With patience, I could have been your wife."

"And now?"

Shouting outside.

It is her turn to sigh. She pulls his head to her swollen belly. "Now it is all for naught. The Half-breeds are massing for attack and the people say we shall be wiped out. I have heard the most horrid tales this spring. We have been lied to, Alexander."

"So how would you have it then, if things could be according to your will?"

She looks down at him. "I would be your wife, my love. Though there be nothing between my husband and myself but a contract, I must honour this, and therefore him, until the parting of this life. I love you and have done so ever since I met you. I have wondered and worried about where you were in this great awful land: alive and in the arms of some woman, or lying dead upon a plain with arrows in your back. There has not been a night since you left me when my tears were not the herald of Morpheus."

"So come life or death, I cannot have you — yet again you will reject me?"

She kisses the top of his head and rests her own upon his. "Some things are beyond choice, beyond the heart's desire. I so do love you."

Wiping away his tears, Alexander leaves her and steps into the courtyard.

"The Half-breeds are coming," a lookout with a spyglass shouts from a tower.

—◡—

Twenty men march north along the shore of the Red River. Most are Highlanders and HBC employees, strong and grim, but uncertain, holding their muskets at uncomfortable angles as if they are not quite sure of their purpose.

"They are done up all in feathers and war paint, sir," a man informs the governor after speaking with a Stony scout. "And they are all on horseback."

"This is a powerful force," Alexander says. "Sixty at least I made out when last I spied them. We must wait for the cannon."

"Nonsense. There will be no battle today. I gave the peasants a good hurrah at the fort, but when I read my proclamation, the Savages will disperse."

"A proclamation?"

"Certainly. I am the law in Assiniboia and with a king's authority at my back, they will obey, I assure you."

"And if they do not?"

"Why, if that fortunate chance presents itself, no mere Savage can withstand my stout Highlanders. We shall feed them a world of sorrow."

"Excuse me, Governor," interrupts an officer, hurrying up. "We have come upon settlers fleeing the attack."

"Attack, what attack? What are you talking about, man?"

"Right here, sir," he says, bringing forward two women, pale and teary-eyed, gasping for breath, their skirts torn and muddied.

"Mr. and Mrs. Murray, sir. And Mr. Sutherland. All taken prisoner," one of the women says. "Oh, it were terrifying, those awful savages. Screeching and wailing something fierce. They bound 'em and took 'em they did."

"Aye, I saw it wit me own eyes," the other woman adds, her eyes proving their veracity by bulging from her head.

"They did, eh?" says Semple. "Well, I shall have something to say about that. Move on, men! Mr. McKenzie, Mr. Pritchard, bring that rabble up will you? Form a line there, smartly now. Where are those laggards with the field-piece? Blast them, I shall not wait. Move on!"

~

They enter a grove of wizened oaks, and as Alexander walks beneath their hoary, twisted limbs; a flock of magpies takes wing in a clatter of black and white plumage. He pauses, listening to the leaves rattle in the hot air, dappled by flickering light and shadow. As the Highlanders gather around, a wind lifts from the prairie with a roar, carrying away many of their hats and filling their eyes with sand. When they can at last see through the settling dust, a line of Half-breed horsemen waits not a hundred yards away.

Governor Semple moves to the front of his column. They are outgunned, at least three to one. He pulls his proclamation out of his pocket.

Alexander watches the Half-breeds move along their flank, aware of the danger they are in; he has faith in neither their position nor Semple's authority. His heart grieves when he sees many men opposite that he knows by name, people who mean far more to him than these foolish Highlanders.

A Half-breed leaves his line, nudging his horse toward Semple. He wears a beaded deerskin vest with a scarlet sash wrapped about his waist, the tasseled ends flapping in the wind. Feathers dangle from the barrel of a musket draped across the horse's back.

"I am Boucher," he says to Semple, in a tone thick with insolence. He looks down at the small sortie, the cannon his people feared nowhere in evidence. "What do you want, old man?"

"What the hell is this?" says Semple. "What do you mean by speaking to me this way? Do you know who I am?"

"I care not. You are English pig, and that is enough." Boucher leans over, spitting beside his horse.

"Why, you son of a dog, I'll have you whipped; get down from there." Semple grabs for the reins, and Boucher's startled horse rears with a cry onto its hind legs.

A shot goes off beside Alexander. Another follows, and the Highlanders let loose a scattered, disorganized volley. When the gun smoke at last blows clear, a cheer goes up, and muskets lift in triumph; there is not a Half-breed still sitting on a horse.

Alexander throws himself into the waving grass. "Get down," he shouts to the exulting men, but is ignored. Seeing several valuable prizes among the Half-breed horses, many Highlanders begin running towards them. Alexander flings out his rifle, tripping Declan.

"What the devil …?" Declan begins, turning towards Alexander. His eyes widen. "You! By Christ …" Another volley erupts from around them, and many Highlanders go down. One man, shot through the eye, collapses onto Declan. "What the hell? What is going on?"

Alexander worms his way towards him. Gunfire surrounds them now, balls whining furious and hot. "Fool. I warned you," he says, around the shot carried in his mouth. He spits a ball into the smoking barrel of his carbine. "They have us now."

Semple kneels in the grass, stunned and uncomprehending while blood pumps from his thigh. A Half-breed runs him through the breast with a spear and he falls onto his back, the protruding shaft waving with the last tremors of his heart. Behind his prostrate men, Cuthbert Grant carries the black Half-breed flag, exhorting them in the battle. Alexander takes aim and fires, sees him flinch. "Just a nick, Grant, but that'll learn you not to be so damned cocky," he says under his breath. Beside him, Declan shoots wildly at a hidden foe. Alexander spits in another ball. "Get out of here. There's not a chance. For your life!"

Declan's face is a ghastly yellow and marked with a long, red weal where a ball has creased his cheek. "I … I believe I have pissed myself," he says, looking down at the dark stain in his breeches. He looks up again, and both men suddenly laugh. There is the sound of approaching hooves, and a Half-breed runs through the line, turves flying. Spying Declan, he levels his musket; Alexander's carbine barks, and the man flies backwards off his horse.

"Now!" says Alexander. Declan stares at him a moment, shaking, then begins an awkward backward shuffle on his belly through the grass.

Shots become scattered, as few of Semple's men remain alive either as targets or as defenders. Alexander reloads as fast as he is able, the Baker hot in his hands. Whenever a Half-breed head pops up, he sends a ball whistling through a hat or nicking off a feather.

Soon all survivors who are able have crept away and he finds himself in the absurd position of his carbine being the only response to the shooting around him. The Half-breeds are crawling closer, their balls clipping grass stems and thudding into the ground beside him, sprinkling him with dirt. He is almost obscured by a fog of Half-breed powder smoke, and his ears ring with the reports. A man rises to get a clearer shot, and Alexander takes a bead on his nose; he freezes as he recognizes Jacque, remembering his words: "I wanted to with all my heart, my friend, but not here, not now. I will spill your blood another day."

A puff of smoke from Jacque's gun, and Alexander's world bursts in a riot of burning, red light.

Rose lies on her back, her knees high. Her face glares puffy and red, sweat glittering on her forehead. The small window has been covered, the only light from a sputtering tallow dip resting on a nearby table. Several women surround her, scurrying about and pretending to help. The popping of distant gunfire carries into the room, bringing with it the faint hellfire reek of burning powder. With each new volley, Rose cries out and strains, her body convulsing; her head rocks from side to side. Women take each of her hands as if to comfort, to give her strength, but they are not really with her, focused as much as she at the sounds of battle and the sound of their men cut down with the ease of running buffalo.

With each shot a contraction waves through her, leaving her gasping. As blood spills scarlet over the waving, yellow grass, so too it flows from her womb, following the emerging child.

Hands wring in concern as the head crowns, announced by a wail of grief and pain. A deer hide is placed before the emerging life: a head, an arm, a red fist clenched tight. While the last fleeing man falls into the grass with his heart pierced by a ball, the infant slides onto the wet cloth accompanied by a warm, living flow.

The dying man's shriek mingles with the cries of the child, and in that small dark room on the prairie, birth and death are conjugated.

Alexander lies on his back and stares up at the day's blue firmament that seems without end, his eyes taking him to a height that seems to continue on forever. He wonders if heaven indeed exists in that blue depth; even the clouds and the wheeling hawk above him seem hopelessly earth-bound when compared to the heights he feels within his breast. As life prepares to abandon him, he reaches a bloodied hand skyward, feeling impossibly remote from that high, lovely place.

Epilogue

The Métis sit upon their horses, the settlers and Company men filing out through the fort gates, their dragging feet lifting a saffron-coloured cloud of dust. A few children cry. Now and then, a widow shrieks and faints, seeing the damp scalps — red, brown, or yellow — hanging from several of the Half-breeds' horses. Above them all, the new flag of the Métis nation snaps in the rising wind.

Rose walks with Declan limping beside her. She lifts her pale face to see Cuthbert Grant at the head of his men, presiding over the surrender and abandonment of Fort Douglas. His grey eyes meet hers, and with a great effort of will she returns his gaze; tears gather, but she refuses them freedom. She pulls her infant tighter to her breast and looks to the horizon, Declan's arm moving around her. Together with the rest of her people, they shuffle from the fort.

Do you want to hear sung
A song that is true?

Last June the 19th
The band of *bois-brûlés*
Arrived like a band of warriors.

Arriving at la grenouillère,
We took three prisoners.
Three prisoners from the Orkneys,
Who are here to steal our homeland.

We were about to dismount
When two of our men arrived.
"Here are the English,
Who are coming to attack us!"

Right away we turned around,
And we trapped the band of grenadiers.
They are caught; they all dismounted.

We acted like honourable folks.
We sent an ambassador.
"Mr. Governor, would you stop for a moment?
We want to speak with you."

The governor who was enraged.
He told his men to shoot.

The governor who thought himself emperor,
He tried to take tough action.
Having seen go by all the *bois-brûlés*,
He set out to scare them
Having set out to rout them.
He made a mistake and got himself killed.

He well got killed
A number of his grenadiers
We killed almost all his army
From this mistake
Four or five escaped.

Oh, if you only had seen these Englishmen
And the *bois-brûlés* after them.
From hill to hill the English stumbled.
And the Bois-Brûlés let out shouts of joy!

And who has composed this song?
It is Pierriche Falcon this good lad.
It has been made and composed
About the victory that we have won.

— Métis National Anthem by Pierre (Pierriche)
   Falcon

Acknowledgements

The writing of any full-length work of fiction is an arduous task, especially when writing about a location and period where there were few literate witnesses, and even fewer records kept. The explosion of information on the Internet has helped writers a great deal, but most of the research for this novel was done when the Internet had yet to find its wings. It was a slow, plodding process.

Part of the challenge was not only discovering the information, but also locating it in the proper time and place. I tried wherever possible to use the correct language of the era, but when quoting Aboriginal terms, at times I had to reference modern sources because I could not find records from that early period. Even if I could, often the language had specific dialects; those speaking Swampy Cree on the coast might be quite different from those inland. Sometimes it just becomes an educated guess.

But I had a lot of help. I'd like to thank Hilda Fitzner for sending me her hand-written dictionary of common Swampy Cree terms and expressions. I'd also like to thank the knowledgeable staff of Fort

Carlton Provincial Park in Saskatchewan, who showed me many small details of life during the fur trade that I had not found elsewhere

This book couldn't have happened without the firm and wise hand of Bernice Lever who edited my manuscript before submitting it to Dundurn. She greatly improved the manuscript, and even suggested Dundurn as a perfect fit for the book. One is always very grateful for the publisher who first takes a chance on an unknown author, and I know Bernice's support facilitated that. It is a debt I shall never be able to fully repay.

Lastly, as we all know, the real power lies behind the throne. I likely would have spent my declining years labouring in salt mines or marching on foreign battlefields if my ever-patient, ever-supportive, lovely wife had not deigned to allow me to play the Bohemian and dedicate a large chunk of my life to drinking too much and chasing ideas in fiction. Livers can be replaced, but stories are priceless. I hope this work proves worthy of her faith.